A SCRIPTURAL
Discussion of Light

A Scriptural

Discussion of Light

By
Allen J. Fletcher

CFI
Springville, Utah

© 2007 Allen J. Fletcher

ISBN 13: 978-1-59955-032-9

Published by CFI, an imprint of Cedar Fort, Inc., 2373 W. 700 S., Springville, UT, 84663
Distributed by Cedar Fort, Inc. www.cedarfort.com

LIBRARY OF CONGRESS CATALOGING-IN-PUBLICATION DATA

A scriptural discussion of light / Allen J. Fletcher.
    p. cm.
    ISBN 978-1-59955-032-9
    1. Church of Jesus Christ of Latter day Saints--Doctrines. 2. Mormon Church—Doctrines. 3. Light and darkness in the Bible. 4. Jesus Christ—Mormon interpretations. I. Title.

    BX8635.3.F54 2007

    230'.9332—dc22

Cover design by Nicole Williams
Cover design © 2007 by Lyle Mortimer
Edited and typeset by Kimiko M. Hammari

Printed in the United States of America

10 9 8 7 6 5 4 3 2 1

Printed on acid-free paper

Contents

Acknowledgments

I would like to thank my wife, Elaine, for her love and support as I have done the research and the writing of this book. She has been my sounding-board and my confidant. I acknowledge the valuable contributions of my brother-in-law Vernon Jubber, without which this work never could have been produced. Rick Cartier, a CES colleague, helped with the editing; Terrence Smith, Larry Varty, and David Bullock offered valuable suggestions. Finally, I would like to express love and appreciation to my father, Nyal A. Fletcher, for his generous contributions to my research over the years.

Introduction

This project began long ago, when as a new teacher in the Church Educational System, I grew curious about words in the scriptures. I was especially drawn to Doctrine and Covenants 84:45 and knew that it held a key—if only I could find out what it was—to the meaning of the wonderful and oftentimes mysterious passages of the language of God in the scriptures. I felt that it was a "mother-lode" scripture.

D&C 84
45 For the **word** of the Lord is **truth**, and whatsoever is **truth** is **light**, and whatsoever is **light** is **Spirit**, even the **Spirit** of Jesus Christ.

I worked with the words and concepts of that scripture, trying them over and over in different ways. I made charts and developed formulas and labored to understand their significance, yet I always felt that the real message was just beyond the horizon.

Gradually, the Spirit of the Lord distilled into my mind and into my heart the things that I will share with you here. On occasion, the enlightenment has been quite dramatic and dynamic. At other times, it has been a simple peace. Now that I know what I know, I can't seem to remember a time when I did not know. These things are part of the fiber and fabric of my existence. This work is my testimony.

A note about this book

I take full responsibility for this work. I am not introducing anything new. I am not propounding new doctrine or new revelation. I am just uncovering what is already in the scriptures. Anyone could do it. If we think that we know all there is to know about a subject in the scriptures, we are in for a great surprise. And just because we have found one or two wonderful correlations and relationships, we need not suppose that more will not be found—many more, hundreds more, thousands more. Should such a discovery be a surprise to anyone? The author of these scriptures is infinite and eternal, and so are his words. Someone once said: "The boundaries of what we know are limited, whereas the boundaries of our ignorance are infinite."

Elder Richard G. Scott made the following statements:

> First, let's discuss different ways of learning from the scriptures. One way is . . . to analyze and unite related scriptures. Then on a separate sheet of paper, prepare a statement of principle that embodies the truths contained in those scriptures. Where these two things are carefully and consistently done, then you can be instructed through inspiration as you search the scriptures.
>
> Point out how risky it is to use a single scripture and expect that it communicates all that is needed.
>
> Effort to study the scriptures and unite common concepts from like scriptures will qualify one to receive further inspiration and guidance through pondering the scriptures.
> (Richard G. Scott, "Helping Others to Be Spiritually Led," [BYU: Doctrine and Covenants and Church History Symposium, August 11, 1998]. Published by the Church of Jesus Christ of Latter-day Saints, Salt Lake City, Utah, 1998, 4, 6, and 8)

President Packer of the Quorum of the Twelve Apostles also made this insightful comment:

> Individual doctrines of the gospel are not fully explained in one place in the scriptures, nor presented in order or sequence. They must be assembled from pieces here and there. They are sometimes found in large segments, but mostly they are in small bits scattered through the chapters and verses.
>
> You might think that if all the references on baptism, for instance, were assembled in one chapter of each standard work, and all references on revelation in another, it would make the learning of the gospel much simpler. I have come to

be very, very grateful that scriptures are arranged as they are. Because the scriptures are arranged the way they are, there are endless combinations of truths that will fit the need of every individual in every circumstance. (Boyd K. Packer, "The Great Plan of Happiness," (BYU: CES Symposium, August 10, 1993], 1–2.)

I struggled to know how to write my experience. I finally decided to present it in an experiential way—which means, rather than coldly writing about doctrines and concepts, I have simply told a story. It is a story of two couples who meet together periodically and share their scriptural studies. The development of what they learn follows the unfolding of my own learning about this subject. My great hope is that my weakness in writing does not get in the way of the beauty and purity of the concepts.

Special note to the reader

As you go through the experience of this book, you may occasionally find some of the examples to be a bit lengthy or repetitive. Be patient. This book is not just a book about light, but how to learn about light—or any other scriptural subject for that matter. It is almost a workbook on how to use the scriptures to learn about the scriptures. The many examples are necessary to create exposure to the scriptural language of light.

Many teaching and learning methods are demonstrated in this work, such as reading, searching, comparing, pondering, visualizing, listening, reflecting, questioning, explaining, discussing, sharing, and writing. Other skills include cross-referencing, keyword studies, charting, and using the Topical Guide and the Bible Dictionary. Also included are instances attesting to the value of computer skills, especially with the scripture programs and their ability to facilitate scripture searches.

CHAPTER 1

God Is Light

Steve and Joan Terry sat in Frank Gray's office. They had wanted to attend a fireside given by Frank a few nights before, where he had talked about principles from the Doctrine and Covenants, but they were unable to go. They had been intrigued with what others were saying about the fireside, especially about a scriptural understanding of light. They had set up an appointment with Frank to discuss their questions, and he had invited them to spend some time with him in discussion.

"Frank," Steve said. "We're sorry that we couldn't attend your fireside, but we've heard that you spoke of the gospel being centered on the idea of light and its effects and blessings. We would like to know more about that. Could you help us understand more?"

"Thanks for your interest," Frank said. "I'll try to help you, but let me say at the outset that there is no one way to see the scriptures. They have multiple implications and layer upon layer of meaning. With that in mind, is it all right if I begin by asking you a question or two?"

"Certainly," Steve said.

"Our bodies get hungry, and we do lots of things to satisfy that hunger. Some people do silly things to satisfy hunger. What happens to a body that is fed improper food?"

"It begins to break down and not perform normally," Steve said.

"The behavior of the body is a fairly good indicator of nutrition, isn't it? Just as our physical bodies require appropriate physical food, our spirits require appropriate spiritual food. Some people do very strange things to satisfy their spiritual hungers. What happens to a spirit that is fed improper food?"

1

"I think that we see evidence of that all over," Steve said. "People do strange things. Their emotions get bent out of shape, communications break down—unhappiness results."

"What do you think spiritual food is, Joan?" Frank asked.

"It would be having the Spirit of the Lord, wouldn't it?"

"That's what I think," Frank said.

"But wait!" Joan said. "In starting to answer our question about light, you've changed the subject and are now talking about spirit. I don't understand the relationship of those two things."

"That leads us to the all-important question," Frank said. "What is spirit?"

"I've always understood the spirit to be the power that comes from God to help man live righteously," Steve said.

"That's a good answer. There are many names for that power in the scriptures, Steve. Let's look at section 84 verse 45 of the Doctrine and Covenants and see if we can identify some of those names."

D&C 84
45 For the **word** of the Lord is **truth**, and whatsoever is **truth** is **light**, and whatsoever is **light** is **Spirit**, even the **Spirit** of Jesus Christ.

"What names can you see?"

"I see the word of the Lord and truth and light and spirit," Joan said.

"What is the relationship of those names, Joan?"

"They all come from Jesus Christ."

"That's true. What is the relationship of each word to each of the other words?"

"As I look at them," Steve said, "I think . . . that they must all mean the same thing. It says the word of the Lord *is* truth, truth *is* light, and light *is* spirit. And the word *whatsoever* is intriguing," Steve added, as he began to look deeper. "It suggests to me that every part or every instance or every occurrence of truth *is* light, and every part of light *is* spirit. I've never considered that before. It's exciting."

"Yes, it is," Frank continued. "So, if we wanted to follow the theme of our discussion, what is the spirit-food that we all need?"

"Well, Frank," Joan said. "I see now why you started this discussion about light with spirit. The words are interchangeable. They mean the same thing. The spiritual food we need is his word, or in other words his truth, or in other words his light, or in other words his spirit."

"When the scriptures use the word *light* with these other words, *truth*, *spirit*, and so forth," Steve asked, "do you think they intend to convey the idea of *real* light, or is it just a symbolic or figurative expression?"

"That is a very good question, Steve. Let's look at section 131 verse 7," Frank said.

D&C 131

7 There is no such thing as immaterial matter. All **spirit** is matter, but it is more fine or pure, and can only be discerned by purer eyes.

"What does this tell us about the nature of the spirit or light we're discussing, Joan?"

"I'm beginning to see things I've never even thought about before, Frank. If I understand this correctly, the light or spirit that works upon us is real matter."

Steve leaned forward and said, "Frank, do you mean that when we feel the spirit or light from God that it is a real substance working in us, and not just our having a good feeling?"

"That is the way I understand it, Steve."

"That helps me understand that we can never produce those good feelings ourselves. They are projected toward us and placed in us as a real force for good—light acting upon us."

"If this is real light, how come we can't see it?" Joan asked. Then, catching herself, she said, "Oh, I see. The answer is right here in the scripture. It is more fine or pure and can only be seen by purer eyes."

Frank thumbed through his scriptures. "There are a couple of other verses that speak of this. Here, let me show them to you."

D&C 6

21 Behold, I am Jesus Christ, the Son of God. I am the same that came unto mine own, and mine own received me not. I am the **light** which shineth in *darkness*, and the *darkness* comprehendeth it not.

D&C 88

7 Which truth shineth. This is the **light** of Christ. As also he is in the sun, and the **light** of the sun, and the power thereof by which it was made.

---

8 As also he is in the moon, and is the **light** of the moon, and the power thereof by which it was made;
9 As also the **light** of the stars, and the power thereof by which they were made;
10 And the earth also, and the power thereof, even the earth upon which you stand.
11 And *the* **light** *which shineth, which giveth you* **light**, *is through him who enlighteneth your eyes, which is the same* **light** *that quickeneth your understandings;*

"Notice in these verses that part of the light that shines from God can be seen, and part of it cannot. Can you see the difference, Steve?"

"Well, we can certainly see the sun and the moon and the stars, but it would appear from this last verse that there is some kind of dimension or continuum of light that contains an invisible spectrum as well as a visible one. The invisible spectrum seems to be the part that works on our minds and helps us to understand."

Joan, almost interrupting her husband, said, "Would this be like the light spectrum that we understand in science, where we have infrared rays on one end which we can't see, then visible light toward the center, then gamma rays toward the other end which we again can't see?"

"I have wondered about that same thing, Joan. I am sure there must be a correlation," said Frank.

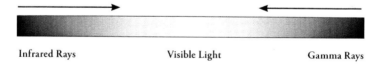

Infrared Rays   Visible Light   Gamma Rays

"To increase our understanding of light, we need to read what John says about God," Frank said. "Would you please read this verse, Joan?"

1 John 1
5 This then is the message which we have heard of him, and declare unto you, that *God is* **light**, *and in him is no* ***darkness*** *at all.*

"What does this verse add to our understanding of light, Joan?"

"Well, first of all, it says that God is light. To me that means that God doesn't just dwell in light or use light, but that he *is* light—he is a being of light. And second, it explains something about that light. It is a light in which there is no darkness at all. It must be the ultimate, the finest, the purest, the highest, and the most infinite form of light in the universe."

"I agree, Joan," said Frank. "Brigham Young said that God is the very 'Fountain of light' itself, that 'the spirit of truth . . . will lead to God, the Fountain of light.'" (*Teachings of the Presidents of the Church: Brigham Young* [Salt Lake City: Intellectual Reserve, Inc., 1997], 34).

"Steve, would you would please read this next verse?"

D&C 88

12 Which **light** *proceedeth forth from the presence of God to fill the immensity of space . . .*

"What do you see here, Steve?"

"Not only is God light, but light goes forth from him to fill the immensity of space. I'm getting an idea how little I know about this."

"I agree that we know very little," said Frank. "Perhaps if we compare his infinite light to the light that comes from the sun—the part of the light that we can see—we might be able to increase our knowledge of that part which we can't see. I have a drawing here, Joan. I wonder if you could describe what is going on."

"The light from the sun comes into the prism from the left and exits at the right. The prism bends the ray of light and separates it into its colors."

"What does this teach us about light, Steve?"

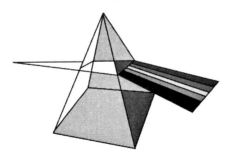

"It shows that light is composed of parts—red, orange, yellow, green, blue, purple—and that a prism can separate the light into those various parts, or that it can allow us to see the various parts."

"Even though the parts are different colors, Steve, are they still light?"

"Yes."

"So the names of the colors are names that are given to various parts of the light, or we could say various manifestations of the light. With that understanding of the light that we can see, Joan and Steve, we should be able to apply it to the nature of the light of God that we can't see, as we talked about in D&C 88:11. Let's first of all look at another scripture."

> **2 NEPHI 31**
> 3 For my soul delighteth in plainness; for after this manner doth the Lord God work among the children of men. For *the Lord God giveth* **light** *unto the understanding; for he speaketh unto men according to their language, unto their understanding.*

"In this verse, Joan, what is God giving?" Frank asked.

"God is giving light."

"Where is that light going?"

"To the understanding of men."

"Steve, how is he giving light to the understanding?"

"He is speaking words in their language."

"So, what is the relationship of the words he is speaking in their language to his light?

"His words are light," Steve said. "That's what we learned earlier. The word of the Lord is light."

"Is there any way that we can apply what we learned about the prism to this information, Steve?" Frank asked.

"Let me see if I can make sense of it," Steve said. "Light goes forth from the presence of God to man. Man is incapable of understanding that light in its fulness or all at once, so it passes through some kind of prism where it can be separated into or manifested in its several parts. These component parts are far easier to grasp than the whole, and when they are manifested to men, they are given names in his language so that men can understand them. Would that be close?

"Yes, Steve, and what might the prism be?"

"I am not sure, Frank."

"Let's look at one more scripture."

> **2 NEPHI 33**
> 1 And now I, Nephi, cannot write all the things which were taught among my people; neither am I mighty in writing,

> like unto speaking; for *when a man speaketh by the* **power** *of the Holy Ghost the* **power** *of the Holy Ghost carrieth it unto the hearts of the children of men.*

"The prism is the Holy Ghost," Steve said.

"Yes," replied Frank. "The pure light of God—on its way to us—in some way passes through the 'wisdom and judgment' of the Holy Ghost (see Moses 6:61). We can envision it being slowed down, simplified, separated into some of its component parts, and conveyed to us incrementally in a manner that we can understand. And what is it that God wants us to ultimately understand, Joan?"

"The light in which there is no darkness at all. I see now that the words and commandments of God to us in this world are simplified manifestations of that total light."

"Yes," said Frank. "With the understanding we now have, we could render our drawing something like this:"

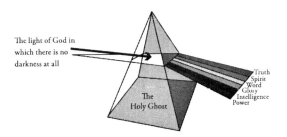

The light of God in which there is no darkness at all

The Holy Ghost

Truth
Spirit
Word
Glory
Intelligence
Power

"The prism is almost like the lens or pupil of an eye," Joan said. "Light passes through it and is transformed so that we can make meaning out of it. That's really what the Holy Ghost does for us, isn't it?"

"Yes, Joan. Thank you for that insight," Frank said. "I want to come back to that point later. Once we catch the vision of this principle, we can see it all through the scriptures. Notice in this next verse that God is giving commandments, or we might say light or lights by the means of speaking words after the manner of the language of men so that they can come to an understanding."

D&C 1

24 Behold, I am God and have spoken it; these **commandments** are of me, and were given unto my servants in their weakness, after the manner of their language, that they might come to understanding.

"Words are really just symbolic ideas in the first place," Joan said, "and the very same object or concept in one culture is given a different name in another, so words are simply a way to make meaning. I know that our meaning is not God's meaning, but it is interesting to understand that he uses our words to convey his meaning. It is incredible to understand that his sole purpose of speaking in our language is to bring us to a comprehension of his light."

"Thank you, Joan. Now that we have come to this point," Frank said, "I would like to go back to verse 45 of section 84 and look at it again."

D&C 84
45 For the **word** of the Lord is **truth**, and whatsoever is **truth** is **light**, and whatsoever is **light** is **Spirit**, even the **Spirit** of Jesus Christ.

"As we pointed out earlier, these four major key words are identical and, we might also add, interchangeable." I like to use diagrams, so I'll just draw one here to help us keep that interchangeableness in mind.

Word = Truth = Light = Spirit

We can refer to it from time to time to help us remember that if we see one of these words in a verse, it's possible to exchange it for one of the others to help expand our understanding. Sometimes the scriptures themselves do this very thing. Let's look at an example:

---

1 JOHN 1
10 If we say that we have not sinned, we make him a liar, and *his* **word** *is not in us.*
1 JOHN 1
8 If we say that we have no sin, we deceive ourselves, and *the* **truth** *is not in us.*
JOHN 11
10 But if a man walk in the night, he stumbleth, because *there is no* **light** *in him.*

2 NEPHI 33
2 But behold, there are many that harden their hearts against the Holy **Spirit**, that it *hath no place in them;* wherefore,

---

they cast many things away which are written and esteem them as things of naught.

"What do you see, Steve?" asked Frank.

"The Lord uses each of the four words interchangeably, just like you said. I had no idea that these things even existed in the scriptures."

"Let's look at another example," Frank continued. "Here is an interesting verse from the Book of Mormon:"

ALMA 5

7 Behold, he changed their hearts; yea, he awakened them out of a deep sleep, and they awoke unto God. Behold, they were in the midst of darkness; nevertheless, *their souls were illuminated by the* **light** *of the everlasting* **word**; yea, they were encircled about by the bands of death, and the chains of hell, and an everlasting destruction did await them.

"Notice what happens when we apply what we have learned. Listen to this statement: 'Their souls were illuminated by the light of the everlasting word.' Imagine how many different ways that could be said:

Their souls were illuminated by the:
- word of the everlasting truth
- word of the everlating light
- word of the everlasting spirit
- truth of the everlasting word
- truth of the everlasting light
- truth of the everlasting spirit
- light of the everlasting truth
- light of the everlasting spirit
- spirit of the everlasting truth
- spirit of the everlasting light

"Now, the scriptures themselves do not contain every one of these word variations," Frank said. "And if we had time, we could discuss possible reasons for that, but we can find the variations if we put the four words on a chart and then work the statements from the chart. I have an example here. Notice how I placed the four words horizontally across the top and the same four words vertically down the side. I have written the words in each box that line up from the words on top and on the side. This gives us a logic pattern. Some of the usages make more sense than others, such as 'the truth of the word,' but even 'the word of the word' makes sense when you think of the 'word' of the scriptures, as coming from the 'word' of the Lord, or the 'spirit' that you feel as coming from the 'spirit' of the Holy Ghost."

"I'm impressed that so much can be learned from comparing and analyzing the scriptures," Joan said. "This is so far beyond the understanding I had when we came in here. Is that how you feel, Steve?"

	WORD	**TRUTH**	**LIGHT**	**SPIRIT**
WORD	Word Word	Truth Word	Light Word	Spirit Word
TRUTH	Word Truth	Truth Truth	Light Truth	Spirit Truth
LIGHT	Word Light	Truth Light	Light Light	Spirit Light
SPIRIT	Word Spirit	Truth Spirit	Light Spirit	Spirit Spirit

"It sure is, Joan. And you know, while I look at that chart, I keep wondering, and I just have to ask, how far can that go? In other words, if these four words are interchangeable, how many more are interchangeable with them?"

"That's a good question, Steve," said Frank. "And that brings us right to our next point. Knowing that the above four words are interchangeable, look at this verse:"

D&C 93
36 The **glory** of God is **intelligence**, or, in other words, **light** and **truth**.
37 **Light** and **truth forsake that** evil **one**.

"Are there any words here that you could add to the basic four, Joan?"

"Well, we know that light and truth are the same, and here it is said that the glory of God is light or truth, and it also says that glory is intelligence, and it also says that light and truth forsake evil. So I think we could add those to the list."

"Steve, would you write the list as we begin to discover it?" Frank asked.

"Sure will," Steve said.

Steve began to write out the words that they had discovered so far.

Word = Truth = Light = Spirit = Glory = Intelligence = Forsakes evil

"Here is another verse," Frank said.

D&C 93
24 And **truth** is **knowledge** *of things as they are, and as they were, and as they are to come.*

"I am going to revise the way I am making this list," Steve said. "Perhaps if I do it in a chart form, it will be more accurate.

Steve began drawing boxes and lines connecting the boxes together:

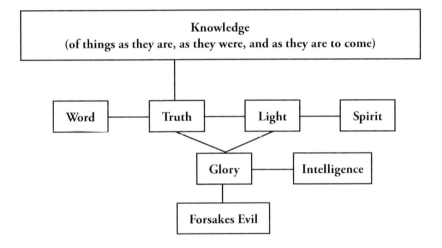

"That makes it easier to visualize, Steve," Frank said. "I see that you didn't just write the word *knowledge*, but 'knowledge of things as they are, as they were, and as they are to come.' There is a great difference as I'm sure we can all appreciate. Let's add one more verse."

MOSES 1
39 For behold, this is my **work** and my **glory**—to bring to pass the immortality and eternal life of man.

"Here we see that the word *glory* may be equated with the word *work*, and the work is 'to bring to pass the immortality and eternal life of man.' So, Steve, you could add those things to your chart," said Frank.

"But wait, Frank," Joan said. "How can you be so sure that the word *glory* can be equated with the word *work*? The conjunction *and* does not always indicate that two words mean the same thing."

"That is a great point, Joan," Frank answered. "There are at least two ways to show that these words are equivalent. The first is through other scriptures that show that the work of God is light (see 2 Nephi 31:3; Alma 26:3,15; D&C 11:19). If the glory of God is light, as we have shown, and his work is light, as these other verses show, then his glory and his work are light and may be equated. The second way is through the concept that whatsoever is of God is light (see D&C 50:14), and surely his work is of him; therefore it is light."

"Now I understand why it's sometimes hard to keep all the commandments," Joan said.

"Why is that?" asked Steve as he continued to draw on the chart.

"Because I see that light is work—hard work!" Joan said, laughing.

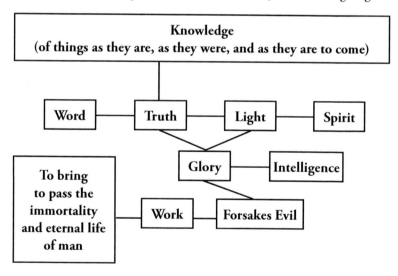

"Earlier we read a scripture that said God is light," Steve said. "I remember reading in 1 John 4:8 that God is love. Are there other references in the scriptures that say God is such and such? Because if there are, they would equate to light, truth, spirit, and love, and could be added to the list."

"I think if we look in the Topical Guide and the Bible Dictionary or in one of the computer scripture-databases, we could discover many references like that," Frank said. "I made a list like that somewhere—let me just look . . . oh, here it is."

God is **holy** ....Psalm 99:9
God is **pure** ....Proverbs 30:5
God is **good** ....Psalm 73:1
God is **merciful**... D&C 3:10
God is **everlasting**...................................... Genesis 21:33
God is **gracious**................................... 2 Chronicles 30:9
God is **almighty**..Revelation 15:3
God is **eternal** ....1 Nephi 12:18
God is **life** ....John 11:25
God is **Alpha** and **Omega** ....Revelation 21:6
God is **endless**... D&C 19:4
God is **just** .... Revelation 15:3

"I can plainly tell that study like that would take a lot of time and thinking," Joan said.

"Yes, it does take a lot of time," Frank replied. "But remember this is only one way to look at the scriptures, and I suppose in the eternal scheme of things, it is very elementary."

"It's not elementary to us," Joan said.

"I would like to share with you an experience," Frank said. "I began, many years ago, to make a chart similar to the one we have begun today. I took four sheets of letter-size paper (it was pink because that was the only paper I could find at the time) and taped them together lengthwise, which I thought would be plenty adequate.

"I wrote *Word of the Lord* in the center of the first one, *Truth* in the center of the second one, *Light* in the center of the third one, and *Spirit* in the center of the fourth one. Then I drew a line between them, showing that they were all connected with each other. I then began to add words as I discovered their interchangeableness. For example: going out from *Word*, I added, *voice, mind, commandment, scripture*, and so forth, showing that the word of the Lord is the voice of the Lord, the mind of the Lord, the commandment of the Lord, and the scripture of the Lord. Going out from *Truth* I added *knowledge, wisdom, endless, understanding*, and so forth. Going out from *Light*, I added *glory, power, intelligence, understanding*, and so forth. And going out from *Spirit*, I added *life, joy, peace, freedom*, and so forth. I was careful to make sure that I did not invent connections but simply recorded them. I put every word in a little box with its reference and a line from that box to the word it connected to. I had to add more and more pages. I spent nearly two years, off and on, doing it. When I was done—and I say done, advisedly because a work like this will never end—the chart was huge." *(Note: This is a greatly reduced picture of the chart.)*

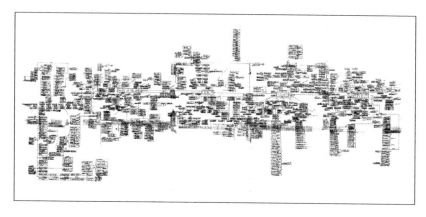

"What a project!" Joan said.

"Can we see the chart?" said Steve.

"Yes, I have it over here," Frank said as he reached into the corner between his desk and the wall. He brought out a tube from which he took a roll of slightly tattered pink paper.

"It's really worn and not very pretty to look at," he said as he unrolled it for Joan and Steve to look at.

"This is incredible! Are you going to prepare it for publication?" Steve asked.

"No, I did it only to understand the principles I've shared with you, and it is probably only of value to me."

"I would like to have a copy of this," Steve said.

"The real value is not in the finished chart, Steve, but in the principles that unfold while you are doing it. I wouldn't want to rob you of that experience. You have had a bit of a taste of that today."

"This is an intriguing chart, Frank. Could you share with us some of the things you learned by doing it? I mean, apart from what you have already told us," Joan said.

"Let me just tell you a couple of things, and then we can break for lunch. First, I found various connections that invariably led back to one of the original four words. Second, I realized that every major key word of the scriptures would eventually go somewhere on that chart. All these scriptural words are connected and are part of one great whole. I knew then that there is only one light and only one darkness.

"I next came to the conclusion that God is not saying a thousand different things—he is saying only one thing a thousand different ways. I next realized that if all these words are manifestations of the fulness of the light or spirit of God, then we, as the children of God, if we are faithful, can one day have a fulness of all the things listed on that chart. Another thing that impressed itself upon my mind was the question, what is spiritual death? The answer to that was shocking to me. It is to *die* as to all those qualities and manifestations listed on the chart. That is something I never want to experience."

"Thank you very much, Frank," Joan said. You have certainly opened our eyes this morning."

"Yes, you have," Steve said, "and I appreciate what you have done. I would feel a lot better if I could have a copy of that chart."

"Steve! You have all the tools you need to construct one of your own," Joan said, "and I think it would be fun to do it together."

"Let's meet back here at one o' clock this afternoon," Frank said, "and we can continue with some of these ideas."

"Sounds good," Steve said.

They arose, shook hands, and went down the hall to the cafeteria to have lunch.

Understanding Light

Joan, Steve, and Frank had just finished their lunch and had stepped back into Frank's office. They were talking about the beautiful setting of the building and the coziness of the fireplace in the lounge where they ate. Steve, almost interrupting the conversation, said, "I was looking at the light as it shone across the table while we were eating, and I thought about the colors of the rainbow. It made me appreciate the condescension of God."

"What do you mean, Steve?" his wife asked.

"Well, according to our discussion, God, in all his fulness, is willing to bestow his light upon us and give it to us in varying degrees.[1] He gives names—from our language—to these separations so that we can begin to understand them. I thought about it like this: If the light of God came down and acted upon me so that I had faith, then the manifestation of light in that instance could be called faith. If it acted on me to be charitable, then the manifestation could be called charity. In those instances, light seems to be given a name based upon what it does or what a person does when he has it. And if I were a German, the name of the manifestation would be something else. So what I am trying to say is, if we compare it to the colors of the rainbow, the name red, for example, is not light at all; it is a name we give to a certain appearance of light. Similarly, charity, in actuality, is not light; it is a word in our language that describes something that light does. So the Lord is willing to attach names from our ordinary language to manifestations of his eternal light, and that seems like a condescension. Am I getting close to an understanding, Frank?"

"Boy, Steve, you must not have eaten much of your lunch if you thought of all that," Joan said.

"I appreciate your thoughts very much, Steve," Frank said. "Following your logic, then, light could do all that it does, even if it had no names at all in our language. I suspect the names that are given to its manifestations are not anywhere near adequate to explain or describe it, but the Lord has permitted the names so that we might come to an understanding."

"Yes," said Steve, "and they just might also be a way of identifying and even measuring our growth. If light moved upon us, and we had no way of identifying or naming the experience, we might not even comprehend what the light is doing to us."

"That sounds like an experience with the Lamanites in the Book of Mormon," Frank said, "where they 'were baptized with fire and with the Holy Ghost, and they knew it not' (3 Nephi 9:20)."

"Then thank goodness for the names," Joan said.

"Speaking of names," Frank said, "look at this scripture:"

2 PETER 1
5 And beside this, giving all diligence, *add* to your **faith virtue**; and to **virtue knowledge**;
6 And to **knowledge temperance**; and to **temperance patience**; and to **patience godliness**;
7 And to **godliness brotherly kindness**; and to **brotherly kindness charity**.
8 For *if these things be in you, and abound, they make you that ye shall neither be barren nor unfruitful in the* **knowledge** *of our Lord Jesus Christ.*

"Here in this scripture, we see names given to the process of progression in discipleship. Now, look at how the Lord says virtually the same thing in a different scripture."

D&C 50
24 That which is of God is **light**; and he that receiveth **light**, and continueth in God, receiveth more **light**; and that **light** groweth **brighter** and **brighter** until the perfect day.

2 NEPHI 31
3 For the Lord God giveth **light** unto the understanding; for he **speaketh** unto men **according to their language**, unto their understanding.

The first scripture is a perfect example of the Lord speaking words to us, 'after the manner of our language,'—faith, virtue, knowledge, temperance, and so forth. The second scripture verifies that all these words are really different names given to various manifestations of the light. The last verse ties the concept of both words and light together. This is another witness that the Lord is not saying different things but is saying the same thing different ways—'add light to your light, and then add more light to your light."

"So," Joan interjected, "if we watched a person move from belief to faith, it would be just as correct to say 'he is receiving light.' And if he moved from faith to repentance, it would be just as correct to say 'he is receiving more light.' Why does the Lord use so many different ways to say things? It might be better if he just said it—straight out."

"Yes, but different people understand in different ways, and the Lord is concerned with reaching everyone. He almost has to speak in as many different ways as possible so as to reach the greatest range of people— both those who are righteous and those who are not. After one particular method of wording in a scripture, the Lord said this:

D&C 19

7 Again, it is written eternal damnation; *wherefore it is more express than other scriptures, that it might work upon the hearts of the children of men*, altogether for my name's glory.

"Steve, I have thought a lot about what you said earlier, that if a manifestation of the light of God acting upon you produced faith, then the light in that instance could be called faith, and so with charity and other attributes. I have wondered if that process might also work in the opposite direction. Have you ever operated a mechanical color wheel?"

"We used to have one in our science lab at school," replied Steve.

"Do you remember how it worked?"

"Yes. A flat wheel with all the colors of the rainbow on its face was attached to a gear box, and by turning a handle, the wheel would spin. When it reached a certain speed, the colors would fade into white."

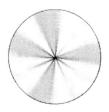

Color wheel
On the left, the wheel is still. On the right, it is
rotating in quick motion.

"You remember our earlier discussion about the prism and the rainbow," Frank said. "The prism separates the light into its component parts, or colors. The mechanical color wheel reverses this process, blending the colors back into their original form of white light.

"In this same likeness, it seems to me that if a person had received light and had acquired in some degree a number of its attributes—faith, charity, love, virtue, knowledge—the Lord could do something in him, like the turning of the color wheel, so that he might experience, if even for a moment, a glimpse of white or pure light, or light in which there is no darkness at all (see 1 John 1:5)."

"Aren't there accounts in the scriptures that tell of people being . . . I think the word is *quickened* by the Lord?" Joan asked.

"That's very perceptive," Frank said. "Yes, there are. Let's study some verses that have that word in them."

PSALM 119
40 Behold, *I have longed after thy* **precepts**: **quicken** *me in thy* **righteousness**.
PSALMS 119
107 I am afflicted very much: **quicken** *me, O Lord, according unto thy* **word**.
PSALMS 119
93 *I will never forget thy* **precepts**: *for with them thou hast* **quickened** *me*.
JOHN 6
63 *It is the* **spirit** *that* **quickeneth**; the flesh profiteth nothing: the words that I speak unto you, they are spirit, and they are life.
D&C 88
11 And the light which shineth, which giveth you light, is through him who enlighteneth your eyes, which is the same **light** *that* **quickeneth** *your understandings*;

D&C 138

29 And as I wondered, *my eyes were opened, and my under-standing* **quickened**, *and I perceived* that the Lord went not in person among the wicked and the disobedient who had rejected the truth, to teach them;

"What do you see here, Steve?"

"Well, it says that if we have in us the precepts of God, we can be quickened either by the spirit, the word, righteousness, or the light of God—which of course we now know all mean the same thing," Steve answered.

"What seems to be the effect of that quickening, Steve?"

"It says that we could see, understand, or perceive."

"The Lord makes reference to this idea when he says a person may receive 'pure knowledge, which shall greatly enlarge the soul' (D&C 121:42), and as the prophet Joseph describes, it is 'feeling pure intelligence flowing into you, [giving you] sudden strokes of ideas' (HC 3:381). Other scriptures refer to it as 'the spirit of prophecy and of revelation.'" (See Jacob 4:6, Jacob 1:6, Alma 9:21, Alma 12:7, and D&C 8:3.)

"Do you have a dictionary handy, Frank?" Steve asked.

"Yes, there is one right here."

Steve turned the pages for a few seconds. Then, finding what he was looking for, he said, "Now I understand that the Lord was saying this very thing in verse 8 of that first scripture we read in 2 Peter."

---

2 PETER 1

5 And beside this, giving all diligence, *add* to your **faith virtue**; and to **virtue knowledge**;

6 And to **knowledge temperance**; and to **temperance patience**; and to **patience godliness**;

7 And to **godliness brotherly kindness**; and to **brotherly kindness charity**.

8 For *if* **these things** *be in you, and* ***abound***, *they make you that ye shall neither be barren nor unfruitful in the* **knowledge** *of our Lord Jesus Christ.*

"He is saying," Steve said, "that if the precepts or attributes of light, which are faith, virtue, knowledge, temperance, and so forth are in us, and *abound*—that is the word I just looked up—and it means to grow,

21

increase, or intensify, and in one sense of the word, to speed up, which is pretty close to 'quicken,' then, we will be fruitful in the knowledge or light of Christ, which of course is the light 'in which there is no darkness at all.'"

If a person has in him some of the attributes of the spirit, just like the various colors of the rainbow, the Lord could quicken him so as to experience, if only briefly, pure light, pure intelligence, or pure knowledge flowing into him.

"There is a remarkable verse that speaks of the experience of being filled with light and even becoming white as a result of it," Frank said.

---

3 NEPHI 19
25 And it came to pass that Jesus blessed them as they did pray unto him; and his **countenance** did smile upon them, and the **light** of his **countenance** did **shine** upon them, and behold they were as **white** as the **countenance** and also the garments of Jesus; and behold the **whiteness** thereof did exceed all the **whiteness**, yea, even there could be nothing upon earth so **white** as the **whiteness** thereof.

"This is all quite wonderful, you know," Joan remarked. "We wanted to know more about light, but we had no idea there was so much to know. The more we delve into this, the more I feel the deep stirrings of power. Of course I always knew there was power there, but I never thought that I would ever begin to have some idea about it. I know it's time to let you get back to your work, but I feel that we could discuss this all day. And by the way, thank you so much for lunch."

"I'm thoroughly overwhelmed with the implications of this information," Steve said. "Thank you for helping us to understand. I'll never see the scriptures the same. Could we please do this again? I know there is so much more."

"I have enjoyed our meeting," Frank said. "Yes, there is so much more. If you would like, I could meet with you for a while on Saturday morning over at the stake center. I have a meeting at eleven thirty, but I could meet with you before that."

"That would be great," Joan said. "Let's say nine o' clock in one of the classrooms. We will have a lot more questions by then."

"Oh, and by the way," Steve said as they were leaving, "I would still like to have a copy of that chart."

Joan elbowed Steve in the ribs and gave him the "look" as the two of them walked down the hall to the front exit.

Notes

1. Elder Packer said, "The First Presidency has written, 'There is a universally diffused essence which is the light and the life of the world, "which lighteth every man that cometh into the world," which proceedeth forth from the presence of God throughout the immensity of space, the light and power of which God bestows in different degrees to "them that ask him," according to their faith and obedience (Boyd K. Packer, "The Light of Christ," *Ensign*, April 2005, 8 9).

CHAPTER 3

Receiving Light

Saturday morning came, and Steve and Joan went to the stake center to meet Frank. They were excited because they had done some homework and were anxious to discuss their findings.

Frank came just a minute or two before nine o' clock, and after warm greetings, they found a classroom to meet in just down the hall from the bishop's office. When they were comfortably seated, Joan said, "I can't wait to tell you what we have found. We've been reading and searching and making lists, and we want to share some of it with you."

"I'm happy for you," Frank said. "What have you got?"

"You remember when we left your office," Joan continued. "I said that I felt a deep stirring of power connected with this study. Well, I went home and began searching the word *light*, and almost the first thing I found was that light is the very power of God."

D&C 88

12 Which **light** proceedeth forth from the presence of God to fill the immensity of space—

13 The **light** which is in all things, *which giveth life to all things*, which is the law by which all things are governed, even *the* **power** *of God* who sitteth upon his throne, who is in the bosom of eternity, who is in the midst of all things.

"Yes!" Steve interjected, "and it also says that light is the power that gives life to everything. And here is another verse that says the same thing in a different way."

D&C 88

50 *I am the true* **light** that is in you, and that you are in me; otherwise ye could not **abound**.

"In other words," Steve continued, "we live because of the power of his light—and incidentally, there is that word *abound* again."

"Those are noteworthy discoveries," Frank said. "Thank you for sharing them with me. What you have said leads right into the concept that I have been thinking about. Look at this scripture:"

D&C 84

46 And the **Spirit** giveth **light** to every man that cometh into the world; and the **Spirit enlighteneth** every man through the world, that hearkeneth to the voice of the **Spirit**.

"If the Lord gives his spirit, or light, to every man that is born, is that enough, or do we need more light than that? And if so, why?"

"We definitely need more light than that," Joan said. "The last part of that verse emphasizes that the Spirit gives light to every man that hearkens to the voice of the Spirit. I found an insight into that in one of the scriptures I looked at this morning."

D&C 50

24 That which is of God is **light**; and he that receiveth **light**, and continueth in God, receiveth more **light**; and that **light** groweth brighter and brighter until the perfect **day**.
25 And again, verily I say unto you, and I say it *that you may know the* **truth***, that you may chase* **darkness** *from among you.*

"We need an increase of light in order to become perfect like God, and also, as the last verse says, so that we can come to know the light and chase darkness away from us."

"Yes," Frank said. "We must chase darkness away from us if we are to have 'light in which there is no darkness at all.'"

"Speaking of that, we found a scripture that shows the distinct contrast between God and Satan," Steve said. "Look at this:"

MOSES 1

13 And it came to pass that Moses looked upon Satan and said: Who art thou? For behold, I am a son of God, in the similitude of his Only Begotten; and where is thy **glory**, that I should worship thee?

14 For behold, I could not look upon God, except his **glory** should come upon me, and I were transfigured before him. But I can look upon thee in the natural man. Is it not so, surely?

15 Blessed be the name of my God, for his **Spirit** hath not altogether withdrawn from me, or else where is thy **glory**, for it is *darkness* unto me? And I can judge between thee and God; for God said unto me: Worship God, for him only shalt thou serve.

"Moses had seen God in all his glory and had to be transfigured in order to even be able to look at him. He was so overcome that he fell down and was without strength. When he had gained some of his strength back, Satan came to him and commanded that he worship him."

"What a reply Moses gave," Steve continued. "He asked Satan where his light was—he could see him with his normal eyes—and saw that he was a being of darkness."

"With that understanding," Joan said, "we could reason that if God is light in which there is no darkness at all, Satan and his plan must lead to darkness in which there is no light at all."

"And that is just what this verse says that I found in John 8:44," Steve said. "Jesus, speaking of the devil, said:"

JOHN 8:44

44 He was a murderer from the beginning, and abode not in the **truth**, because there is no **truth** in him.

"I also found these statements from President Smith and President Kimball," Steve continued.

> Satan has great knowledge and therefore power, but he has *no intelligence, or light of truth, which is the Spirit of Christ*. Because of his knowledge he has influence among the children of men. Without knowledge he would be without power. *If he had intelligence, or the light of truth, which comes only from God, he could not possibly be the adversary of all righteousness.* (Joseph Fielding Smith, *The Way to Perfection: Short Discourses on Gospel Themes* [Salt Lake City: Genealogical Society of Utah, 1931], 231; emphasis added)

In the realms of perdition or the kingdom of darkness, where there is no light, Satan and the unembodied spirits of the pre-existence shall dwell together with those of mortality who retrogress to the level of perdition. These have lost the power of regeneration. They have sunk so low as to have lost the inclinations and ability to repent, consequently the gospel plan is useless to them as an agent of growth and development. (Spencer W. Kimball, *The Miracle of Forgiveness* [Salt Lake City: Bookcraft, 1969], 117; emphasis added)

"It's exhilarating to hear you talk about these things," Frank said. "I appreciate your insights very much."

"To carry on with that same level of thinking," Frank continued, "we know that God is the only source of light, and that he imparts of that light to give us life. Then when we arrive at the age of accountability, he gives us agency to see what we will do with the light that we have. Nephi says that we are then . . ."

---

2 NEPHI 2

27 . . . free to choose **liberty and eternal life**, through the great Mediator of all men, or to choose captivity and death, according to the captivity and power of the devil.

"That is the same choice that Moses had," Joan said.

"Yes," said Frank, "and what would be the consequence if a person did not choose light?"

"The scripture says that he would be in captivity which leads to death," Steve said.

"There is a very special reason why choosing darkness is so devastating to us," Frank said. "Could you please read these verses from section 93, Steve?"

D&C 93

23 *Ye* were also in the beginning with the Father; that which is **Spirit**, even the **Spirit** of **truth**;

32 And every man whose **spirit** receiveth not the **light** is under *condemnation*.

33 For man is **spirit** . . .

"What do we learn here, Steve?"

"Well, it says we were spirits of truth or light in the beginning with the Father. And now, on the earth, if we do not receive light from God, we are rejecting what we really are."

"And what are we, Steve?"

"We are beings of light."

"Here is a scripture that I read this morning that fits right in with what we are talking about," Joan interjected.

D&C 1

33 And he that repents not, from him shall be taken even the **light** which he has received; for my **Spirit** shall not always strive with man, saith the Lord of Hosts.

"That is serious business," Steve said. "To reject light is to reject what we really are. It sure makes you want to stay on the path of light, doesn't it?"

"Now that we understand that God is 'light in which there is no darkness at all,' and that we are beings of light as well, though currently in a very embryonic and mortal state, we need to understand how God has arranged for us to receive and increase in light," Frank said. "Let's look at a few scriptures on that."

D&C 63

64 *Ye receive the* **Spirit** *through prayer.*

D&C 103

36 All **victory** and **glory** is brought to pass unto you through your *diligence, faithfulness, and prayers of faith*

PSALM 119

130 *The entrance of thy* **words** *giveth* **light**; it giveth understanding unto the simple.

ALMA 5

7 *Their souls were illuminated by the* **light** *of the everlasting* **word**.

ALMA 17

2 Now these sons of Mosiah . . . *had searched the scriptures diligently,* that they might know the word of God.

3 But this is not all; they had given themselves to much prayer, and fasting; *therefore they had the* **spirit** *of prophecy, and the* **spirit** *of revelation, and when they taught, they taught with* **power** *and authority of God.*

D&C 68

4 And *whatsoever they shall speak when moved upon by the*

Holy Ghost shall be scripture, shall be the will of the Lord, shall be the mind of the Lord, shall be the **word** of the Lord, shall be the voice of the Lord, and the **power** of God unto salvation.

"Steve, what can you see in these scriptures, as avenues for receiving light?"

"I'll just make a little list here, Frank," Steve said.

- Prayer
- Diligence, faithfulness, and prayers of faith
- Searching the scriptures
- Hearing the word of God through his servants
- Fasting
- Being moved upon by the Holy Ghost

"What is the difference between 'prayer' and a 'prayer of faith'?" Joan asked.

"I think it is a matter of sincerity and what we really intend to do with the answer," Frank replied. "It's called real intent in a number of places in the scriptures." (See 2 Nephi 31:3, Moroni 6:8, 7:6, 9, 10:4.)

"I guess I need to work on my prayers," Joan said, "but I certainly have found wonderful enlightenment in reading the scriptures these last few days. I am convinced more than ever that light comes to us through the words of the Lord."

"I am too," Frank said. "One of the most graphic representations of that principle is found in Facsimile Number Two in the book of Abraham. Why don't we turn there for a few minutes and have a look at it. It's found on page thirty-six."

There was a short rustling of pages as they found what they were looking for.

Facsimile No. 2 from the book of Abraham

"This document and others like it were used by ancient prophets and others to demonstrate the idea of the transmission of light from God to man," Frank said. (See Hugh Nibley, "One Eternal Round," FARMS Tape series, Tape 11, September 26, 1990.)

"I have looked at these facsimiles and have never been able to make heads or tails out of them," Steve said. "What do you mean 'a transmission of light'?"

"And why is it round?" Joan interjected.

"Those are both good questions," Frank replied. "The document has to be round, precisely because it represents a transmission of light."

"I don't understand," Joan said.

"Well, what is round and transmits light?" Frank asked.

"Oh, I see, the sun," Joan replied. "Is that what Facsimile Number Two represents—the sun?"

"It represents the sun and more," Frank said. "Many of these documents were even painted yellow. Do you remember the scripture we studied earlier that spoke of the light of Christ? It said that 'he is in the sun and the light of the sun and the power thereof by which it was made.' It also said that the light that lights the sun is the same light that lights our understanding. In other words, the light of the Savior which is the source of the sun's light can, under certain conditions, be made manifest to the understanding of man. The principle of these things is actually shown on the facsimile itself. First of all, look again at the document. You've said that it is the sun, but what else does it look like?"

"I can't tell," Joan said.

"Look into your husband's eyes, and then look back at the document."

"It looks like the pupil of his eye!" Joan exclaimed.

"That's exactly what it is," Frank said. "Why do you think that the sun would have an eye superimposed over it?"

"I'm not sure," Steve replied.

"Let's look at figure number seven on the facsimile and see if it can help to answer the question."

There was a pause while Steve and Joan searched the document.

"Here it is," Joan said. "It's upside down and on the top left side. It has a bird figure in it."

Facsimile No. 2 from the book of Abraham
(upside down)

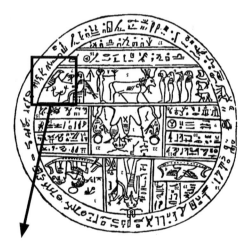

Fig. 7. The sign of the Holy Ghost unto Abraham, in the form of a dove

"There's an explanation of that bird figure (Figure Seven) over on the opposite page of your scriptures, Joan. Could you please find that and read it for us?"

Joan read for a moment and then said, "It's the Holy Ghost in the form of a dove."

"Thank you, Joan. Now, notice that the dove is holding something with out-stretched arms. Can you tell what it is, Steve?"

"It has to be symbolic because a dove has wings, not arms," Steve replied. "I can't tell what he is holding."

"I think it's an eye," Joan said. "An Egyptian eye. I saw one something like that on a chart our son brought home from school."

"It is an eye," said Frank. "Why do you think the Holy Ghost would be represented as holding out an eye?"

"Well, the Holy Ghost shows you things," Joan said. "And when we talked about the prism, which we compared to the Holy Ghost, we said that it was like the lens or pupil of an eye. Sort of like he gives you an eye to look through to make the things of God understandable."

"Now I get it," Steve said. "The incomprehensible light coming from God, which is represented by the sun in the facsimile, must be viewed through the eye of the Holy Ghost in order for it to be made understandable."

"Yes," Frank said. "And then we must consider the writing on the surface. The words written there are a manifestation of that incomprehensible light behind them. One author said that the ink with which these types of documents were written was made from the soot of pure olive-oil lamps burned for light—a further representation of the transmission of light through the word." (See Dee Jay Nelson and David H. Coville, *Life Force in the Great Pyramids* [Marina del Ray: DeVorss & Company, 1977], 1. See also Exodus 27:20; 25:6; 39:37; Numbers 4:16.)

"Not everyone gets a chance to see into the glory of God," Frank continued. "So it is a blessing when the knowledge gained by those who do is written for the benefit of others. The Prophet Joseph Smith said it like this:"

D&C 76

12 By the power of the **Spirit** our eyes were opened and our understandings were enlightened, so as to see and understand the things of God—

28 And while we were yet in the **Spirit**, the Lord commanded us that we should *write* the vision.

"There is just one problem," Joan continued. "The words on our facsimile are still not understandable to me—they're Egyptian!"

Everyone laughed.

"That was not a problem for Abraham, but it's a continuing problem for us," Frank said. "Thank goodness for the Prophet Joseph Smith for giving us the most important information."

"But even though the words are Egyptian, you have helped me appreciate that the light of God can be transmitted to us through the word," Joan said. "Having that idea in my mind will certainly help me in my scripture study."

The background disk of our Facsimile No. 2 (sometimes painted yellow in similar representations) represents the pure light of God. The drawings and writings upon the disk by their shape and content represent the "eye" of the Holy Ghost transforming the light behind it into the word. The intent of all this seems to signify that when a person reads the words by the Holy Ghost, the words carries the meaning of the pure light of God into the mind.

"There is another thing that we must consider if we are to understand the principle of receiving light," Frank said. "Let's read together these next verses from section 93. They tell us about the Savior as he came into mortality. Joan, would you please start with verse 12?"

D&C 93

12 And I, John, saw that *he received not of the* **fulness** *at the first, but received* **grace** *for* **grace**.

"What is this talking about, Steve?"

"It says that the Savior did not have a fulness of light at the first of his earth life but obtained it little by little."[1]

"That's right, but notice the wording. It says: he received light for light. What can that mean, Joan?"

"I'm sorry; I just read the sentence and didn't realize how significant the wording was. It must mean that he received light, and for what he did with that light, he received more light."

"Why is that significant?" Frank asked.

"Because he had to be faithful to the light he received in order to receive more," Joan answered.

"That is true. Now, let's read the next verse."

D&C 93

13 And *he received not of the* **fulness** *at first, but continued from* **grace** *to* **grace**, *until he received a* **fulness**.

"What is the difference between light for light and light to light, Steve?" asked Frank.

"Well, it must mean that he received light and then was faithful and received more, and then he continued the process. He didn't stop. He kept doing it over and over until he had the fulness."

"That's very insightful, Steve," Frank said. "Just the way you said that reminded me of the statement of the Savior in John 8:31."

JOHN 8:31

If ye *continue* in my **word**, *then* are ye my disciples indeed.

"It puts a lot of responsibility on us, doesn't it?" Joan said.

"It does," said Frank. "The next couple of verses speak of the baptism of the Savior and tell us that the Holy Ghost came down upon him. And when it did, something wonderful happened. Could you please read verses 15 through 17?"

D&C 93

15 *The heavens were opened, and the Holy Ghost descended upon him in the form of a dove, and sat upon him,* and there came a voice out of heaven saying: This is my beloved Son.

16 And I, John, bear record that *he received a* **fulness** of the **glory** of the Father;

17 And *he received all* **power**, *both in heaven and on earth, and the* **glory** *of the Father was with him, for he dwelt in him.*

"This is awesome! It is just what we've been studying about," Joan said. "The Holy Ghost came upon him in the form of a dove and gave to him the fulness of the light of the Father. Or if we used the idea in Figure Seven of Facsimile Number Two, the Holy Ghost gave him the whole eye to comprehend the fulness of God."

"Thank you, Joan," said Frank. "The Holy Ghost can only give to mortal men on the earth a very small portion of that eye, but he gave the fulness to the Son of God. That is just what section 84 verse 45 confirms."

D&C 84

45 For the **word** of the **Lord** is **truth**, and whatsoever is **truth** is **light**, and whatsoever is **light** is **Spirit**, even the **Spirit** of **Jesus Christ**

"It tells us that the word, the truth, the light, and the spirit of the Lord—this is speaking of the Father—became 'even' (exactly) the word, the truth, the light, and the spirit of the Son. Now, the next two verses have to do specifically with us. Will you please read them, Steve?"

D&C 93

19 *I give unto you these sayings* that you may understand and know how to worship, and know what you worship, *that you may come unto the Father in my name, and in due time receive of his* **fulness**.
20 *For if you keep my* **commandments** *you shall receive of his* **fulness**, *and be* **glorified** *in me as I am in the Father; therefore, I say unto you, you shall receive* **grace** *for* **grace**.

"What insights do you get from this?" Frank asked Steve.

"We have the promise that if we are faithful, in due time we can receive the same fulness that Christ received, but we have to do it grace for grace and continue in it, the same as he did."

"What will we have when we have the same fulness that Christ has, Joan?" asked Frank.

"I think that our word, our truth, our light, and our spirit will be exactly the word, the truth, the light, and the spirit of Jesus Christ and his Father."

"I like how you've put that together. Thank you so much for your insights. To summarize this area, then," Frank said, "could you share what you have written on your list as avenues for receiving light, Steve?"

Steve held up his list:

- Prayer
- Fasting
- Diligence, faithfulness, and prayers of faith
- Being moved upon by the Holy Ghost
- Searching the scriptures
- Being true to the light we already have and living worthy of more
- Hearing the word of God through his servants

"That is a very important list, and I think we are all more aware now of what is in store if we are true to the light," Frank said.

"I know I am," Steve replied as they gathered up their papers and prepared to leave. "I can't begin to tell you what it has meant that you would share your knowledge with us. We really appreciate it."

"It makes me want to hurry home and keep studying," Joan said, "and you can be sure that we will keep our eyes and hearts open for inspiration. Thank you so much."

"You are both welcome. It's been a pleasure. Let me know how your study goes."

"We will," Steve said, "and by the way, you know that I would love to have copies of your material."

"Steve!" Joan exclaimed. "It's up to us to do our own work."

"Maybe someday I'll publish a book," Frank said as he smiled and shook their hands.

"I have one more question before we leave," Steve said. "There must be many things about light that we don't understand, but one thing that interests me is the effect that it has on us when it comes into us. Do you have any insights or scriptures about that?"

"There are many," Frank replied, "but if you were to read Alma chapter 32, from about verse 28 to the end, remembering that the 'word' is light, I think you would see some very interesting things, especially in light of what we have already talked about."

"No pun intended," Joan quipped. "By the way, could we invite you and your wife to dinner on Friday night? We would love to have you."

"That sounds great!" Frank replied. "I'll talk to Karen and see if we are free and then call you."

"Thanks again," Steve said as they walked down the hall toward the exit.

Notes

1. Notice that we have substituted the word *light* for *grace*. In this substitution and in all others in this work where we substitute the word *light*, some may think we are reducing the rich and poignant meanings of scriptural words to the more mundane concept of scriptural light. We are not suggesting that the original word meanings be forsaken; we are simply showing that these words can be understood as manifestations of light. Is light mundane? Does the act of pointing out that words of scripture that are representations of various functions of eternal light lessen their meaning? Light is the very essence of God himself. It is the unfathomable power by which suns and galaxies are made. We are not simply playing word games. We are suggesting when we make such substitutions that we are then enabled to appreciate more the meaning behind the original scriptural words—to show that the words have reference to the actual light of God in fervent action—the life-giving particles of pure matter emanating from God upon his children, motivating them to do the works of righteousness among themselves, and transforming their persons into the image of Christ in the same manner and to the same extent that it transformed him into the image of his Father. We have such a tendency to read scriptural words with a yawn—without attaching a great deal of meaning to them. This present work, if nothing else, should help us to focus on the fact that the words of God are alive and have behind them all the force and power of heaven.

D&C 33:1

1 Behold, I say unto you, my servants Ezra and Northrop, open ye your ears and hearken to the voice of the Lord your God, whose word is quick and powerful, sharper than a two-edged sword, to the dividing asunder of the joints and marrow, soul and spirit; and is a discerner of the thoughts and intents of the heart.

A poignant reminder, is it not, that while we are so often passively reading the word of God, it is actively reading us! (A fact of which Facsimile No. 2—the "eye" of God looking out upon us from the pages of scripture—should keep us continually aware.)

One might say that the gospel should not be reduced to just one word as we have done when we substitute the word *light* for so many other words. But reconsider. What is the gospel? It is everything that comes from God reduced to just one word. Jesus often expressed his fulness in just one word: "I am the same that leadeth men to all good" (Ether 4:12). "Behold, I am the Law" (3 Nephi 15:9). We are only doing what God himself has done when we substitute the word *light* for many other words. He said, "That which is of God is light" (D&C 50:24). In other words, it is acceptable to call every single thing that comes from him "light," even every single word. If we then say that grace or charity is light, is that a reduction? Look at the understanding that comes to charity if we were to say, that which is of God is charity, or to grace if we were to say that which is of God is grace. Yet that understanding is true. And could we not say the same thing of faith, hope, and wisdom, and if we were to say further that these words may be interchanged with light, would that not also be acceptable inasmuch as they are all light—all attributes of one great light?

The Effect of Light in Us

Joan and Steve returned to their normal, everyday lives, yet somehow they were both different. They were much more aware of the wonder of the gospel and the presence of the spirit, especially when they read the scriptures. They were also more aware of situations where that spirit or light was dim or absent. It gave them great determination to learn more and to stay in the light. Their new understanding continued to motivate them, and while they wanted to shout it to the whole world, it seemed sacred and almost beyond words.

They continued their studies in the scriptures, often sharing with each other some new insight or enlightenment. Their family scripture study was more important than ever because of the slower pace of reading and how insightful it was to ponder while someone else read. They always kept a notebook handy.

One evening, after the children were in bed, they were sitting in the study and Steve said, "When we last met with Frank, we talked about some of the avenues for receiving light. Do you remember the list that I made as we read those verses?"

"Yes, Steve, I do," Joan said, "though I can't remember all the things that were on it."

"Well, I have been really trying to do those things, as I know you have, and it's very fulfilling, but I need to work harder. Also, I've been thinking that we haven't read the chapter that Frank suggested to us, and I really want to concentrate on what to look for as the spirit works in us. It was Alma 32, verse 28 to the end. He asked that we remember as we read that the word is light. Have you got time to read that with me?"

"Yes," Joan said, "but before we do, I have had an experience that I would like to share with you. I was sitting by a sister in Relief Society on Sunday, and we shared a scripture. We read it, and then as we re-read it, I substituted the word *light* for *good*—it seemed the most natural thing in the world for me to do. She asked me why I did that. I explained that many of the words in the scriptures are interchangeable and that while we could use any number of substituted words, the word *light* is probably the one that we can visualize the best. It's pretty hard to visualize truth or spirit or good, but we can visualize light. I'm not sure I explained it very well, and I am not sure she understood what I was talking about."

"What scripture were you reading?" Steve asked

"Here, I'll show you."

ETHER 4

12 And whatsoever thing persuadeth men to do **good** is of me; for **good** cometh of none save it be of me. I am the same that leadeth men to all **good**; he that will not believe my words will not believe me—that I am; and he that will not believe me will not believe the Father who sent me. For behold, I am the Father, I am the **light**, and the life, and the truth of the world.

"It sure seems plain to me," Steve said. "I enjoy how you study and the things you share with me. Thanks, Joan. I had an interesting experience also. I attended priesthood meeting and went to the High Priest group. The instructor was quoting from some source he had found, and I wrote down two of the quotes he gave. Here is what they said."

> 1. The glory of God is intelligence; and when that intelligence is felt in any compartment of creation, there is an application of truth and law which may *figuratively* be called light.
> 2. Truth is *closely associated* with light or the Spirit in a number of scriptures, for example, D&C 84:45.

"I groaned when I heard the words *figuratively* and *closely associated,*" Steve said. "I knew that whoever wrote those things didn't really understand the scriptures . . . A week ago I didn't either. I didn't say a word."

"I guess we can be thankful for what we know and not try to impose our way of seeing things on others," Joan said. "Frank told us there are many ways of seeing the scriptures. Let's see what Alma has to say."

Steve opened the scriptures, read the verses out loud to Joan and then said, "Let's go back now and highlight every word in these verses that can be interchanged with light and then read the verses as if light was the original word, and see what we can learn."

(Note: On the left below are the verses in their original form with words highlighted that can be interchanged with the word light. On the right are the same verses with the highlighted words actually changed to the word light so that the meanings can be compared. This pattern will occur a number of times throughout this work.)

ALMA 32

28 Now, we will compare the **word** unto a seed. Now, if ye give place, that a **seed** may be planted in your heart, behold, if it be a true **seed**, or a good **seed**, if ye do not cast it out by your unbelief, that ye will resist the **Spirit** of the Lord, behold, it will begin to swell within your breasts; and when you feel these swelling motions, ye will begin to say within yourselves—It must needs be that this is a good **seed**, or that the **word** is good, for it beginneth to enlarge my soul; yea, it beginneth to enlighten my understanding, yea, it beginneth to be delicious to me.

31 And now, behold, are ye sure that this is a good **seed**? I say unto you, Yea; for every **seed** bringeth forth unto its own likeness.

34 . . . ye also know that it hath sprouted up, that your under-standing doth begin to be **enlightened**, and your mind doth begin to expand.

35 O then, is not this real? I say

ALMA 32

28 Now, we will compare the **light** unto a seed. Now, if ye give place, that a **light** may be planted in your heart, behold, if it be a true **light**, or a good **light**, if ye do not cast it out by your unbelief, that ye will resist the **light** of the Lord, behold, it will begin to swell within your breasts; and when you feel these swelling motions, ye will begin to say within yourselves—It must needs be that this is a good **light**, or that the **light** is good, for it beginneth to enlarge my soul; yea, it beginneth to enlighten my understanding, yea, it beginneth to be delicious to me.

31 And now, behold, are ye sure that this is a good **light**? I say unto you, Yea; for every **light** bringeth forth unto its own likeness.

34 . . . ye also know that it hath sprouted up, that your under-standing doth begin to be **enlightened**, and your mind doth begin to expand.

35 O then, is not this real? I say

unto you, Yea, because it is **light**; and whatsoever is **light**, is good, because it is discernible, therefore ye must know that it is good; . . . 37 And behold, as the **tree** beginneth to grow, ye will say: Let us nourish it with great care, that it may get root, that it may grow up, and bring forth **fruit** unto us. And now behold, if ye nourish it with much care it will get root, and grow up, and bring forth **fruit**. 38 But if ye neglect the **tree**, and take no thought for its nourishment, behold it will not get any root; and when the heat of the sun cometh and scorcheth it, because it hath no root it withers away, and ye pluck it up and cast it out. 39 Now, this is not because the **seed** was not good, neither is it because the **fruit** thereof would not be desirable; but it is because your ground is barren, and ye will not nourish the **tree**, therefore ye cannot have the **fruit** thereof. 40 And thus, if ye will not nourish the **word**, looking forward with an eye of faith to the **fruit** thereof, ye can never pluck of the **fruit** of the tree of **life**. 41 But if ye will nourish the **word**, yea, nourish the **tree** as it beginneth to grow, by your faith with great diligence, and with patience, looking forward to the **fruit** thereof, it shall take root; and behold it shall be a **tree** springing up unto everlasting **life**. 42 And because of your diligence and your faith and your patience with the **word** in nourishing it, that it may take root in you, behold, by and by ye shall pluck the **fruit** thereof, which is most

unto you, Yea, because it is **light**; and whatsoever is **light**, is good, because it is discernible, therefore ye must know that it is good; . . . 37 And behold, as the **light** beginneth to grow, ye will say: Let us nourish it with great care, that it may get root, that it may grow up, and bring forth **light** unto us. And now behold, if ye nourish it with much care it will get root, and grow up, and bring forth **light**. 38 But if ye neglect the **light**, and take no thought for its nourishment, behold it will not get any root; and when the heat of the sun cometh and scorcheth it, because it hath no root it withers away, and ye pluck it up and cast it out. 39 Now, this is not because the **light** was not good, neither is it because the **light** thereof would not be desirable; but it is because your ground is barren, and ye will not nourish the **light**, therefore ye cannot have the **light** thereof. 40 And thus, if ye will not nourish the **light**, looking forward with an eye of faith to the **light** thereof, ye can never pluck of the **light** of the tree of **light**. 41 But if ye will nourish the **light**, yea, nourish the **light** as it beginneth to grow, by your faith with great diligence, and with patience, looking forward to the **light** thereof, it shall take root; and behold it shall be a **light** springing up unto everlasting **light**. 42 And because of your diligence and your faith and your patience with the **light** in nourishing it, that it may take root in you, behold, by and by ye shall pluck the **light** thereof, which is most precious, which is sweet above all that is sweet, and which is white above all that is white, yea, and pure above all that is pure; and ye shall feast upon this **fruit** even until ye are filled, that ye hunger not, neither shall ye thirst.

43 Then, my brethren, ye shall reap the rewards of your faith, and your diligence, and patience, and long-suffering, waiting for the **tree** to bring forth **fruit** unto you.

precious, which is sweet above all that is sweet, and which is white above all that is white, yea, and pure above all that is pure; and ye shall feast upon this **light** even until ye are filled, that ye hunger not, neither shall ye thirst.

43 Then, my brethren, ye shall reap the rewards of your faith, and your diligence, and patience, and long-suffering, waiting for the **light** to bring forth **light** unto you.

As they read the highlighted words, they began to discover the wonder of the message behind the words—a marvelous underlying language in the scriptures. They could quickly see the principle that they had learned earlier in D&C 50:24—that light grows in us and becomes brighter and brighter if we are faithful, until it reaches the perfect light, which is of course the light in which there is no darkness at all.

They also found some answers to Steve's question about the effects of light as it works in us. They made a list:

1. Light enlarges the soul and enlightens the understanding, and begins to be delicious.
2. It is discernible.
3. If we nourish the light with light, it will bring forth more light.
4. Light brings forth unto its own likeness—springing up unto everlasting light.
5. Light is most precious and sweet above all that is sweet, white above all that is white, and pure above all that is pure; we can feast upon this light even until we are filled, that we hunger not, neither shall we thirst.
6. We can have the reward of our faith, diligence, patience, and long-suffering, waiting for the light to bring forth light unto us.

Through one of the cross-references, they found their way to Alma 19:6. This is an account of the conversion of the Lamanite king, Lamoni, who had never experienced the workings of the power of God in his life. As they read and highlighted this verse, they were amazed at the understanding:

ALMA 19
6 Ammon . . . knew that king Lamoni was under the **power** of God; he knew that the *dark veil of unbelief* was being cast away from his mind, and the **light** which did **light** up his mind, which was the **light** of the **glory** of God, which was a marvelous **light** of his **goodness**—yea, this **light** had infused such **joy** into his soul, the **cloud of *darkness*** having been dispelled, and that the **light** of **everlasting life** was **lit** up in his soul, yea, he knew that this had overcome his natural frame, and he was carried away in God.

"This has to be one of the most powerful descriptions of the effect of light upon the human soul in all scripture," Steve said. "The 'light of God,' it says, 'infuses light into the soul, and there lights up the light of everlasting light.'"

"It strikes me as interesting," Joan said, "that the dispelling of the cloud of darkness by the light was exactly what happened to Joseph Smith in the sacred grove. His account says: 'It [the light] no sooner appeared than I found myself delivered from the enemy which held me bound' (JSH–1:17)."

"That is a great correlation," Steve said. "One of the things that impresses me is that the light that was infused into the king's soul, and which lit up eternal light there, is called joy. This adds meaning to the verse we know so well in 2 Nephi."

2 NEPHI 2	**2 NEPHI 2**
25 Adam fell that **men** might be; and **men** are, that they might have **joy**.	25 Adam fell that **lights** might be; and **lights** are, that they might have **light**.

Joan contemplated for a moment and then said, "I am continually amazed where this study leads, Steve. For a moment, I was taken aback when you wrote: 'Adam fell that lights might be,' but then I remembered the study we did earlier, that 'man is spirit' (D&C 93:33, see above). You were one step ahead of me. So Adam fell that spirits or lights might come to earth, and they have come here that they might have more light."

"Just think of some of the scriptures that speak of joy," Steve said, "and when you realize that they are speaking of light, it becomes very insightful." (See 1 Nephi 8:12; Mosiah 4:3; Alma 33:23; 36:20; 36:24, Helaman 5:44, 3 Nephi 17:17; 28:10, D&C 11:13; 18:16.)

"Speaking of lights coming to earth for the purpose of gaining more light," Steve continued. "I remember in one of our priesthood manuals a quote by the Prophet Joseph Smith about enlargement. I'm not sure where the manual is, but I'll get on the computer and open up our scripture program and see if I can find the quote."

While Steve booted up the computer, Joan added a number of words to the chart that she was making—similar to the one Frank had made. Every word was like a revelation.

"I've found the quote," Steve said after a few minutes. "It is in *Teachings of the Prophet Joseph Smith.*"

> *Intelligence* is eternal and exists upon a self-existent principle. It is a *spirit* from age to age, and there is no creation about it. All the *minds and spirits* that God ever sent into the world are susceptible of *enlargement.* (Joseph F. Smith, *Teachings of the Prophet Joseph Smith,* [Salt Lake City: Deseret Book, 1938], 354; emphasis added)

"That is so powerful, Steve. I found two scriptures the other day that relate to this," Joan said. "One calls God the Father of lights (plural), and the other calls his children the children of light."

D&C 67
9 That which is **righteous** cometh down from above, from the *Father of* **lights**.
John 12
36 While ye have **light**, believe in the **light**, that ye may be the *children of* **light**. These things spake Jesus.

"It's almost overwhelming, isn't it?" Steve said. "Look at these two verses I marked yesterday without realizing their significance:

---

2 Corinthians 3
18 But we all, with open face beholding as in a glass the **glory** of the Lord, are changed into the same **image** from **glory** to **glory**, even as by the **Spirit** of the Lord.

> **Alma 5**
> 14 And now behold, I ask of you, my brethren of the church, have ye **spiritually** been born of God? Have ye received his **image** in your **countenances**?

"We are being asked in these scriptures if we are engaged in adding the light of God to our light. 'Have ye received his light in your light?' That seems to be the whole purpose of our lives here."

"I am convinced of that!" Joan said.

"Repentance requires significant changes," Steve said, "and of course the stages could go in either direction depending on one's faithfulness—toward the light or toward the darkness. The Book of Mormon certainly demonstrates that. It really makes me want to hold onto the light."

After a few moments of thought and contemplation, Joan said, "We have been talking about the effect of light in us, Steve, and I just found this scripture in the Topical Guide."

> **D&C 88**
> 67 And if your **eye** be *single* to my **glory**, your whole bodies shall be filled with **light**, and there shall be *no **darkness** in you*; and that body which is filled with **light** comprehendeth all things.

"It seems to say that if the light that is in us is in accord with the light that is in God, our bodies will be filled with light. I don't really understand that, Steve, do you?"

"No, I don't, but let's continue and look up some of the other key words on the computer and see what we can find. Let's type in the words *glory* and *body*."

They waited for the computer to search these words, and then Joan said, "It looks like there are seven references that have those two key words. Let's choose D&C 88:27–32."

> **D&C 88**
> 27 For notwithstanding they die, they also shall rise again, a **spiritual** body.
> 28 They who are of a celestial **spirit** shall receive the same body which was a natural body; even ye shall receive your bodies, and your **glory** shall be that **glory** by which your bodies are **quickened**.

29 Ye who are **quickened** by a portion of the celestial **glory** shall then receive of the same, even a **fulness**.
30 And they who are **quickened** by a portion of the terrestrial **glory** shall then receive of the same, even a **fulness**.
31 And also they who are **quickened** by a portion of the telestial **glory** shall then receive of the same, even a **fulness**.
32 And they who remain shall also be **quickened**; nevertheless, they shall return again to their own place, to enjoy that which they are willing to receive, because they were not willing to enjoy that which they might have received.

"Let's look at the first verse:

27 For notwithstanding they die, they also shall rise again, a **spiritual** body.

"What do you think this is saying, Joan?"

"It seems to be saying that even though we die, we will rise again with a 'light' body, or I assume, a body of light."

"That sounds interesting but I don't know what it means. Let's go to the next verse."

28 They who are of a celestial **spirit** shall receive the same body which was a natural body; even ye shall receive your bodies, and your **glory** shall be that **glory** by which your bodies are **quickened**.

"Who do you think it's referring to when it says '*they* who have a celestial light'?"

"It must mean those who have that light here on the earth," Joan replied, "because it says they will receive their bodies back. That won't happen until after they die."

"So those who follow the celestial light while they are on the earth will get their bodies back; and then it says that their light shall be the light that their bodies are quickened or lighted with. There is a footnote that says to see Ephesians 5:14."

EPHESIANS 5
14 Wherefore he saith, Awake thou that sleepest, and arise from the dead, and Christ shall give thee **light**.

"Speaking of being lighted in the resurrection, it uses that word *quicken* again," Joan said. "As we saw earlier, it means to expand and get things in motion."

"It also must mean to 'fill up,'" Steve said, "because D&C 88:67, the scripture that we just read, says: 'your whole body shall be filled with light.'"

"How do you fill up a body with light?"

"I don't know," Steve said. "Let's read on."

---

29 Ye who are **quickened** by a portion of the celestial **glory** shall then receive of the same, even a **fulness**.

"This is interesting," Joan said. "It says that those who are quickened, put in motion, motivated, or filled by a relatively small amount of celestial light here on earth will then have a fulness of that same light in the resurrection. That suggests to me that if we are in accord with his light now, we will receive a fulness of that same light then."

---

30 And they who are **quickened** by a portion of the terrestrial **glory** shall then receive of the same, even a **fulness**.

"This is very intriguing," Steve said. "Those who follow a lesser light while they are here on the earth will then be filled with a fulness of that same lesser light there."

ALMA 34
34 That same **spirit** which doth possess your bodies at the time that ye go out of this life, that same **spirit** will have power to possess your body in that eternal world.

"It says the same thing for the telestial light as well," Joan said.

---

31 And also they who are quickened by a portion of the telestial **glory** shall then receive of the same, even a **fulness**.

"This must be something like a wattage system," Steve said. "The celestial like a hundred watts, the terrestrial like sixty watts, and the telestial like thirty."

MARK 4

8 And other (**seeds**) fell on good ground, and did yield **fruit** that sprang up and increased; and brought forth, some **thirty**, and some **sixty**, and some an **hundred**.

"That's a good way to look at it, Steve," Joan said. "The hundred watts could be compared to the light in which there is no darkness at all. A state of darkness in which there is little or no light seems to be represented in the next verse:"

32 And they who remain shall also be quickened; nevertheless, they shall return again to their own place, to enjoy that which they are willing to receive, because they were not willing to enjoy that which they might have received.

"It sounds like they are quickened but with some force below any of the degrees of light previously spoken of."

"Now the question remains, how is a body filled with light in the resurrection?" Steve said.

"Maybe you could look that up in the computer program as well," Joan said.

"Okay, I will look up *resurrection* and *light*, or *spirit*," Steve said.

The computer churned for a few minutes and then Steve said, "Wow! Look at this statement by the Prophet Joseph Smith."

As concerning the resurrection . . . all will be raised by the power of God, having *spirit* in their bodies, and not *blood*.
(HC 4:555–6; emphasis added)

"Here are two more:"

Flesh and blood cannot inherit the kingdom of God, or the kingdom that God inherits or inhabits, but the flesh without the blood, and the *Spirit* of God flowing in the veins instead of the blood. (Kent P. Jackson, comp. and ed., *Joseph Smith's Commentary on the Bible* [Salt Lake City: Deseret Book, 1994], 170–1; emphasis added)

God Almighty himself dwells in *eternal fire*. Flesh and blood cannot go there, for all corruption is devoured by the fire. Our God is a consuming *fire*. When our flesh is *quickened* by the *Spirit*, there will be no blood in the tabernacles. Some dwell in higher *glory* than others . . . . Immortality dwells in everlasting *burnings* . . . . All men who are immortal dwell in everlasting *burnings*. (Kent P. Jackson, comp. and ed., *Joseph Smith's Commentary on the Bible* [Salt Lake City: Deseret Book, 1994], 51; emphasis added

"So, a resurrected body is filled with light in the same manner that a mortal body is filled with blood," Steve said. "Light fills the veins and arteries! I had no idea."

"Neither did I! What would a person look like if he were filled with light?" Joan asked.

"Well, now that you mention it, I can think of a couple of examples," Steve said. "The prophet Joseph in describing the Angel Moroni, said:

JS–HISTORY 1
32 Not only was his robe exceedingly white, but his whole person was **glorious** beyond description, and his **countenance** truly like **lightning**. The room was exceedingly **light**, but not so very bright as immediately around his person.

"He also described the Father and the Son, and Nephi described the Son descending out of heaven:"

JS–HISTORY 1
17 When the **light** rested upon me I saw two Personages, whose **brightness** and **glory** defy all description, standing above me in the air.
1 NEPHI 1
9 And it came to pass that he saw One descending out of the midst of heaven, and he beheld that his **luster** was above that of the **sun** at noon-day.

"Will we actually look like that someday, Steve?"

"I think that's what it's all about, Joan. Only in that state will we have all power and be able to comprehend all things."

MATTHEW 13
43 Then shall the righteous **shine** forth as the **sun** in the kingdom of their Father. Who hath ears to hear, let him hear.

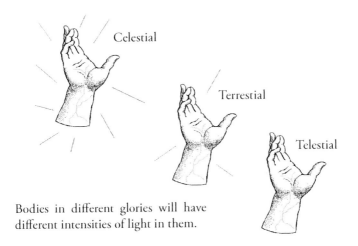

Celestial

Terrestial

Telestial

Bodies in different glories will have different intensities of light in them.

"Well, Steve, this has been quite a night. I never dreamed that there would be so much information under the surface in the scriptures. Our simple question to Frank was to ask him about the scriptural meaning of light. When you think of what we knew then, and what we are understanding now, it's nothing short of a miracle."

"It is, Joan. I feel that we have been greatly blessed, and I feel very humble before the Lord. I hope I can live up to the things that we have learned."

Steve and Joan retired, feeling a peaceful sense of love and a connection with each other and with God. The feelings while saying their prayers together were beyond what either had ever experienced before. They knew that the Spirit of the Lord was acting upon them, and they were willing to respond.

The next day, after the children were off to school, Joan was again studying her scriptures. She was thinking back over all the concepts she had learned. One thing that began to weigh heavily on her mind was the consequences a person would suffer if he rejected the light of God. She remembered Frank speaking of spiritual death and how that had shocked him. It would be a death to all the attributes of the light. She was trying to make a chart something like his, and she knew that Steve was happy she was doing it, because he seemed to want a copy so bad.

She decided to look up a few scriptures dealing with the idea of rejecting light. Her searching lead her to D&C 93:

D&C 93	D&C 93
31 Behold, here is the agency of **man**, and here is the condemnation of **man**; because that which was from the beginning is plainly manifest unto them, and **they** receive not the **light**. 32 And every **man** whose **spirit** receiveth not the **light** is under condemnation.	31 Behold, here is the agency of **light**, and here is the condemnation of **light**; because that which was from the beginning is plainly manifest unto them, and **lights** receive not the **light**. 32 And every **light** whose **light** receiveth not the **light** is under condemnation.

"Man is light," she said to herself, "and the agency of light, and the condemnation of light is that it can resist or reject more light, and if it does, it is condemned."

Hmmm . . . I wonder what the condemmation is, she thought.

She continued searching.

D&C 1

33 And he that repents not, from him shall be taken *even* the **light** which he has received; for my **Spirit** shall not always strive with **man**, saith the Lord of Hosts.

D&C 82

3 For of him unto whom much is given much is required; and he who sins against the greater **light** shall receive the greater *condemnation*.

JOHN 3

19 And this is the *condemnation*, that **light** is come into the world, and **men** loved **darkness** rather than **light**, because their deeds were evil.

"Here are the answers," she said. "A man (who is light) who does not repent shall have taken from him the light he has received. There's that word *even* again—I remember it meant 'exactly' or the 'exact amount.' So this is saying that he will have all the light that he has ever received taken away. And he that has had the greater light will have the greater darkness. This must be the darkness in which there is little or no light at all. How awful that would be. I can't even begin to imagine it."

Joan turned the pages and searched for the word *darkness*. One reference she found was in the book of Jude. These verses spoke of those who reject light after having received it:

Jude 1

11–13 Woe unto them! for . . . they are . . . wandering **stars**, to whom is reserved the ***blackness*** of ***darkness*** for ever.

"That's just what a meteorite is," she thought. "It flares brightly for a time, and then it dies. What an awful end to a spirit of light. I can't wait to share these things with Steve."

More Light about Light

That evening, Joan explained to Steve what she had learned about those who resist or reject the light and how it had made her feel. Steve had said that that information helped him to understand another scripture that is read in priesthood meetings all the time but had never impacted him until now. They looked it up and Steve read it to Joan. Then he re-read it, substituting the word light in the appropriate places.

D&C 58

27 Verily I say, **men** should be anxiously engaged in a **good** cause, and do many **things** of their own free will, and bring to pass much **righteousness**;

28 For the **power** is in them, wherein they are agents unto themselves. And inasmuch as **men** do **good** they shall in nowise lose their reward.

29 But he that doeth not **anything** until he is **commanded**, and receiveth a **commandment** with doubtful heart, and keepeth it with slothfulness, the same is *damned*.

D&C 58

27 Verily I say, **lights** should be anxiously engaged in a **light** cause, and do many **lights** of their own free will, and bring to pass much **light**;

28 For the **light** is in them, wherein they are agents unto themselves. And inasmuch as **lights** do **light** they shall in nowise lose their reward.

29 But he that doeth not **any light** until he is **lighted**, and receiveth a **light** with doubtful heart, and keepeth it with slothfulness, the same is *darkened*.

I keep getting the impression that this is very serious business, Steve," Joan said. "And I also keep remembering that we were in that group that 'shouted for joy' before we came here. So, we have a lot of work to do (see Job 38:7)."

"Listen to you!" Steve said. "Every word you speak is *light*."

"Perhaps that's what it means to 'speak with the tongue of angels,' Steve."

"I've never made that connection before. What does it mean?"

"Well, look at this verse I found while I was studying:

---

2 Nephi 32
2 Do ye not remember that I said unto you that after ye had received the Holy Ghost ye could **speak** with the **tongue** of angels? And now, how could ye **speak** with the **tongue** of angels save it were by the Holy Ghost?
3 Angels **speak** by the **power** of the Holy Ghost; wherefore, they **speak** the **words** of Christ . . .

"I believe I understand, now," Steve said. "When we speak by the light that comes from the Holy Ghost, we are speaking by the same light that the angels are speaking . . ."

" . . . because they also speak by the Holy Ghost," they said in unison.

In that moment of enlightenment, tears came to their eyes, and it seemed to them that they had been quickened in their understanding. When they had regained their composure, Steve said, "That scripture sure had a great impact on me."

"Me too," Joan said. "We were truly edified by the Spirit."

On Friday night, Frank and his wife, Karen, according to arrangements, knocked on the Terrys' door and were greeted warmly by Steve and Joan. The Terrys had not met Karen formally before but had seen her at stake conferences and other functions. She was a delightful conversationalist, and in no time they felt very comfortable together. They had a wonderful dinner, and many questions were asked about family, relatives, places they had lived, and interests and callings in the Church.

At one point, Joan asked Karen how she felt about the studies her husband was doing.

"I don't understand things like he does," Karen said, "but we have been studying the scriptures together for a long time. We think a lot alike, and I have marked my scriptures much like his. I know one thing—we don't realize how focused we can become in the scriptures until we try to explain what we know and feel to someone else."

"I found that out at church last Sunday," Joan said, "I tried to share something about light with a sister sitting next to me, and I know she didn't understand at all what I was saying."

"I had an interesting experience last month when I went visiting teaching," Karen said. "The husband of the lady I teach is not a member of the Church, but he is often there when I visit. I was sharing a thought from the lesson about the word of God being truth, and I quoted D&C 84:45—'the word of the Lord is truth, and truth is light, and light is spirit'—you know that one. He leaned over and said, 'That was a nice bit of doctrine, but it is from the Mormon scriptures. If you can show me that in the Bible, I will believe it.' Well, I was surely taken aback."

"What did you do?" Joan asked.

"I went home, got on the computer, and searched for those words in the Bible. It took me a long time, and I was worried that maybe I could not find them in a way that he could relate to. Some were in the New Testament and some on the Old, but, sure enough, they were all there. I prepared a little hand-out for him."

Karen reached for her handbag, took out a sheet of paper, and showed it to Joan.

D&C 84:45	Correlations from Bible Sources
1. For the **word** of the Lord is **truth**, and	1. JOHN 17 17 Sanctify them through thy **truth**: thy **word** is **truth**.
2. whatsoever is **truth** is **light**, and	2. PSALM 43 3 O send out thy **light** and thy **truth**. JOHN 3 21 But he that doeth **truth** cometh to the **light**.
3. whatsoever is **light** is **Spirit**,	3. DANIEL 5:14 14 I have even heard . . . that the **spirit** of the gods is in thee, and that **light** . . . is found in thee.
4. even the **Spirit** of **Jesus Christ**.	4. 1 JOHN 5 6 And it is the Spirit that beareth witness, because the **Spirit** is **truth**. 2 CORINTHIANS 11:10 10 **Truth** of **Christ** is in me. JOHN 8:12 12 Then spake **Jesus** again unto them, saying, I am the **light** of the world. PSALMS 119:130 130 The entrance of thy **words** giveth **light**. JOHN 6:63 63 The **words** that I speak unto you, they are **spirit**.

"This is impressive. Have you shared it with him yet?" Joan said.

"No, I am going back next Tuesday night."

"Well, good luck!"

Steve and Frank had moved into the family room and were getting seated. Joan and Karen also went in and sat down. Frank asked how the studies had been going, and Steve and Joan shared with him and his wife many of the things that they had learned and felt since their last meeting. They expressed thanks again for the scriptural enlightenment, especially what they had learned from the verses in Alma 32 that he had suggested.

When they had finished, Frank said, "Where to now? Do you have questions that I could help you with?"

"I've noticed a particular phenomenon as I have studied the scriptures that I would like to ask you about," Steve said. "On my lunch breaks, I have turned on my laptop computer and searched various major key words that relate to light, spirit, truth, and so forth. Something that I've seen that I don't understand is the number of phrases with paired words."

"What do you mean, Steve?" Joan said.

"Well, I see phrases like light and truth, power and glory, and sometimes, light of truth, or spirit of truth. I know from our studies that both words on each side of the phrase mean the same thing, but I don't understand exactly why they are used."

"Perhaps I could share an insight here," Frank said. "I have seen that same thing and have asked that same question. I did a computer search a while ago and began recording the phrases that were used and how many times they appeared in the scriptures. I have a copy of that research in my briefcase. Let me get it for you."

Some paired-word phrases in the scriptures and the number of times they occur:

authority and power 3	power and glory 4
calling and election 2	prophecy and revelation 2
charity and love 2	revelation and prophecy 3
faith and charity 4	right and truth 1
faith and diligence 3	righteousness and peace 2
fruit and works 1	righteousness and truth 3
gift and grace 1	righteousness and truth 3
gifts and callings 3	spirit and light 1
gifts and power 6	spirit and truth 12
glory and honor 8	truth and holiness 1
glory and power 2	truth and judgment 2
goodness and grace 1	truth and justice 1
goodness and mercy 2	truth and life 1
goodness and truth 1	truth and light 2
grace and favor 2	truth and love 1
grace and glory 1	truth and peace 3
grace and mercy 6	truth and righteousness 4
grace and peace 1	truth and righteousness 4
grace and truth 11	truth and uprightness 2
honor and glory 2	virtue and holiness 2
judgment and truth 7	wisdom and truth 2
just and true 10	word and truth 6
justice and judgment 10	word and work 1
justice and mercy 3	
justice and truth 1	**Number of paired-word phrases shown:** 64
kindness and truth 1	
kingdom and dominion 1	**Total number of times they appear:** 233
kingdom and glory 2	
kingdom and ministry 1	
kingdom and power 2	
life and truth 1	**Note:**
light and glory 1	1. This is not an exhaustive list.
light and knowledge 4	2. This list could include phrases such
light and spirit 2	as word and the truth, power and
light and truth 7	with authority, in spirit and in
love and truth 2	truth, revelation upon revelation,
mercy and grace 3	and so forth, since they are
mercy and justice 3	variations of the same principle.
mercy and truth 12	3. There are *hundreds* of phrases like
peace and truth 4	these in the scriptures.
power and authority 31	

Steve and Joan studied the paper that Frank handed to them and both expressed surprise at the number and frequency of phrases that were listed.

"But what does it all mean?" Joan asked.

"It holds the key to understanding something of the very nature of God and how he works," Frank said.

"But how?" Joan replied. "Don't keep us in suspense!"

"Do you have a small chalkboard I could write on?" Frank asked.

"Yes, there is one in our son's room," Steve said. "I will get it."

Steve set up the chalkboard and handed some chalk to Frank.

Frank took the chalk and said, "Let's go back to one of the initial scriptures that we started with when we first met."

He wrote on the board:

---

1 JOHN 1
5 God is **light**, and in him is no *darkness* at all.

"Now, let's link another scripture to this one that describes something about that light," Frank continued. He wrote again:

D&C 93
36 The **glory** of God is **intelligence**, or, in other words, **light** and **truth**.
37 **Light** and **truth** forsake that *evil one*.

"With the understanding we've gained from our study, this verse tells us that the light of God is light *and* light. Like Steve said, it has the same meaning on both sides of the phrase.

"But what does light *and* light mean?" Joan said.

"The key is the word *and*, and the concept is that you are adding two things together. It may be expressed as light *plus* light."

There was a moment of silence as the concept sunk deep into Steve and Joan's heart.

"So the glory or light of God is not just light. It is light + light, a light + light principle," Joan said. "And that principle is what forsakes evil."

"That is what the Lord is saying in D&C 93," Frank said.

D&C 93
39 And that **wicked** one cometh and taketh away **light** <u>and</u> **truth**, through disobedience, from the children of men, and because of the tradition of their fathers.

---

40 But I have commanded you to bring up your children in **light** *and* **truth**.

42 You have not taught your children **light** *and* **truth**, according to the commandments; and **that wicked one hath power, as yet, over you**, and this is the cause of your affliction.

"The problem with so many of us," Karen reflected, "is that when we receive light, we often add darkness to it by wrong choices, and 'light + darkness' is not what the light of the Lord is all about."

"Thanks, Karen," Frank said. "We are either growing in light or in darkness. Look at these verses:"

HELAMAN 6
34 And thus we see that the Nephites did begin to *dwindle* in **unbelief,** and grow in **wickedness** *and* **abominations**, while the Lamanites began to *grow* exceedingly in the **knowledge** of their God; yea, they did begin to keep his **statutes** *and* **commandments**, and to walk in **truth** *and* **uprightness** before him.

PROVERB 16
6 By **mercy** *and* **truth** *iniquity* is purged: and by the *fear* of the Lord men depart from *evil*.

"I can see now why the word *light* by itself is not enough to explain the light of the Lord," Steve said. "It is a growing, moving, and dynamic thing, and one or two applications of it in our lives would never prepare us sufficiently to become like God."

"The Lord says that very thing in numerous ways," Frank said.

JOHN 8
31 If ye *continue* in my **word**, *then* are ye my disciples indeed;

D&C 50
24 That which is of God is **light**; and he that receiveth **light**, and *continueth* in **God**, receiveth *more* **light**; and that **light** *groweth brighter and brighter* until the perfect **day**.

1 TIMOTHY 1
7 For God hath not given us the **spirit** of **fear**; but of **power**, *and* of **love**, *and* of a **sound mind**.

"Notice how uniquely the Lord has given us the light + light principle in verse 7," Frank pointed out.

"God has not given us the light of darnkess but of light + light + light," Joan repeated. "That is one of the most significant concepts I have ever learned. The light of God is light + light + light . . . and I suppose that goes on for ever and ever."

"That is what Abraham meant, I am sure, when he spoke of our eternal progression," Karen said.

ABRAHAM 3

26 And they who keep their *first* estate shall be **added** upon; and they who keep not their *first* estate shall not have **glory** in the same **kingdom** with those who keep their *first* **estate**; and they who keep their *second* estate shall have **glory added** upon their heads *for ever and ever.*

"As you can see, the light + light principle is often, but not always, given in simple paired phrases," Frank explained. "Key words may simply have commas between them, or they may be joined together with words like *and, in, with, by, upon, to,* and *through.* Or they may be constructed in other more complex and intricate ways. There are hundreds of them. You just have to keep your eyes open as you read. Let me show you a few more examples. They are a mixture of various types of the light + light principle."

---

1 NEPHI 19

13 They . . . turn their hearts aside, rejecting **signs** *and* **wonders,** *and* the **power** *and* **glory** of the God of Israel.

D&C 50

9 Wherefore, let every man beware lest he do that which is not in **truth** *and* **righteousness** before me.

1 NEPHI 16

28 I, Nephi, beheld the pointers which were in the ball, that they did work according to the **faith** *and* **diligence** *and* **heed** which we did give unto them.

1 NEPHI 1

14 Thy throne is high in the heavens, and thy **power,** *and* **goodness,** *and* **mercy** are over all the inhabitants of the earth.

JOHN 14

6 Jesus saith unto him, I am the **way,** the **truth,** *and* the **life:** no **man** cometh unto the **Father,** but by **me.**

D&C 124

18 It is my will that my servant Lyman Wight should continue in preaching for Zion, . . . and he shall beget **glory** *and* **honor** to himself and unto my name.

Revelation 2

19 I know thy **works**, *and* **charity**, *and* **service**, *and* **faith**, *and* thy **patience**, *and* thy **works**; and the last to be more than the first.

Alma 7

24 And see that ye have **faith**, **hope**, *and* **charity**, and then ye will always abound in **good** works.

Ether 12

28 I will show unto them that **faith**, **hope** *and* **charity** bringeth unto **me**—the **fountain** of *all* **righteousness**.

D&C 4

6 Remember **faith**, **virtue**, **knowledge**, **temperance**, **patience**, **brotherly kindness**, **godliness**, **charity**, **humility**, **diligence**.

D&C 88

40 For **intelligence** cleaveth unto **intelligence**; **wisdom** receiveth **wisdom**; **truth** embraceth **truth**; **virtue** loveth **virtue**; **light** cleaveth unto **light**; **mercy** hath compassion on **mercy** and claimeth her own; **justice** continueth its course and claimeth its own; **judgment** goeth before the face of him who sitteth upon the throne and governeth and executeth all things.

D&C 46

33 And ye must practise **virtue** *and* **holiness** before me *continually*. Even so. Amen.

D&C 42

61 If thou shalt ask, thou shalt receive **revelation** *upon* **revelation**, **knowledge** *upon* **knowledge**, that thou mayest know the **mysteries** *and* **peaceable** things—that which bringeth **joy**, that which bringeth **life eternal**.

"I would never have imagined how these things all work together," Steve said. "Though I guess by now we should be getting the message."

"And the core of that message," Frank added, "is that while God is providing light + light for man, it is the duty and privilege of man to exercise the light + light principle toward his fellow men and God."

MATTHEW 25:21	MATTHEW 25:21
21 His **lord** said unto him, Well done, thou **good** and **faithful** servant: thou hast been **faithful** over a few **things**, I will make thee **ruler** over many **things**: enter thou into the **joy** of thy **lord**.	21 His **lord** said unto him, Well done, thou **light** + **light** servant: thou hast been **light** over a few **lights**, I will make thee **light** over many **lights**: enter thou into the **light** of thy **lord**.

"That brings tears to my eyes," Joan said. "I can hardly believe the unity and harmony of all these scriptures that have been written at different times and in different places. It is a witness to me that man did not write these things."

"I feel the same way, Joan," Steve said. "And now that we have gained some understanding of the meaning of words as they point to the light *and* light principle, what about the paired words that have *of* between them? There must be a light *of* light principle. I haven't seen any of them in the examples you've shown us, Frank."

"I have deliberately avoided those constructions until now," Frank said, as he took the chalk and wrote the following on the board:

light *of* truth   spirit *of* power   word *of* power
spirit *of* truth   spirit *of* glory   word *of* life

"These phrases and many more like them point to another level of understanding of God and his light," Frank continued. "To arrive at that understanding, I want to speak now for a few minutes about God the Father and Jesus Christ in the premortal state. There are five principles that I would like to set forth:

"First: God the Father is a resurrected and immortal being, whose body is filled with infinite and eternal light. His light is founded upon the principle of light + light. He became God through that principle, and he desires his children to become like him through that same principle."

D&C 93
36 The **glory** of God is intelligence, or, in other words, **light** *and* **truth**.
Moses 1
39 For behold, this is my **work** *and* my **glory**—to bring to pass the **immortality** *and* **eternal life** of man.

Discourses of the Prophet Joseph Smith, p. 40–41
Here, then, is eternal life—to know the only wise and true God; and you have got to learn how to be gods yourselves, and to be kings and priests to God, the same as all gods have done before you, namely, *by going from one small degree to another, and from a small capacity to a great one; from* **grace** *to* **grace***, from* **exaltation** *to* **exaltation**, until you attain to the resurrection of the dead, and are able to dwell in everlasting **burnings**, and to sit in **glory**, as do those who sit enthroned in everlasting **power**.

"Second: The immortality and eternal life of man required passing through mortality where sin and death exist. God the Father cannot dwell nor deal personally and directly with his children in a fallen mortal world. No unclean thing can dwell in his light. That light would destroy them."

EXODUS 19
21 And the **Lord** said unto Moses, Go down, charge the people, lest they break through unto the **Lord** to gaze, and many of them *perish.*

"Third: The Father chose his firstborn spirit Son—who had the capacity to make the journey into mortal life—to be a substitute for him. He gave him a fulness of his eternal light and glory, and appointed him to be the means of taking that light—little by little, into this mortal world."

BRUCE R. MCCONKIE, *THE PROMISED MESSIAH,* P. 51
The **gospel** *of* **God** became the **gospel** *of* **Jesus Christ**; And so the very plan of salvation itself—to signify that salvation comes through Christ—was named after the One who was "Beloved and Chosen from the beginning" (Moses 4:2).
JOHN 1
14 And the **Word** was made flesh, and dwelt among us, (and we beheld his **glory**, the **glory** as of the only begotten of the **Father***,) full* of **grace** *and* **truth**.

"Fourth: The cost to Jesus of bringing that light into the fallen world was to be an infinite and eternal sacrifice of suffering and death. The agreement to make that sacrifice paved the way for the light + light principle to come into effect for us."

2 NEPHI 11

7 For if there be no **Christ** there be no **God**; and if there be
no **God** we are not, for there could have been no creation.
But there is a **God**, and he is **Christ**, and he cometh in the
fulness of his own time.

"Fifth: Because Jesus was appointed by the Father to be the carrier
of his light into this world, he became the Light of his Father's Light to
all mankind, or in other words, the Light of Light. The Holy Ghost, as
the eternal witness, is the Light of the Light of the Father and the Son.
He also, therefore, is the Light of Light. Not only are their names and
titles expressive of the light of light principle, but so also is the work
they do. The light of light principle, therefore, points more specifically
to the idea of the administration of light from one level to another.

"As their names, titles, and principles pass into this mortal world
(through the prism, as it were) and are expressed in our language, they
take on the form of paired-word phrases with the word *of* between them,
hence the titles."

the Prince *of* Peace	the Spirit *of* Truth
the Lamb *of* God	the Light *of* Truth
the King *of* Kings	the Bread *of* Life
the Son *of* Man	the Messenger *of* the Covenant
the Prince *of* Life	the Word *of* Life
the Spirit *of* Power	the Spirit *of* Glory
the Spirit *of* Life	the King *of* Glory (and so forth)

"In this same manner," Frank continued, "we have references to the
kingdom they have established and the work of that kingdom."

the Kingdom *of* God	the Glory *of* Zion
the Spirit *of* God	the Gospel *of* Christ
the Power *of* God	the Church *of* Christ
the Kingdom *of* Heaven	the Power *of* Redemption
the Kingdom *of* Christ	the Gospel *of* Peace
the knowledge *of* Salvation	(and so forth)
the City *of* Zion	

"You remember the list I showed you earlier of paired-word phrases
that showed the light + light principle?" Frank asked.

"Yes," Steve and Joan answered in unison.

"Well, here is another list showing paired-word phrases with the light *of* light principle:

Some scriptural phrases with paired-words having *of* between them, and the number of times they appear in the scriptures

beauty of holiness	4	power of priesthood	1
city of holiness	1	spirit of adoption	1
city of Zion	2	spirit of Christ	5
faith of Christ	21	spirit of council	2
faith of God	9	spirit of Elias	1
faith of Jesus	4	spirit of faith	3
gospel of Abraham	1	spirit of freedom	2
gospel of Christ	20	spirit of glory	1
gospel of God	7	spirit of God	57
gospel of Jesus	8	spirit of grace	2
gospel of peace	3	spirit of holiness	2
gospel of repentance	6	spirit of inspiration	1
gospel of salvation	1	spirit of Jesus Christ	2
joy of Christ	1	spirit of judgment	3
joy of faith	1	spirit of knowledge	3
joy of holiness	1	spirit of life	5
kingdom of heaven	59	spirit of meekness	7
kingdom of God	121	spirit of prayer	2
kingdom of Christ	1	spirit of promise	8
kingdom of glory	2	spirit of prophecy	23
kingdom of Zion	1	spirit of revelation	11
knowledge of Christ	2	spirit of wisdom	5
knowledge of God	14	strength of God	1
knowledge of salvation	1	strength of Israel	2
knowledge of wisdom	1	strength of salvation	1
life of men	1	strength of Zion	2
life of God	8	truth of Christ	3
light of Christ	4	truth of God	4
light of God	2	truth of holiness	1
light of Israel	3	way of holiness	1
light of life	1	wisdom of God	16
light of men	2	word of Christ	7
light of truth	6	word of exhortation	3
Man of Council	1	word of faith	2
Man of Holiness	2	word of God	144
mountain of holiness	1	word of Jesus	2
power of God	80	word of knowledge	3
power of deliverance	2	word of life	2
power of resurrection	1	word of prophecy	2
power of Christ	3	word of righteousness	1
power of heaven	1	word of truth	9
power of spirit	1	word of wisdom	6
power of godliness	2		

Notes about the chart on page 67
Number of paired-word phrases shown. 85
Total number of times they appear 772

---

1. This is not an exhaustive list.
2. There are hundreds of phrases with these and other kinds of paired-words in the scriptures. We have included only phrases like power of spirit. We could have included power of my spirit or power of the spirit or word of my power, and so forth. The list goes on and on and on.

Again Steve and Joan were surprised.

"How is it that we have read the scriptures so many times and have passed over such valuable information?" Joan said. "I can't believe how rich the scriptures are and how little of them we see."

"Let me just show you a few more scriptures that demonstrate that both the Savior and the Holy Ghost are seen as the 'light that comes from the Father's light,'" Frank said.

The Savior

D&C 93
26 The **Spirit** *of* **truth** is of **God**. I am the **Spirit** *of* **truth**, and John bore record of me, saying: *He received a fulness of* **truth**, yea, *even of all* **truth**;
D&C 84
45 For the **word** of the **Lord** [i.e., the Father] is **truth**, and whatsoever is **truth** is **light**, and whatsoever is **light** is **Spirit**, *even* the **Spirit** of **Jesus Christ**.
[or in other words: the word, the truth, the light and the spirit of the Father is exactly the word, the truth, the light, and the spirit of the Son.]
D&C 93
11 And I, John, bear record that I beheld his **glory**, as the **glory** of the Only *Begotten* of the **Father**, *full of* **grace** *and* **truth**, *even* the **Spirit** *of* **truth**, which came and dwelt in the flesh, and dwelt among us.

68

The Holy Ghost

JOHN 15
26 But when the **Comforter** is come, whom I will send unto you from the **Father**, *even* the **Spirit** *of* **truth**, which *proceedeth from the* **Father**, he shall testify of me:
John 16
13 Howbeit when he, the **Spirit** *of* **truth**, is come, he will guide you into all **truth**: for he shall not speak of himself; but whatsoever he shall hear, that shall he speak: and he will shew you things to come.
14 He shall **glorify** me: for he shall *receive of mine*, and shall shew it unto you.
15 All things that the **Father** hath are *mine*: therefore said I, that *he shall take of mine*, and shall shew it unto you.

"These five principles," Frank concluded, "and the way they translate into the wording of our scriptures are to me one of the greatest witnesses of the truth that we could ever have. Now, I have done all the talking. Do you have comments or insights?"

Steve, Joan, and Karen sat spellbound as the reality of what Frank had shared impacted them. It was a while before they could respond. Finally Steve said, "What infinite love the Lord has for us. I had no idea that such incredible things have gone on behind the scenes. It makes me want to know more, to understand them better, to be one with them, to have the light that they have, and to be faithful to the light I already have."

"I haven't looked at them in depth," Karen said, "but my quick calculations of the lists you have shown us add up to more than a thousand times that these paired-word phrases occur in the scriptures. I have seen some of them but certainly not all of them, and I am beginning to believe you, Frank. The lists must be endless. I noticed that you didn't have the references by the words. It would be good for me to see the references; I could then look them up."

"That's a good suggestion," Frank said. "It's a lot of work. I searched them on the computer and counted the instances, but I didn't take the time to list all the references. Maybe you could help me with that."

Karen smiled one of her "knowing" smiles.

"It seems that we are limited in our discovery of these words, only by our inability to recognize or comprehend them," Steve said. "It brings us back to your earlier observation, Frank, that the Lord is not saying a thousand different things; he is only saying one thing a thousand different ways."

"What impacts me," Karen added, "is that it is important to understand not only *what* is being said but *how* it is said. The structure of the wording, particularly with the light + light principle, in some cases tells me as much or more than the words themselves. In fact, the actual English words sometimes get in the way of understanding. When I fully concentrate and accept the fact that the Lord is fundamentally trying to teach me about light, the English words seem to disappear, or become transparent, and the light shines through them."

It was evident that all were deeply touched by what had been discussed during the evening. As they moved around putting things away, there was a reserved quiet and a reverence in each heart.

When they gathered at the door to say good-bye, Joan said, "Have you ever looked at one of those 3-D pictures that you have to concentrate to see?"

"Yes, we have," Frank said, smiling at his wife. "We're not too good at seeing them, though."

"At first all you see is a mass of color and form," Joan said. "And then—all at once—you see the picture. Once you have seen it, you see it every time. In fact, it becomes impossible not to see it—even if you try. That is how I am beginning to see the scriptures. I have seen a picture emerge from the form and print of the scriptural pages. That picture becomes more and more clear, and I suppose that I will never look at the scriptures without seeing it. You, Frank, have helped me to see that picture. Thank you so much. And thanks to you, Karen. It has been a grand visit."

"Thanks for inviting us," Frank said.

"I, too, appreciate all you have done for us," Steve said. "Shall we do this again sometime?"

"Call us, and we can arrange a time," Frank said.

"By the way," Steve said, "I still want copies of some of your research."

Steve got another jab in the ribs from his wife.

The next evening Frank and Karen were sitting in their living room, relaxing. Dinner was over, and the children were putting together a puzzle their grandparents had sent them. Karen turned to Frank and said, "Do you remember my comment as we left Joan and Steve's house last night, about the structure of many scriptural words and how they are fundamentally teaching us about light?"

"Yes, I remember."

"I read some verses this afternoon that helped me see more clearly that the Lord wants us to understand his wording. In the first one, he is speaking about his creations and says:

D&C 29
30 All things . . . I have **created** by the **word** of my **power**, which is the **power** of my **Spirit**.

"I pondered this for a long time. The first thing that came clear to me is that the Lord wants us to know that when he says 'the word of my power,' it is the same thing as when he says 'the power of my spirit.' These expressions are interchangeable. It's as if he's saying, 'Don't miss this! It is a principle I want you to understand.'

"Next, I knew that *word*, *power*, and *spirit* can each be interchanged with *light*, so I transposed the statement into the idea of light, like this: 'all things . . . I have lighted by the light of my light.'

"The bottom line here for me is, there are many ways in which the Savior expresses the idea of giving 'light' by his' light.'"

"That makes sense to me," Frank said. "And what about the other verse?"

"The Lord speaking about the devil's desires says:

D&C 29
36 The devil . . . rebelled against me, saying, Give me thine **honor**, which is my **power**.

"Here he tells us that when Satan asked for his honor he was asking for his power. And just to confirm that, the Lord says the same thing in another place:

Moses 4
3 Wherefore, . . . Satan rebelled against me, and sought . . . that I should give unto him mine own **power**.

"In other words, the Lord wants to make sure we understand that the words *honor* and *power* are interchangeable. Knowing that, we can see the 'light + light principle' when we use the word *honor* with other words that are also interchangeable with light. For example, the Lord said the following about Lyman Wight:

D&C 124

18 He shall beget **glory** and **honor** to himself and unto my name.

"And he said this about the temple:

D&C 124

34 For therein are the keys of the holy priesthood ordained, that you may receive **honor** and **glory**.

"When we understand these things, we can see how it all relates to the light + light principle, and I'm just beginning to appreciate how significant it is."

"I'm continually impressed with the way the scriptures affect you, Karen. It must be satisfying to discover such motivating things."

"Well, I know you know more about it than I do, but you are right; it is such a thrill to have the scriptures opened to you."

A few days later Karen and Frank were finishing up a family history project in the study when Karen said, "I've been thinking a lot about the Savior since our discussion with Steve and Joan, and I can't help wondering about his name, the name Christ. There must be a very significant meaning to that name. We haven't ever discussed it."

"I think if you look in the Bible Dictionary you'll find its meaning," Frank said.

Karen turned the pages of her scriptures and said, "It means 'the anointed.' Help me understand that."

"Look in Gospel Explorer on your computer and see if there is an explanation."

Karen typed in the word *Christ* and clicked a few buttons that led to one of the Bible Dictionaries and found the following:

CHRIST, noun [Greek, *anointed*, from, to anoint.]

THE ANOINTED; an appellation given to the Savior of the world, and *synonymous with the Hebrew MESSIAH*. It was a custom of antiquity to consecrate persons to the sacerdotal [priestly] and regal [kingly] offices by *anointing them with oil.* (Noah Webster, *American Dictionary of the English Language, 1828*; emphasis added)

Christ. *Anointed,* the *Greek translation of the Hebrew word rendered "Messiah"* (q.v.), the official title of our Lord, occurring *five hundred and fourteen times in the New Testament.* It denotes that *he was anointed or consecrated* to his great redemptive work

To believe that "Jesus is the Christ" is to believe that he is the Anointed, the Messiah of the prophets. (Easton's Bible Dictionary; emphasis added)

A scripture to show that the Hebrew word *Messiah* (*Messias* in the New Testament) and the Greek word *Christ* are the same:

JOHN 4

25 The woman saith unto him, I know that Messias cometh, which is called Christ: when he is come, he will tell us all things.

She then looked up the words *anoint* and *oil* in the scripture database.

EXODUS 29

7 Then shalt thou take the anointing oil, and pour it upon his head, and anoint him.

2 KINGS 9

3 Then take the box of oil, and pour it on his head, and say, Thus saith the LORD, I have anointed thee king over Israel.

"If Christ is the 'anointed one' and the idea of anointing relates to oil, what is the oil, and how and by whom was Jesus anointed?"

"Do you remember the parable of the ten virgins and who had oil in their lamps?" Frank asked.

"Yes, but I've never understood just exactly what the oil represents."

"Try looking up the words *oil* and *light*," Frank suggested.

Among the verses that came up, Karen found this one:

> **Exodus 27**
> 20 And thou shalt command the children of Israel, that they bring thee *pure oil olive* beaten for the **light**, *to cause the lamp to burn always.*

"I should have suspected that oil represents light," Karen said. "It's a logical conclusion."

"The Lord expands the meaning of these things in the Doctrine and Covenants," Frank said.

> **D&C 33**
> 17 Wherefore, be faithful, praying always, having your *lamps* trimmed and *burning*, and **oil** with you, that you may be ready at the coming of the Bridegroom—
> **D&C 45**
> 56 And at that day, when I shall come in my glory, shall the parable be fulfilled which I spake concerning the ten virgins.
> 57 For they that are wise and have received the **truth**, and have taken the **Holy Spirit** for their guide, and have not been deceived.

"The idea of anointing, then," Karen observed, "seems to do with receiving light from God to perform a special or significant mission or assignment."

"Isaiah, through prophecy, gave us the words of the Savior about his anointing," Frank said.

> **Isaiah 61**
> 1 The **Spirit** of the Lord GOD *is upon me*; *because* the LORD hath **anointed** me to preach good tidings unto the meek.

"There's my answer," Karen said. "It was the Father who anointed the Son. But how and when did he do it?"

"When Jesus began his ministry, he did a very curious thing in relationship to this prophecy," Frank continued.

> **Luke 4**
> 14 And Jesus returned in the **power** of the **Spirit** into Galilee:
> 16 And he came to Nazareth, where he had been brought up:

and, as his custom was, he went into the synagogue on the sabbath day, and stood up for to read.

17 And there was delivered unto him the book of the prophet Esaias [Isaiah]. And when he had opened the book, he found the place where it was written,

18 The **Spirit** of the **Lord** is upon me, *because he* hath **anointed** me to **preach** the **gospel** to the poor; he hath sent me to heal the brokenhearted, to preach deliverance to the captives, and recovering of sight to the blind, to set at liberty them that are bruised,

20 And he closed the book, and he gave it again to the minister, and sat down. And the eyes of all them that were in the synagogue were fastened on him.

21 And he began to say unto them, *This day is this scripture fulfilled in your ears.*

"It says that Jesus came into Galilee in the light of the Light, which to me means that he came in the light of the Father. Then, through the words of Isaiah, he says that the light of the Father was upon him because the Father had already anointed or lighted him to light the light to the poor, the brokenhearted, the captives, the blind, and the bruised. He is bearing witness to those whose hearts were ready that he was the anointed one, the Messiah, the Christ. That touches me so deeply, Frank. What a witness!"

"Yes, and as he says, that anointing had happened earlier. It came at his baptism when the Holy Ghost descended upon him as is described by John:

D&C 93

15 And I, John, bear record, and lo, the heavens were opened, and the **Holy Ghost** descended upon him in the form of a dove, and sat upon him, and there came a voice out of heaven saying: This is my beloved Son.

16 And I, John, bear record that he received a *fulness* of the **glory** of the Father;

17 And he received all **power**, both in heaven and on earth, and the **glory** of the Father was with him, for he dwelt in him.

"Luke in the book of Acts also confirms this."

ACTS 10

38 God **anointed** Jesus of Nazareth with the **Holy Ghost** and

with **power**: who went about doing **good**, and healing all that
were oppressed of the **devil**; for God was with him.
Acts 4
26 The rulers were gathered together against the *Lord*, and
against his **Christ**.
27 For . . . against thy holy child Jesus, whom thou hast
anointed . . . the people of Israel, were gathered together.

"When we look at all that information," Karen said, "no wonder the
Savior said in so many places, 'I am the light.'"

"He made that formal statement eleven times that we have record of,
but as you know, the scriptures are full of other references to him as the
source of light. We have seen many but consider these further examples:

Ephesians 5
14 Arise from the dead, and **Christ** shall give thee **light**.
2 Corinthians 4
4 The god of this world hath blinded the minds of them . . . lest
the **light** of the glorious **gospel** of **Christ**, who is the image of
God, should **shine** unto them.
Moroni 7
18 And now, my brethren, seeing that ye know the **light** by
which ye may judge, which **light** is the **light** of **Christ**, see
that ye do not judge *wrongfully*;
19 Wherefore, I beseech of you, brethren, that ye should search
diligently in the **light** of **Christ** that ye may know **good** from
evil; and if ye will lay hold upon every **good** thing, and con-
demn it not, ye certainly will be a **child** of **Christ**.

"In addition to these types of declarations, there are many others
made in the underlying language of light which we have been discussing.
Let's look at an example or two of those:

Alma 38
9 There is no other way or means whereby man can be saved,
only in and through **Christ**. . . . Behold, he is the **word** *of*
truth *and* **righteousness**.

"This verse emphasizes that Christ is the light of light + light, rein-
forcing again what *kind* of light he is. It reminds us that:

D&C 93
36 The **glory** of God is intelligence, or, in other words, **light** *and* **truth**.

"This next verse says the same thing a different way:

COLOSSIANS 1
27 God would make known . . . this mystery . . . which is **Christ** in you, the **hope** *of* **glory**:

"We learned earlier that the name Christ and the name Messiah are the same. The Book of Mormon tells us about the light of the Messiah and then indicates that he is Christ.

2 NEPHI 3
5 He obtained a promise . . . that the **Messiah** should be made **manifest** unto them in the latter days, in the **spirit** *of* **power**, unto the bringing of them out of ***darkness*** unto **light**—yea, out of hidden ***darkness*** and out of captivity unto **freedom**.
2 NEPHI 25
19 The **Messiah** cometh in six hundred years from the time that my father left Jerusalem; and . . . his **name** shall be **Jesus Christ**, the Son of God.

"Once we understand that the name Christ (or Jesus Christ) means light," Frank continued, "it opens up a whole new avenue of perception in the scriptures for us. Let me share some insights with you."

"I would love that," Karen said.

"When we are baptized into the Church," Frank continued, "we take upon us the name of Christ.

MORONI 6
3 None were received unto baptism save they took upon them the **name** of **Christ**, having a determination to serve him to the end.

"So, then, as we have just discovered, we not only take upon us his literal name, but we have actually entered into his light.

ALMA 26
15 Yea, they were encircled about with everlasting *darkness* and *destruction*; but behold, he has brought them into his everlasting **light**.

"Adam, immediately following his baptism, was given this instruction:"

MOSES 5
8 Wherefore, thou shalt do all that thou doest in the **name** of the **Son**, and thou shalt repent and call upon God in the **name** of the **Son** forevermore.

"I'm beginning to see the picture," Karen said. "I have always wondered how we could do everything we do, in the name of the Son, but now I see that one meaning is to do all that we do in his light—to continue in his light."

"I think that is why the sacrament prayer is worded as it is," Frank said.

D&C 20
77 . . . witness unto thee, O God, the Eternal Father, that they are *willing* to take upon them the **name** of thy Son.

"It implies that we are willing to continually take upon us the light of Christ, until we are able to receive a fulness. There is a great scripture that expounds on that thought:

D&C 18
21 Take upon you the **name** of **Christ**, and speak the **truth** in soberness.
22 And as many as repent and are baptized in my **name**, which is **Jesus Christ**, and endure to the end, the same shall be **saved**.
23 Behold, **Jesus Christ** is the **name** which is given of the **Father**, and there is none other **name** given whereby man can be **saved**;
24 Wherefore, all men must take upon them the **name** which is given of the **Father**, for in that **name** shall they be **called** at the last **day**;
25 Wherefore, if they know not the **name** by which they are **called**, they cannot have **place** in the **kingdom** of my **Father**.

D&C 18
21 Take upon you the **light** of **Christ**, and speak the **light** in soberness.
22 And as many as repent and are baptized in my **light**, which is **Jesus Christ**, and endure to the end, the same shall be **lighted**.
23 Behold, **Jesus Christ** is the **light** which is given of the **Father**, and there is none other **light** given whereby man can be **lighted**;
24 Wherefore, all men must take upon them the **light** which is given of the **Father**, for in that **light** shall they be **lighted** at the last **light**;
25 Wherefore, if they know not the **light** by which they are **lighted**, they cannot have **light** in the **light** of my **Father**.

"King Benjamin said it this way:

Mosiah 5
9 And it shall come to pass that whosoever doeth this shall be found at the right hand of God, for he shall know the **name** by which he is **called**; for he shall be **called** by the **name** of **Christ**.

Mosiah 5
9 And it shall come to pass that whosoever doeth this shall be found at the right hand of God, for he shall know the **light** by which he is **lighted**; for he shall be **lighted** by the **light** of **Christ**.

"I love the scriptures," Karen said. "They are so profound when the Lord gives us eyes to see what is there."

"There are other references to the name of Christ that we should see," Frank said.

Mosiah 5
7 And now, because of the covenant which ye have made ye shall be called the **children** of **Christ**, *his sons, and his daughters*; for behold, this day he hath **spiritually** *begotten you*; for ye say that your hearts are changed through faith on his **name**; therefore, ye are born of him and have *become his sons and his daughters*.

Mosiah 5
7 And now, because of the covenant which ye have made ye shall be called the **lights** of **Christ**, *his sons, and his daughters*; for behold, this day he hath *begotten you* into his **light**; for ye say that your hearts are changed through faith on his **light**; therefore, ye are born of him and have *become his sons and his daughters*.

"King Benjamin also said:

MOSIAH 15
11 All those who have . . . believed that the **Lord** would redeem his people, and have looked forward to that **day** for a remission of their sins, I say unto you, that these are his **seed**, or they are the heirs of the **kingdom** of God.
12 For these are they whose sins he has borne; these are they for whom he has died, to redeem them from their transgressions. And now, are they not his **seed**?

"Paul and James have added:

EPHESIANS 5
8 For ye were sometimes *darkness*, but now are ye **light** in the **Lord**: walk as **children** of **light**:
James 1:17–18
The **Father** of **lights** . . . begat . . . us with the **word** *of* **truth**, that we should be a kind of firstfruits of his creatures.

"When I read these things, I think about the use of the word *Christian*, which was given to members of the Church by their enemies both in New Testament and Book of Mormon times. One commenter said that they were called Christians because they were Christ-like. They spoke, acted, and suffered like Christ. 'As they did this, they grew in Christ-likeness, and as the world noticed this, they began to mock them by referring to them as Christians—little Christs. (A sermon preached by Doug Van Meter on Acts 11:19-26 at Brackenhurst Baptist Church on Sunday morning, October 6, 2002)

"The Book of Mormon says the following about Christians:

ALMA 46
15 All those who were true believers in **Christ** took upon them, gladly, the **name** of **Christ**, or **Christians** as they were called, because of their belief in **Christ** who should come.

"What an honor to be called 'little Christs'—little lights—children of the light," Karen said.

"Paul summed it up well," Frank said, "when he wrote:

GALATIANS 4
19 My *little children*, of whom I travail in birth again until **Christ** be **formed** in you.

"But there are still more references in the scriptures that give us insight into his name," Frank said. "Look at this verse:

Luke 10

17 And the seventy returned again with joy, saying, Lord, even the *devils* are subject unto us through thy **name**.

"It is a commandment to actually say his name as we pray and perform ordinances. We are doing this, or saying this, 'in the name of Jesus Christ,' but the Lord warns that we have to qualify in order to use his name, because to say or use his name is equivalent to using his light—that is why the devils were subject to the Seventy. And if we use the name and do not have the light, we are under condemnation."

D&C 63

61 Wherefore, let all men beware how they take my **name** in their lips—

62 For behold, verily I say, that many there be who are under this condemnation, who use the **name** of the Lord, and use it in vain, having not **authority**.

63 Wherefore, let the church repent of their sins, and I, the Lord, will own them; otherwise they shall be cut off.

64 Remember that that which cometh from above is sacred, and must be spoken with care, and by constraint of the **Spirit**; and in this there is no condemnation, and ye receive the **Spirit** through prayer; wherefore, without this there remaineth condemnation.

"That gives you pause," Karen said. "To use the name, one must have the Spirit, or in other words, one must have the light in order to use the light."

"That is exactly what the Lord told the ancient Israelites," Frank said.

Isaiah 48

1 Hear ye this, O house of Jacob . . . which swear by the **name** of the **Lord** . . . but not in **truth**.

"The same type of instruction is given by the Savior to the Nephites:"

---

3 NEPHI 18
19 Therefore ye must always pray unto the Father in my **name**.

"We so often just say the name but never imagine that we are required to be 'in the light' in order to use it," Karen said.

"But there is a promise," Frank said. "If we do all that we do 'in the light,' we will in time receive a fulness of that light."

D&C 93
19 I give unto you these sayings that you may understand and know *how* to worship, and know *what* you worship, that you may come unto the **Father** in my **name**, and in due time receive of his **fulness**.

Ether 4:19
19 And blessed is he that is found faithful unto my **name** at the last **day**, for he shall be lifted up to dwell in the **kingdom prepared** for him from the foundation of the world.

"Elder Dallin H. Oaks spoke on one occasion of taking upon us the name of Christ," Frank continued. "He gave some inspired information which I will paraphrase for the sake of brevity. He spoke of many references in the Old Testament to the name of the Lord in connection with temples. The Lord told the children of Israel that when they entered the Promised Land that:

DETERONOMY 12
11 There shall be a place which the LORD your God shall choose to cause his **name** to dwell.

"Many times thereafter the prophets referred to the future temple as a house 'for the name' of the Lord God of Israel (see 1 Kings 3:2, 5:5, 8:16-20, 29, 44, 48; 2 Chronicles 2:4, 6:5-10, 20, 34, 38). Following the dedication of the temple, the Lord told Solomon:

---

1 KINGS 9
3 I have hallowed this house, which thou hast built, to put my **name** there for ever.

"Likewise, in the Doctrine and Covenants the Lord refers to temples as houses built 'unto my holy name' (see D&C 124:39; 105:33; 109:2–5). The Prophet Joseph Smith in the dedicatory prayer of the Kirtland Temple asked the Lord for a blessing upon

---

D&C 109

26 Thy people upon whom thy **name** shall be put in this house.

"And a short time later the Lord said:

D&C 110

7 For behold, I have accepted this house, and my **name** shall be here; and I will **manifest** myself to my people in mercy in this house.

"All of these references to temples as a house for the name of the Lord clearly involve something far more significant than a mere inscription of his sacred name on the structure. The scriptures speak of the Lord's putting his name in a temple because he gives authority for his name to be used in the sacred ordinances of that house. (See Dallin H. Oaks, "Taking Upon Us the Name of Jesus Christ," *Ensign*, May 1985, 81; emphasis added)

"It is my conviction," Frank continued, "that the Lord puts his name on or in a temple, because the sacred ordinances performed therein endow the participants with his Light."

"That gives me grand feelings all over," Karen said, "and incidentally, it is a confirmation of something I read just the other day. I was reading an article by Elder Carlos E. Asay about the temple. Let me just find it."

Karen reached over to a bookshelf and retrieving a binder, said, "Here it is. I copied it out of the August 1997 *Ensign*, on page 18. He spoke of the temple garment, or garment of the holy priesthood, worn by members of The Church of Jesus Christ of Latter-day Saints who have received their temple endowment. He said that the descriptive terms used for the sacred vestments given to Aaron and his sons and others to minister in ancient tabernacles and temples also apply to the modern temple garment. They are, he said, 'accompanied by expressions such as 'precious garments,' 'glorious garments,' 'garments of honor,' 'coats of glory,' and 'garments of salvation.' . . . The honor, glory, and precious nature of sacred garments . . . transcend the material of which they are made. Their full worth and beauty are appreciated and regarded as precious or glorious when viewed through the "eye of faith"' (Alma 5:15). These expressions certainly suggest to me that the garment is a representation of being 'dressed in light.'"

"Exactly," Frank responded. "And that is exactly how God is portrayed by David in the book of Psalms."

PSLAM 104

1 Bless the LORD, O my soul. O LORD my God, thou art very great; thou art *clothed* with **honour** and **majesty**.

2 Who *coverest* thyself with **light** as with a *garment*: who stretchest out the heavens like a curtain.

"When you said that we are endowed with light in the temple," Karen said, "it made me think of the Savior's words to some of the Saints in the New Testament."

REVELATION 3

4 Thou hast a few names even in Sardis which have not defiled their garments; and they shall walk with me in **white**: for they are worthy.

5 He that overcometh, the same shall be clothed in **white** raiment; and I will not blot out his **name** out of the **book** of **life**, but I will confess his **name** before my Father, and before his angels.

"The appearance of these garments must be akin to those of the saints in the Book of Mormon," Frank said.

---

3 NEPHI 19

25 And it came to pass that **Jesus blessed** them as they did pray unto him; and his **countenance** did smile upon them, and the **light** of his **countenance** did **shine** upon them, and behold they were as **white** as the **countenance** and also the **garments** of **Jesus**; and behold the **whiteness** thereof did exceed all the **whiteness**, yea, even there could be nothing upon earth so **white** as the **whiteness** thereof.

"I am sure that all these things are a foreshadowing of the resurrection," Karen said. "I had no idea that so much was included in taking the name of the Savior upon us."

"There's one other thing that I would like to point out about the name of the Savior," Frank said, "and it is emphasized by the apostle Paul and expanded by President Ezra Taft Benson:

Philippians 2
10 At the **name** of **Jesus** every knee should bow.
11 And that every tongue should confess that **Jesus Christ** is **Lord**.

"President Benson said, 'Ultimately every knee will bow and every tongue confess that Jesus is the Christ.'" (*Ezra Taft Benson Remembers the Joy of Christmas*, Salt Lake City: Deseret Book, 1988, 13)

"If we put this in context, it means that ultimately every light (man and woman) will bow and confess that Jesus is the Light. They will ultimately know that he is the Light of the Father, the Light that fills the immensity of space (see D&C 88:12), and The Light that is in every light (man) that has come or ever will come into the world (see D&C 93:2), and as Alma says:"

Alma 12
15 We must come forth and stand before him in his **glory**, and in his **power**, and in his **might, majesty,** and **dominion**, and acknowledge to our everlasting shame . . . that he has *all* **power** to save every **man** that believeth on his **name** and bringeth forth **fruit** meet for repentance.

"Thanks for sharing these things with me," Karen said. "I truly hope that we can take upon us the name of the Savior and be true to him. I want to be in that light with you, Frank, and with our children. We are so blessed to know these things."

"I feel just like you do, so filled with love for the scriptures and for my family. I hope that we will never tire of light + light."

"And you know, the overwhelming thing about all this," Karen said, "is that a study like this could be done with almost every major key word in the scriptures. Whether it be the name of Christ, his grace, charity, love, knowledge, or honor, these things are all made manifest for what they are by realizing that they are different ways of expressing the action of his Light."

"I just have one more thought about light that we could end on to-night," Frank said. "One of the General Authorities during the administration of President Brigham Young did a deep study of light and erroneously concluded in some of his writings and speeches that we are to *worship* light, for that is the attribute that has made God, God.

"Brigham Young publicly corrected him and said 'it was neither rational nor consistent with the revelations of God and with reason and philosophy, to believe that these latter Forces and Powers (light) had existed prior to the Beings who controlled and governed them,' and 'it will readily be perceived, upon reflection, that attributes never can be made manifest in any world except through organized beings.' (See James R. Clark, comp., *Messages of the First Presidency*, vol. 2, 232–8).

"President Wilford Woodruff and his counselor President George Q. Cannon, in a meeting in Salt Lake City on June 11, 1892, stated that 'it was right to Worship the true, and the Living God, and Him only, and not the intelligence that dwelt in Him; that His Son Jesus Christ, or Jehova[h] never taught such doctrine, but always to worship my Father which is in Heaven, and to always pray to the Father in the name of his Son Jesus Christ.' (Fred C. Collier, comp., *Unpublished Revelations* [Salt Lake City: Collier's Publishing Co., 1981], 173–4)

"The bottom line of this for me is that while we are studying light, we should never lose sight of the fact that it is an attribute of Christ. Christ is not an attribute of light. God is light. Light is not God. The desire of our hearts should be to worship God and let him give us light as he sees fit. That light will then outfit us to do whatever he wants us to do."

"That's something valuable to keep in mind," Karen said. "If we were to worship and obtain light independent of God, we would not be accountable to him for the way we use it."

A few additional insights into the name of Christ

3 NEPHI 11
7 Behold my Beloved Son, in whom I am well pleased, in whom I have **glorified** my **name**—hear ye him.
PHILIPPIANS 2
9 Wherefore God also hath highly exalted him, and given him a **name** which is above every **name**:

3 NEPHI 11
7 Behold my Beloved Son, in whom I am well pleased, in whom I have **lighted** my **light**—hear ye him.
PHILIPPIANS 2
9 Wherefore God also hath highly exalted him, and given him a **light** which is above every **light**:

D&C 132
64 I will *magnify* my **name** upon all those who receive and abide in my **law**.
D&C 132:9
9 Will I accept of an offering, saith the Lord, that is not made in my **name**?
Moroni 10
4 Ask God, the Eternal Father, in the **name** of **Christ**, if these things are not **true**;
3 Nephi 27
8 And how be it my **church** save it be **called** in my **name**?
D&C 84
66 In my **name** they shall do many wonderful works;
67 In my **name** they shall cast out devils;
68 In my **name** they shall heal the sick;
69 In my **name** they shall open the eyes of the blind, and unstop the ears of the deaf;
D&C 88
119 Organize yourselves; . . . and establish . . . a house of **God**;
120 That your incomings may be in the **name** of the Lord; that your outgoings may be in the **name** of the Lord; that all your salutations may be in the **name** of the Lord, with uplifted hands unto the Most High.
D&C 109
22 And we ask thee, Holy Father, that thy servants may go forth from this house **armed** with thy **power**, and that thy **name** may be upon them, and thy **glory** be round about them, and thine angels have charge over them;
Matthew 18
20 For where *two or three* are

D&C 132
64 I will *magnify* my **light** upon all those who receive and abide in my **light**.
D&C 132:9
9 Will I accept of an offering, saith the Lord, that is not made in my **light**?
Moroni 10
4 Ask God, the Eternal Father, in the **light** of **Light**, if these things are not **light**;
3 Nephi 27
8 And how be it my **light** save it be **lighted** in my **light**?
D&C 84
66 In my **light** they shall do many wonderful works;
67 In my **light** they shall cast out devils;
68 In my **light** they shall heal the sick;
69 In my **light** they shall open the eyes of the blind, and unstop the ears of the deaf;
D&C 88
119 Organize yourselves; . . . and establish . . . a house of **Light**;
120 That your incomings may be in the **light** of the Lord; that your outgoings may be in the **light** of the Lord; that all your salutations may be in the **light** of the Lord, with uplifted hands unto the Most High.
D&C 109
22 And we ask thee, Holy Father, that thy servants may go forth from this house **lighted** with thy **light**, and that thy **light** may be upon them, and thy **light** be round about them, and thine angels have charge over them;
Matthew 18
20 For where *two or three* are

gathered together in my **name**, there am I in the midst of them.

D&C 42

6 And ye shall go forth in the **power** of my **Spirit**, preaching my **gospel**, *two by two*, in my **name**, lifting up your voices as with the sound of a trump, **declaring** my **word** like unto angels of God.

D&C 132

46 Whatsoever you **seal** on earth shall be **sealed** in **heaven**; and whatsoever you **bind** on earth, *in* my **name** and *by* my **word**, saith the Lord, it shall be eternally **bound** in the **heavens**;

EPHESIANS 1

10 That in the dispensation of the fulness of times he might gather together in one all things in **Christ**, both which are in heaven, and which are on earth; even in him:

gathered together in my **light**, there am I in the midst of them. (light + light)

D&C 42

6 And ye shall go forth in the **light** of my **Light**, preaching my **light**, *two by two*, in my **light**, lifting up your voices as with the sound of a trump, **lighting** my **light** like unto angels of God.

D&C 132

46 Whatsoever you **light** on earth shall be **lighted** in **light**; and whatsoever you **light** on earth, *in* my **light** and *by* my **light**, saith the Lord, it shall be eternally **lighted** in the **light**;

EPHESIANS 1

10 That in the dispensation of the fulness of times he might gather together in one all things in **Light**, both which are in heaven, and which are on earth; even in him:

[Gather together in one all things in **light**]
[All **Light** will be gathered together into one great whole]

The next morning, Frank was up early studying his scriptures. Something had been on his mind all night, and he was trying to bring it into focus. It had something to do with baptism and taking upon us the name of Christ. The scriptures testify that that is what we do when we are baptized:

---

2 NEPHI 31

13 . . . witnessing unto the Father that ye are willing to take upon you the name of Christ, by baptism—yea, by following your Lord and your Savior down into the water, according to his word.

But the question that now formed itself in his mind was, exactly how do we take upon us the name of Christ when we are baptized?

He thought that he should review the words of the baptismal prayer and see if they offered any insight. He found them in D&C 20:

73 The person who is called of God and has authority from Jesus Christ to baptize, shall go down into the water with the person who has presented himself or herself for baptism, and shall say, calling him or her by name: Having been commissioned of Jesus Christ, *I baptize you in the name of the Father, and of the Son, and of the Holy Ghost.* Amen.
74 Then shall he immerse him or her in the water, and come forth again out of the water.

Having reviewed that, he found another scripture:

3 Nephi 11
23 Verily I say unto you, that whoso repenteth of his sins through your words, and *desireth to be baptized in my name*, on this wise shall ye baptize them—Behold, ye shall go down and stand in the water, and in my name shall ye baptize them.
24 And now behold, *these are the words which ye shall say*, calling them by name, saying:
25 Having authority given me of Jesus Christ, *I baptize you in the name of the Father, and of the Son, and of the Holy Ghost.* Amen.
26 And then shall ye immerse them in the water, and come forth again out of the water.
27 And *after this manner shall ye baptize in my name*; for behold, verily I say unto you, that the Father, and the Son, and the Holy Ghost are one; and I am in the Father, and the Father in me, and the Father and I are one.

Nothing was really coming through, and he was about to lay the study aside when all of a sudden the words came off the page. "I baptize you in the name!" He said that two or three times and then said again, "I baptize you in*to* the name." There it was. He had been so caught up thinking that this was a statement of the authority by which the baptism was done that he had not noticed that the statement just before it said, 'having authority' or 'having been commissioned.' This was the first time the reality of this had dawned on him. When we are baptized, we are baptized "into" the name of Christ. Then he saw something else. Jesus said those who were baptized into his name were baptized into the name of the whole Godhead—the name of the Father, and the name of the Son, and the name of the Holy Ghost—because all three have upon them the same name and are one.

Frank could not wait to see if any other scriptures confirm the idea of being baptized *into* the name of Christ. He found these:

GALATIONS 3
27 For as many of you as have been *baptized into* **Christ** have *put on* **Christ**.
ROMANS 6
3 Know ye not, that so many of us as were *baptized into* **Jesus Christ** were baptized *into* his death?
4 Therefore we are buried with him by baptism *into* death: that like as Christ was raised up from the dead by the glory of the Father, even so we also should walk *in* newness of life.
MOSES 6:59
59 Inasmuch as ye were born into the world by water, and blood, and the spirit, which I have made, and so became of dust a living soul, even so ye must be *born again into* the **kingdom of heaven**, of water, and of the Spirit, and be cleansed by blood.

There it was again. Those who are baptized are baptized into Christ. They are immersed into every aspect of him—his name, his light, his death, his resurrection, his kingdom, his eternal life—and into every aspect of the Father and the Holy Ghost as well. Of course he knew that this was only one way to view this principle and that the actual wording of the ordinance had been given by revelation. Still, it opened his understanding and gave him an appreciation he had never had.

Frank couldn't wait to share his feelings with his wife. They enjoyed each other's insights very much.

Even More Light on Light

It was probably not by accident that Joan and Karen bumped into each other at the supermarket about three weeks later. Joan came around an aisle, and there was Karen, bent over, looking at the price of ginger spice. They greeted each other warmly and asked about the latest happenings in their lives. After a few minutes, they found that they had learned so much in their individual study that they agreed to get together that afternoon to share their findings.

"My recent studies," Joan began as they sat in her living room, "have been in the book of Moses and the Old Testament. I was studying about the law of sacrifice and the offering of the sacrificial lamb when, to my surprise, I recognized the light + light principle."

"That sounds interesting. Show me," Karen said.

"Well, first of all I read these verses about Adam and Eve:

MOSES 5

5 And he gave unto them commandments, that they should worship the Lord their God, and *should offer the firstlings of their flocks, for an offering* unto the Lord. And Adam was obedient unto the commandments of the Lord.

6 And after many days an angel of the Lord appeared unto Adam, saying: *Why dost thou offer sacrifices* unto the Lord? And Adam said unto him: *I know not,* save the Lord commanded me.

7 And then the angel spake, saying: *This thing is a similitude of the sacrifice of the Only Begotten of the Father, which is full of* **grace** *and* **truth**.

"Adam and Eve were commanded to offer a lamb in sacrifice to the Lord, and when the angel asked them why they were doing it, they didn't know. The angel then told them that this practice was in the likeness of the sacrifice of the Savior which is (or would be) full of light + light. Now *that* principle we know and can understand—it is because of the Atonement of the Savior that we are able to receive light + light. But the thing that impressed me was the methodology of the offering that demonstrated this principle."

"What do you mean?" Karen asked.

"Look at these scriptures in the Old Testament. They tell *how* the sacrifice was to be carried out.

EXODUS 29

38 Now this is that which thou shalt offer upon the altar; *two lambs of the first year* **day by day continually**.

39 The *one lamb thou shalt offer in the* **morning**; and *the other lamb thou shalt offer at* **even**:

40 And with the one lamb a tenth deal of flour mingled with the fourth part of an hin of beaten oil; and the fourth part of an hin of wine for a drink offering.

41 And the other lamb thou shalt offer at even, and shalt do thereto according to the meat offering of the morning, and according to the drink offering thereof, for a sweet savour, *an offering made by* **fire** unto the LORD.

42 This shall be a **continual burnt offering** throughout your generations at the door of the tabernacle of the congregation before the LORD: where I will meet you, to speak there unto thee.

NUMBERS 28

3 And thou shalt say unto them, This is the *offering made by* **fire** which ye shall offer unto the LORD; *two lambs of the first year without spot day by day*, for a **continual burnt offering**.

4 *The one lamb shalt thou offer in the* **morning**, *and the other lamb shalt thou offer at* **even**.

"I see what you mean," Karen said. "A lamb offered by fire (or light) every morning and every evening on the altar—continually. That is beautiful. The one burned all day and the other all night."

"But there is more!" Joan said. "Look down at verses 9 and 10."

> 9 *And on the sabbath day two lambs of the first year without spot,* and two tenth deals of flour for a meat offering, mingled with oil, and the drink offering thereof:
> 10 *This is the* **burnt offering** *of every sabbath, beside the* **continual burnt offering**, and his drink offering.

"That's fascinating! They were to offer a double portion on the Sabbath—two lambs in the morning and two at night," Karen observed. "That is certainly a graphic way to demonstrate the idea of a perpetual regeneration of light."

"After his resurrection, the Savior elevated the principle of sacrifice to a higher level," Joan said. "Look at these verses:"

> **3 NEPHI 9**
> 19 *And ye shall offer up unto me no more the shedding of blood; yea, your sacrifices and your burnt offerings shall be done away, for I will accept none of your sacrifices and your burnt offerings.*
> 20 *And ye* shall offer for a sacrifice unto me a broken heart *and a contrite spirit. And* whoso cometh unto me with a broken heart and a contrite spirit, him will I baptize with **fire** and with the **Holy Ghost** . . .

"In the beginning," Joan continued, "the sacrifice of a lamb was a similitude of the sacrifice of the Savior—full of light + light. When the Savior commanded us to offer instead an offering of a broken heart and a contrite spirit, that offering became a similitude of the sacrifice of the Savior. It becomes a sacrifice bringing light + light if we offer it every morning and every evening by the power (or fire) of the Holy Ghost upon the altar of prayer."

"That really opens up the meaning," Karen said. "I can tell you've really thought about this. If I understand all this correctly, the Lord has not changed the fact that we should be offering sacrifice; he has simply changed the object that we place on the altar. It is in the offering and the blessing of that offering by the Holy Ghost that we receive light + light, and the Lord expects us to offer a double portion on the Sabbath day. Hence, it should be a day when we receive and then give a double portion of light + light."

"I am so glad that we got together," Joan said. "Now I would like to know what areas you have been studying."

"You know, Joan, I have been back in D&C 84:45 again. I continue to find things there that astound me. Let me show you."

Karen took out a sheet of paper on which was the following diagram.

Word = Truth = Light = Spirit

"You remember Frank showed us and taught us this word relationship from this verse. I keep coming back to it. I have found, among other things, that it is a powerful statement about the nature of God and hence about the nature of man. First of all, let's look at the first word in the statement—*word*. Where does the "word" of the Lord come from, Joan?"

"It obviously comes from him."

"Yes, it does, but let's see if we can be more specific. Look at this scripture:"

D&C 68
4 And whatsoever they shall speak when moved upon by the Holy Ghost shall be **scripture**, shall be the **will** of the Lord, shall be the **mind** of the Lord, shall be the **word** of the Lord, shall be the **voice** of the Lord, and the **power** of God unto salvation.

"I think I see what you are getting at. The word of the Lord comes from his mind."

"Yes! The *word* of the Lord is an expression of what is in the *mind* of the Lord."

"Now," Karen said, "let's hold that thought and build on the next word in the statement. The next word is *truth*."

D&C 93
24 And **truth** is knowledge of things as they are, and as they were, and as they are to come;
Jacob 4
13 For the **Spirit** speaketh the **truth** and lieth not. Wherefore, it speaketh of things as they really are, and of things as they really will be.

"According to this verse, what is truth, Joan?"

"Truth is knowledge of things as they really are," Joan responded.

"Again holding that thought," Karen said, "let's consider the next word—*light*."

D&C 88

12 **Light** proceedeth forth from the presence of God to fill the immensity of space—

13 The **light** which is in all things, which giveth life to all things, which *is the law by which all things are governed*, even the power of God who sitteth upon his throne, who is in the bosom of eternity, who is in the midst of all things.

3 Nephi 15

9 Behold, I am the *law*, and the **light**.

"How does this verse define light?" Karen asked.

"It is the law by which all things are governed."

"Finally," Karen said, "let's consider the last word—*spirit*."

D&C 29

31 . . . by the *power* of my **Spirit** . . .

D&C 123

7 . . . supported and urged on and upheld *by the influence of that* **spirit** which hath so strongly riveted the creeds of the fathers

D&C 138

24 Their countenances shone, and *the* **radiance** *from the presence of the Lord rested upon them*, and they sang praises unto his holy name.

"What do these verses teach us about spirit?" Karen asked.

"It seems that it is a power or influence that radiates out," Joan said.

"Now," Karen continued, "we have enough information to understand something about the nature of God." She turned over the page she was holding. "Here is the information:"

That which is in God's mind,
(His **Word**)

is knowledge of things as they really are with him.
(the **Truth**)

That knowledge is the law by which he governs his affairs.
(the **Light**)

That law is the power or influence that radiates out from him.
(the **Spirit**)"

"That's inspiring!" Joan exclaimed. "It helps me see the unity of the attributes that God possesses. The influence that radiates out from him is a direct result of the law by which he governs himself, and that law is based on his knowledge, and that knowledge comes from his word that originates in his mind."

"To me," Karen said, "the fundamental basis of his whole existence is what is in his mind. Elder B. H. Roberts said that 'behind all the phenomena to be seen in the universe' is the 'majesty and the power of [his] Supreme Mind." (Discourse delivered by Elder B. H. Roberts, at Salt Lake City, Utah, December 12, 1897. Brian H. Stuy, ed., *Collected Discourses*, vol. 5)

"We could almost make another diagram," Joan said, "with the wording like this." (She drew some lines and filled in the words)

Word	=	Truth	=	Light	=	Spirit
The Mind of God		Knowledge of things as they really are		Law by which He governs		Power or influence He radiates

"Now that we see this," Karen said, "can you see how it applies to man as well as to God?"

Joan studied the diagram for a few moments and then said, "Yes, I can. The influence that a man has is directly related to the law by which he governs himself, and that law is directly related to his knowledge, and his knowledge, of course, is what he has stored in his mind."

"I wrote down my understanding of that the other day, and it is very similar to what you have just said," Karen remarked.

She took out another sheet and showed Joan what she had written:

That which is in the mind of a man
(his **Word**)

is knowledge of things as they really are with him.
(the **Truth** *about* him and *in* him, regardless of whether his
knowledge is true or not, and whether he likes it or not)

That knowledge is the law by which he governs his affairs.
(the **Light** at one level or another, or the lack of it)

That law is the power or influence that radiates out from him.
(the **Spirit** he manifests—whether good or evil)"

"As I said earlier," Karen continued, "the fundamental thing is what is in the mind. That is the difference between the power and influence of God and the power and influence of man. I have thought about it this way. If ten people got together in a dark room and exercised and combined all their power and energy, do you think they could generate enough light to read a newspaper?"

"Not a chance," Joan chuckled.

"Yet light goes forth from the person of God to fill the immensity of space (see D&C 88:12). That is the difference between what is in the mind of God and what is in the mind of man."

"It gives you pause when we think how far we have to go," Joan said.

"We have the promise, however," Karen added, "that we can eventually have a fulness. That is the wonder of being children of God."

D&C 93

28 He that keepeth his commandments receiveth **truth** *and* **light**, until he is **glorified** in **truth** and knoweth all things.

D&C 88

67 And if your eye be single to my **glory**, your whole bodies shall be filled with **light**, and there shall be no *darkness* in you; and that body which is filled with **light** comprehendeth all things.

It was remarkable how an increased understanding of the scriptures could elevate the feelings of the heart. Both Joan and Karen were edified by their experience and wished they could have spent many more hours together. They soon realized, however, that the available time was gone. They expressed appreciation for what they had learned from each other and applauded the experience by saying how excited they were to share their new insights with their husbands.

They parted with a hug, a warm "thank you," and a promise to meet again soon.

Steve sat in his car and waited for the light to change. He was going to work early because he liked to ponder the scriptures at his desk before the other employees came to work.

He was pondering a verse that he had read in Alma that morning:

ALMA 32
21 And now as I said concerning faith—faith is not to have a perfect knowledge of things; therefore if ye have faith ye hope for things which are not seen, which are true.

He had tried to put this into his own words:

> If you have faith, you hope for things which are true which you can't see.
> If you have faith, you believe in things which are true which you can't see.
> If you have faith, you believe in things which you can't see which are true.
> If you have faith, you believe in truth which you can't see.
> If you have faith, you believe in things which are not seen which are light.
> If you have faith, you believe in light which you can't see.

Suddenly, the last statement made his heart pound. *Faith is to believe in the light which you cannot see.* That was breathtaking! It takes very little faith to believe in light that we can see, but believing in light that we can't see is different, for if you can't see it, how do you know it is there, and if it is there, how do you know that it is light?

Steve hurried to his office, anxious to get on his laptop and search for more information. He found the following scripture in his Gospel Explorer program:

D&C 10
58 I am the **light** which shineth in *darkness*, and the *darkness* comprehendeth it not.

He knew from the former studies that he and his wife and friends had done, that there is a part of the light of Christ that can be seen by mortal man, but the larger part cannot be seen. The world and all that is in it is literally bathed in the light of Christ, but it is invisible to man. Steve remembered reading some other scriptures on this topic and looked them up:

D&C 88
12 Which **light** proceedeth forth from the presence of God to *fill the immensity of space*—
13 The **light** which is in all things, which giveth life to all things, which is the law by which all things are governed,
D&C 38
7 But behold, verily, verily, I say unto you that mine eyes are upon you. I am in your midst and ye cannot see me;

Steve thought about the power and authority that the Lord says rests upon the leaders of the Church and the glory with which the Saints are armed as they are endowed in the temple (see D&C 107:8, 109:22, 1 Nephi 14:14). He reasoned that this light is independent of the vision and comprehension of mortals—even to those who possess it—unless it is specifically given to them to see it. The Savior expounded upon this:

LUKE 17
20 And when he was demanded of the Pharisees, when the **kingdom** of **God** should come, he answered them and said, The **kingdom** of **God** cometh *not with observation.*

"So how does one believe in light that he can't see?" Steve said to himself.

Something stirred in his memory, and he searched for the words of Korihor when he was contending with Alma:

> **ALMA 30**
> 15 Ye cannot know of things which ye do not see; therefore
> ye cannot know that there shall be a Christ.

Here was the very issue. "Impossible," Korihor says, "to believe in light that you can't see." His next statement was very instructive:

> 43 If thou wilt show me a sign . . . that . . . God . . . hath
> **power** . . . then will I be convinced of the **truth** of thy words.

Steve knew what happened next.

> 50 Korihor was struck dumb, that he could not have
> utterance.

He was struck dumb by the light that he could not see. And then he admitted it.

> 52 I know that nothing save it were the **power** of God could
> bring this upon me;

"So," Steve said again, "how does one start to believe in light that he can't see?

He remembered back to the study he and his wife did of Alma 32. He quickly searched for those words again:

> **ALMA 32**
> 27 If ye will awake and arouse your faculties, even to an ex-
> periment upon my **words**, and exercise a particle of faith, yea,
> even if ye can no more than desire to believe, let this desire
> work in you, even until ye believe in a manner that ye can give
> place for a portion of my **words**.
> 28 Now, we will compare the **word** unto a **seed**.
> 30 . . . as the **seed** swelleth, and sprouteth, and beginneth to
> grow, then you must needs say that the **seed** is **good**;
> 35 O then, is not this real? I say unto you, Yea, because
> it is **light**; and whatsoever is **light**, is **good**, because it is
> *discernible.*

Even though he had studied these words before, they entered his heart with great power, and he felt at that moment like he was in touch with eternity. He was glad that he had experienced at least some of that light.

He continued to marvel that God in all his glory and majesty, in his exalted state of ultimate Light—the light which permeates everything—has hidden himself so completely from man that revelation from him is the only means to discover he is there.

1 Timothy 6
16 [God] Who only hath immortality, dwelling in the **light** which no *man* can approach unto; whom no *man* hath seen, nor can see.

He continued to ponder, and another thought came into his mind.

"If the light that we can't see is infinitely greater than the light that we can see, then there must be a darkness that we can't see that is infinitely greater than the darkness we can see."

He clicked away on his computer and tried to find something about that. He found the following verses that speak about those who go away into darkness because of their wickedness.

D&C 76
44 They shall go away into everlasting punishment, which is endless punishment, which is eternal punishment, to reign with the devil and his angels in eternity, where their worm dieth not, and the fire is not quenched, which is their torment—
45 And the end thereof, neither the place thereof, nor their torment, no man knows;
46 Neither was it revealed, neither is, neither will be revealed unto man, except to them who are made partakers thereof;
47 Nevertheless, I, the Lord, show it by vision unto many, but straightway shut it up again;
48 Wherefore, the end, the width, the height, the depth, and the misery thereof, they understand not, neither any man except those who are ordained unto this condemnation.

There was his answer. There is a darkness out there in eternity somewhere that is as far beyond the capability of mortal man to discern as is the very light in which God dwells. Steve determined right then and there that while he wanted to know and understand all that was possible about the Light of God, he didn't want to know any more than he already knew about the darkness.

0

Light plus Light

The phone rang in Steve's office. He didn't expect to hear Frank's voice when he picked it up. They exchanged cheerful greetings and expressed appreciation to each other for the learning experiences both they and their wives were having. Steve said he wished they could have more time to pursue things together.

"That's what I am calling about," Frank said. "My wife and I have access to a time-share cabin on the lake in Woodbine National Park. Its available next month, Thursday to Saturday, the fifteenth to the seventeenth. There are accommodations for two couples. We wondered if you and Joan might like to join us."

Steve and Joan were excited for the chance to get away for a few days and made all the necessary arrangements. On Thursday morning they drove the three hours to the park, and by noon they were comfortably sitting on the deck of the lake-shore cabin surrounded by beautiful mountains and drinking 7Up with Frank and Karen.

"What a place," Joan said. "It's sad that we don't take time in our lives very often to do this kind of thing."

They fixed a lunch and spent much of the afternoon exploring the lake and some of the trails around the resort.

When they finished dinner in the late afternoon, the subject turned to the study of the scriptures. As they pushed their chairs back from the table, Karen said, "Let's just clean up here and then gather in the living room."

They all worked to put away the food and tidy up. Then they moved into the other room.

"Who would like to begin?" Frank asked.

Steve picked up his quadruple combination edition of the scriptures and said, "Perhaps I could. When I think about the light + light principle, I can't help thinking about our Latter-day scriptures and the miracle of light + light that they are. I have done a little study about them, and perhaps we could begin with a discussion about that."

They quickly agreed, and each went to get their scriptures.

When they were all seated, Steve said: "Let me show you a slide and then we can talk about it."

Steve turned on his laptop computer to which was attached a small projector. He focused the picture on the wall by the fireplace.

The Scriptures Grow Brighter and Brighter

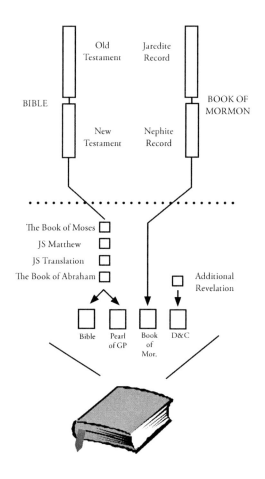

"Let's think first of the Old Testament," Steve said. "The Lord gave revelations to various prophets at various times in history. By a miracle of heaven they were added to each other and preserved and handed on down into the New Testament times. The New Testament was also a series of revelations that were written at various times and in varying places. These records also were miraculously preserved and gathered together. These two records were eventually joined in one, and of that record, the Book of Mormon says:

---

1 NEPHI 13

24 And the angel of the Lord said unto me: Thou hast beheld that the book proceeded forth from the mouth of a Jew; and when it proceeded forth from the mouth of a Jew it contained the fulness of the gospel of the Lord, of whom the twelve apostles bear record; and they bear record according to the truth which is in the Lamb of God.

25 Wherefore, these things go forth from the Jews in purity unto the Gentiles, according to the truth which is in God.

26 And after they go forth by the hand of the twelve apostles of the Lamb, from the Jews unto the Gentiles, thou seest the formation of that great and abominable church, which is most abominable above all other churches; for behold, they have taken away from the gospel of the Lamb many parts which are plain and most precious; and also many covenants of the Lord have they taken away.

29 And after these plain and precious things were taken away it goeth forth unto all the nations of the Gentiles; yea, even across the many waters which thou hast seen with the Gentiles which have gone forth out of captivity.

"While this was happening in the Old World, revelations were given to the Jaredites in the New World. Those records were hid up when the Jaredites were destroyed and then later rediscovered at the time of King Mosiah. He translated them and added them to the records and revelations that had, up to that time, been given to his own people, the Nephites. That combined record was handed down and came forth in our day and was brought side by side with the Bible (light + light). Of course you all know the prophecy in the book of Ezekiel about this happening:

> EZEKIEL 37
> 16 Moreover, thou son of man, take thee one stick, and write
> upon it, For Judah, and for the children of Israel his compan-
> ions: then take another stick, and write upon it, For Joseph,
> the stick of Ephraim, and for all the house of Israel his com-
> panions:
> 17 And join them one to another into one stick; and they
> shall become one in thine hand.

"The sticks, as you know, are the books of the Bible and the Book of
Mormon. When the Book of Mormon was translated, Joseph learned—as
we read above in 1 Nephi 13:26—that the Bible record had lost some of
its most precious parts. He was given a commandment to retranslate the
Bible and restore many of those parts. From that work we received the
book of Moses, the Joseph Smith Matthew material, and the other thousands of insights into the Bible which has become known as the Joseph
Smith Translation. Again, light + light."

*(Author note: I would like to mention that as Joseph translated the Bible,
he published the book of Moses and the Matthew material in the Church's
newspaper. That material became* Church *owned and* Church *published.
However, the rest of his Bible translation materials were still in unpublished
form when he died. When Brigham Young and others went to Joseph's wife,
Emma, to ask for those manuscripts, she would not give them to the Church
but kept them as her own private property. When her son, Joseph Smith III,
became president of the Reorganized Church of Jesus Christ of Latter-day
Saints, she gave them to him, and they became the property of that organization. We will discuss more of this story later.)*

"In the meantime," Steve continued, "the Lord miraculously brought
the ancient Egyptian records of Father Abraham to Joseph Smith. These
he translated and placed side by side with the other records he had translated—more light + light.

"But that is not all; Joseph received the revelations that are contained
in the Doctrine and Covenants. These revelations added more light to the
light already received.

"Now, let's read a prophecy from the Book of Mormon by Joseph who
was sold into Egypt about Joseph Smith in the latter days. Would you
please read this, Joan?"

---

2 NEPHI 3:7–12

Yea, Joseph truly said: Thus saith the Lord unto me: A choice
seer will I raise up out of the fruit of thy loins; and he shall be
esteemed highly among the fruit of thy loins . . . and unto him
will I give power to bring forth my word unto the seed of thy
loins—and not to the bringing forth my word only . . . but
to the convincing them of my word, which shall have already
gone forth among them.
Wherefore, the fruit of thy loins shall write; and the fruit of
the loins of Judah shall write; and that which shall be written
by the fruit of thy loins, and also that which shall be written
by the fruit of the loins of Judah, *shall grow together*, unto the
confounding of false doctrines . . . and bringing them to the
knowledge of their fathers in the latter days, and also to the
knowledge of my covenants, saith the Lord.

"What do these verses say that Joseph Smith is going to do in the
latter days, Joan?"

"He is going to bring forth the word of the Lord from the Nephites
and also convince the people of the truth of the Bible which has *already*
gone forth among the people."

"What will happen to the record of Joseph and the record of Judah in
the last days, Frank?"

"It says that they shall grow together," Frank answered.

"When the Book of Mormon was published and brought side by side
with the Bible, each record had grown in its own individual way, but now
they were growing *toward* each other. I would like to dwell for a moment
on how they have grown and are growing in one, *together*.

"In 1972, acting president of the Quorum of the Twelve Apostles, Spen-
cer W. Kimball, took a proposal to the First Presidency that the Church
have a new edition of the King James Bible. That proposal was approved by
President Joseph Fielding Smith. Three months after President Smith died,
President Harold B. Lee organized a committee that eventually included
Elder Thomas S. Monson, Elder Boyd K. Packer, and Elder Bruce R. Mc-
Conkie. This became known as the Scriptures Publication Committee.

"These brethren were charged with the responsibility from President
Lee to figure out a way to bring about new editions of the standard works
that would be more helpful and would allow the Latter-day Saints to obtain the most possible understanding from the scriptures. (Robert J. Matthews,
"New Editions of the Scriptures," Sidney B. Sperry Symposium, January 30, 1982, 13)

"Elder Kimball sent letters to others and asked them to become part of the committee with a special task: 'to prepare a King James Bible which would include a standardized concordance, dictionary, atlas, and index and . . . have footnotes, ready references, and cross references related to other LDS scriptures.' Its purpose would be to 'assist in improving doctrinal scholarship throughout the Church.' (Lavina Fielding Anderson, "Church Publishes First LDS Edition of the Bible," *Ensign*, October 1979, 12) The project was envisioned as lasting a year or two. It took six years and nine months."

"Why did it take so long?" Karen asked.

"There were thousands of cross-references that needed to be worked out and approved. There were also thousands of Hebrew and Greek clarifications. But there is more. A Latter-day Saint by the name of Robert J. Matthews had had an interest in the Joseph Smith translation materials since the time he was a young boy of eighteen. After as much extensive research as he was able to do, in 1968, when he was forty-two years of age, he was allowed by the Reorganized Church of Jesus Christ of Latter-day Saints to actually see and study the original manuscripts. Because of his work, he was asked by President Kimball, who was now President of the Church, to be on the committee to oversee the work of including as much of the JST material in the new work as the Reorganized Church would allow—they holding the copyright. It was a miracle that this light was allowed to be added to the light of the Bible which was being readied for publication. The fruits of the ancient prophecies and commandments of the Lord to Joseph Smith to restore the most plain and precious parts of the Bible would never have been fully realized at this time if this had not happened. The new edition of the Bible was published in October of 1979.

"It was no sooner off the press than it was determined to re-publish the triple combination in the same format as the new Bible, with cross-references and indexes and all the helps linking it to the Bible. It was during the crescendo leading to these new publications that the Lord revealed that two new revelations should be added to the scriptures (D&C 137 and 138), and then—just near to the time that the triple was to be published—came the marvelous revelation to President Kimball concerning all worthy males being able to hold the priesthood.

"To me, it is the most incredible thing in the world that these four volumes of scripture—now fortified with those things that the Lord wanted us to have in our day, including the words of the Jews and the words of the Nephites, have been published under one cover—a quadruple combination (published in 1981). Of this work, President Packer has said, "The stick or record of Judah—the Old Testament and New Testament—and the stick or record of Ephraim—the Book of Mormon—are now woven together in such a way that as you pore over one you are drawn to the other; as you learn from one you are enlightened by the other. They are indeed one in our hands. *Ezekiel's prophecy now stands fulfilled.*" (Boyd K. Packer, "Scriptures," *Ensign*, November, 1982, 53)

"Now, just before I quit talking, I want to quote a couple of things that Elder Packer and Elder McConkie said about this new revelatory work. Elder Packer spoke about the general attitude of members of the church when the two new revelations were added to the scriptures, and Elder McConkie spoke about attitudes toward the new editions of the standard works:

> I was surprised, and I think all of the Brethren were surprised, at how casually [the] announcement of two additions to the standard works was received by the Church. But we will live to sense the significance of it; we will tell our grandchildren and our great-grandchildren, and we will record in our diaries, that we were on the earth and remember when that took place. (Elder Boyd K. Packer, Address to religious educators, Temple Square Assembly Hall, October 14, 1977)

> We are somewhat saddened, however, that the generality of the saints have not yet caught the vision of what our new scriptural publications contain and are not using them as they should. (Elder Bruce R. McConkie, Regional Representative Seminar, April 2, 1982)

"You can just feel the pain in those statements. They are an echo from the past.

---

2 NEPHI 29
6 Thou fool, that shall say: A **Bible**, we have got a **Bible**, and we need no more **Bible**.

"Essentially these people are saying, 'A light, we have got a light, and we need no more light.'

"Finally, in this concluding statement by Elder Packer, we can sense the prophetic vision and power in these things:

> Do you see, my brethren, do you see, my sisters, the tremendous, monumental work that is rolling forth in this

church and kingdom of God [referring to the new editions of the scriptures]? Do you see a mighty retrenching force preparing this people? Do you see *glory*? You and I, each of us, all of us, have a part in this . . . Do you see the vision of it? Do you see your part in it? Do you not sense a feeling of warmth and *glory* to know that you are a part of such a thing? (Elder Boyd K. Packer, Address to religious educators, Temple Square Assembly Hall, October 14, 1977)

"To me, the 'growing' and 'intertwining' of the scriptures and the impact that they can have on us by the power of the Holy Ghost is at the very heart of the doctrine of light."

D&C 50

24 That which is of God is **light**; and he that receiveth **light**, and continueth in God, receiveth more **light**; and that **light** *groweth* **brighter** and **brighter** until the *perfect* **day**.

A sense of reverence and awe settled over the little group as they contemplated the magnitude of what they had just heard. Each looked at the scriptures they were holding and realized that perhaps they would never look at them the same way again. What a precious gift, what incredible promises, what marvelous light.

The next morning they were up early, bikeriding the trails and enjoying the sunrise. The fresh mountain air was exhilarating, and the scenery was simply good for the soul. They came in for breakfast about eight-thirty, and when they were almost finished, Karen said, "I am so excited to have another day to study with all of you. I want to say how enlightening it was to learn about our scriptures last night. And by the way, Steve, I just have to say again what an incredible presentation that was."

"Thanks, Karen," Steve said. "I was thinking as we were riding along this morning how I would have reacted a few months ago if someone had suggested getting together for three days and studying the scriptures."

"It is a true idiom that we learn to love that which we give our time to," Frank said. "And I'm convinced that this group will never tire of learning about the scriptures."

"I had a thought this morning," Karen said as she showed the others a verse she had found in the Doctrine and Covenants. "The scriptures are not finished growing. Now that they have grown together, they will continue to grow in size because the light of God is always and forever—light + light.

D&C 11

22 But now hold your peace; study my word which hath gone forth among the children of men, and also study my word which shall come forth among the children of men, or that which is now translating, yea, until you have obtained all which I shall grant unto the children of men in this generation, *and then shall all things be added thereto.*

"We still need the records of the lost tribes of Israel, and we also don't have the sealed portion of the Book of Mormon. I am sure that there will be revelations about Adam-ondi-Ahman and the city of Zion. Oh, and I just remembered, we will also have the brass plates. We can look forward to a lot of additions and growth to our scriptures. The Lord told Moses that his words would never cease (see Moses 1:4)."

There was a consensus of feeling on that point.

"Frank," Joan said, "you mentioned something to Steve this morning about light and the Urim and Thummim. I didn't get to hear all of what you said. Will you tell us more?"

"Should we study about that next?" Frank asked.

All agreed, and when they had left the kitchen clean, they retired to the living room to continue their studies.

Steve set up a whiteboard and set out some markers.

"My comment this morning as we were coming into the house," Frank began, "was that the Urim and Thummim was an instrument of light and operated by light. There are some verses of scripture and comments by some of the early brethren that relate to this. Let's look at them and discuss them."

ALMA 37

23 And the Lord said: I will prepare unto my servant Gazelem, *a stone, which shall shine forth in darkness unto* **light**, that I may discover unto my people who serve me . . . the works of their brethren.

MOSIAH 8
17 But a *seer* [one who uses the Urim and Thummim] can know of things which are past, and also of things which are to come, and by them shall all things be revealed, or, rather, shall secret things be made manifest, and *hidden things shall come to* **light**, and things which are not known shall be made known by them, and also things shall be made known by them which otherwise could not be known.

ETHER 3
24 For behold, the language which ye shall write I have confounded; wherefore I will cause in my own due time that *these stones shall magnify to the eyes of men these things* which ye shall write.

"David Whitmer, one of the three witnesses of the Book of Mormon, said that Joseph, when using the Urim and Thummim, would ready himself for translation, and 'then, *a spiritual light would shine forth*, and a parchment would appear before Joseph, upon which was a line of characters from the plates, and under it, the translation in English' (*The Gift of Seeing*, 52; emphasis added).

"Martin Harris, another of the three witnesses and a scribe for Joseph while he translated the first 116 pages of the Book of Mormon, gave this interesting account of the Urim and Thummim:

> After continued translation they would become weary and would go down to the river and exercise in throwing stones out on the river, etc. While so doing on one occasion, Martin found a stone very much resembling the one used for translating, and on resuming their labors of translation Martin put in place (of the Stone) the stone that he had found. He said that the Prophet remained silent unusually long and intently gazing in darkness, no trace of the usual sentence appearing. Much surprised Joseph exclaimed: "Martin! What is the matter? *All is as dark as Egypt.*" Martin's countenance betrayed him, and the Prophet asked Martin why he had done so. Martin said, to stop the mouths of fools, who had told him that the Prophet had learned those sentences and was merely repeating them. (MS 44:78–9, 86–7; Edward Stephenson, *Reminiscences of Joseph, the Prophet* [Salt Lake City: Edward Stevenson, 1893]. Dr. Paul R. Cheesman, *KeyStone of Mormonism* [Provo: Eagle Systems International, 1988], 69)

"Orson Pratt, a member of the Quorum of the Twelve, summed up the matter very well when he said:

> The Urim and Thummim was lighted up by the power of God, and magnified before the eyes of [Joseph], those ancient characters upon the plates of the Book of Mormon . . . (*Journal of Discourses* 21:172-3)

"One of the reasons that these things are important to us in our discussion," Frank continued, "is that a Urim and Thummim is another of the great witnesses to the principle of light + light. Not only does it operate by light, its very name is indicative of that principle."

"What do you mean?" Joan asked.

Frank took a marker and wrote two words on the board:

Ur   Thumm

"Does anyone know what the word *Ur* means?

"Wasn't that the name of the city that Abraham came from?" Karen asked.

"You're right," Frank said, "but let's look up the actual meaning of the word. It's in the Bible Dictionary."

"Here it is," Joan said excitedly. "Wouldn't you know, it means light."

"And the word *Thumm*, which is noted in many of the Biblical commentaries," Frank added, "means 'perfect.'" (See *Strong's Exhaustive Concordance of the Bible* [Crusade Bible Publishers, Inc., 1894, Hebrew and Chaldee Dictionary,] 9-10, 124-125.)

"Hmm, light and perfect," Steve mused. "Taken together, they must mean light that is perfect or perfect light."

"I had no idea that's what those words meant," Joan said.

"But wait!" Karen interjected. "I just realized that you only wrote part of each word on the board. You left off the 'im' endings. What do they mean?"

"I hoped that you would notice that," Frank said. "The Hebrew 'im' makes each word plural."

"Plural?" Joan questioned.

Frank wrote the following on the board as awareness began to dawn on the others.

Ur = light

Ur*im* = lights

Thumm = perfect

Thumm*im* = perfections

"Frank," Joan said, "you just said that the Urim and Thummim demonstrated the light + light principle, so I am assuming that the plural endings mean many lights and many perfections."

"Or in other words, light + light and perfect + perfect," Karen interjected.

"Is that ever interesting," Steve said. "Do you think the words relate to the instrument itself or to what it does?"

"Let's think about that for a moment," Frank replied. "As you said, we are dealing with at least four words here: *Ur Ur* and *Thum Thum*, or in other words, *light light* and *perfect perfect*. If we were to see these four words as defining the instrument and we knew that it took all four of them to make the definition, what might it be?"

"Let me try," Joan said. "A Urim and Thummim is a perfect channel through which perfect light + light comes."

"That is terrific," Frank said. "And the thing that makes it so terrific is that it is almost like the definition that President John Taylor gave in 1883."

> Abraham sought the Lord diligently, and finally he had given unto him a Urim and Thummim, in which he was enabled to obtain a knowledge of many things that others were ignorant of. *I think the meaning of the name of this instrument is Light and Perfection, in other terms, communicating light perfectly*, and intelligence perfectly, through a principle that God has ordained for that purpose.
> (*Journal of Discourses*, 24:262–3)

"I see something else," Karen said. "Steve asked a moment ago if the four words relate to the instrument itself or to what it does. I can see how they relate to the *effect* of the message upon the seer and the people to whom the message comes."

Karen took a marker and drew on the board.

Light + Light   Perfect + Perfect

"As light is communicated through the Urim and Thummim, it enables those to whom it comes to be more perfect—more perfect in understanding and in behavior. That increased level of perfection enables more light to come—which in turn enables more perfection. It seems to suggest continual increase—light and more light, perfection and more perfection, light upon light, and perfection upon perfection.[1]

"It sounds to me like you are quoting the scriptures that Steve ended his presentation with last night," Frank said.

D&C 50

24 That which is of God is **light**; and he that receiveth **light**, and continueth in God, receiveth more **light**; and that **light** *groweth* **brighter** and **brighter** until the *perfect* **day**.

"Remember the verse says that if we receive light from God and continue, it grows brighter and brighter until the perfect day. The last word of the verse, *day*, is of course another word for light. You remember in the Creation, the Lord called the light 'day'—so the word *day*, meaning light, continues the thought of the verse—if we receive light and continue, it grows brighter and brighter until the perfect light, or in other words, a fulness of light."

"And the whole purpose of obtaining a fulness of light," Karen added, "is to be able to become a giver of light + light and perfection + perfection to your eternal posterity."

"That probably explains why the planet on which God resides is a great Urim and Thummim and why this earth in its sanctified state will become a Urim and Thummim to those who live on it, as stated in D&C 130:8–9," Frank said. "Because the business of God, as Karen stated, is to continually give light and perfection to his children. His work is, in effect, a Urim and Thummim principle."

"I'm sure we'll want to come back to these concepts again," Frank added, "but I think we should break for some exercise."

"That's great," Karen said. "Let's get our bikes and take a turn around the lake. We can meet back here for a late lunch about four o' clock."

"The last biker to leave has to do the dishes," Joan called as they all scrambled for their bikes.

Later that evening, as the two couples sat on the deck and listened to the boats on the lake and enjoyed the warmth of the setting sun, Frank asked if any in the group had given any serious thought to the meaning of the word *prepare*.

"I noticed that word when we read the scripture about the Urim and Thummim," Steve said. "The Lord said he would prepare a stone to shine in the darkness, but the word *prepare* didn't register until you just mentioned it."

ALMA 37

23 And the Lord said: I will **prepare** unto my servant Gazelem, *a stone, which shall shine forth in* **darkness** *unto* **light,** that I may discover unto my people who serve me . . . the works of their brethren.

"The word *prepare* or its derivatives," Frank said, "appears 409 times in the scriptures. Some of them obviously relate to mundane things such as preparing chariots or food, but when they relate to the specific work of God, the word means to fill with light. Look in your Topical Guide and see if you can spot some of them."

"Here is one," Joan said. "It is about John the Baptist."

ISAIAH 40

3 The voice of him that crieth in the wilderness, **Prepare** ye the way of the LORD, make straight in the desert a highway for our God.

"And here is one that adds an insight into that one," Steve said.

LUKE 1

17 And he shall go before him in the **spirit** *and* **power** of Elias, to turn the hearts of the fathers to the children, and the disobedient to the **wisdom** *of the* **just**; to make ready a people **prepared** for the Lord.

"I found another one that is very insightful," Karen said.

REVELATION 21

2 And I John saw the holy **city**, new Jerusalem, coming down from God out of heaven, **prepared** as a bride adorned for her husband.

"Here is another one, and I guess because it is so familiar to all of us, we might just pass it by," Joan said.

---

1 Nephi 3

7 And it came to pass that I, Nephi, said unto my father: I will go and do the things which the Lord hath commanded, for I know that the Lord giveth no **commandments** unto the children of men, save he shall **prepare** a way for them that they may accomplish the thing which he commandeth them.

"This one relates to that," Steve added.

---

1 Nephi 10

18 For he is the same yesterday, today, and forever; and the **way** is **prepared** for all men from the foundation of the world, if it so be that they repent and come unto him.

"I found another one," Joan said.

---

2 Nephi 9

43 But the things of the **wise** *and* the **prudent** shall be hid from them forever—yea, that **happiness** which is **prepared** for the saints.

"These scriptures also add a very interesting dimension," Karen said.

Alma 5

28 Behold, are ye stripped of pride? I say unto you, if ye are not ye are not **prepared** to meet God. Behold ye must **prepare** quickly; for the kingdom of heaven is soon at hand, and such an one hath not eternal life.

Alma 34

32 For behold, this life is the time for men to **prepare** to meet **God**; yea, behold the **day** of this life is the **day** for men to perform their labors.

D&C 43

20 **Prepare** yourselves for the great **day** of the Lord.

"They emphasize that light is given to us to prepare for the fulness of light (D&C 84:46)," Karen continued.

"I just thought of an interesting comparison," Joan said. "In the old days people had to get water from a pump. They had to pump the handle up and down to make the water flow, but there was a trick to getting the pump to work. It had to be primed. Guess what it had to be primed with?"

"Water," Karen responded. "That's interesting. To get water you had to prime the pump with water. To get light, you have to prime the pump, so to speak, with light. That is the preparation."

"There are so many insights as we get into this," Steve said. "I found some scriptures about the Savior."

MOSIAH 4

7 I say, that this is the man who receiveth salvation, through the **atonement** which was **prepared** from the foundation of the world for all mankind, which ever were since the fall of Adam, or who are, or who ever shall be, even unto the end of the world.

Ether 3

14 Behold, I am he who was **prepared** from the foundation of the world to redeem my people. Behold, I am Jesus Christ. I am the Father and the Son. In me shall all mankind have **life**, and that eternally, even they who shall believe on my name; and they shall become my sons and my daughters

---

"This verse is especially enlightening," Frank said.

D&C 105

12 For behold, I have **prepared** a great endowment *and* blessing to be poured out upon them, inasmuch as they are faithful and *continue* in humility before me.

"This verse just caught my eye," Karen said.

ALMA 13

7 This high *priesthood* being after the order of his Son, which order was from the foundation of the world; or in other words, being without beginning of days or end of years, being **prepared** from eternity to all eternity, according to his foreknowledge of all things.

"I have never really concentrated on the idea of the priesthood being associated with light," Karen continued, "but with this insight I guess it surely is."

"Should we look at that next?" Frank asked.

"This seems to go on endlessly," Steve said. "I can't believe that we are having such a rich journey. You just wonder where it will go next."

"Well, let me ask you a question or two about priesthood," Frank continued. "What is priesthood?"

"The standard statement about priesthood," Steve said, "is that it's the power of God delegated to man to act for God on earth. We know that the power is light, so it could be said that it is the light of God delegated to man to act for God on earth."

"That's an excellent place to start," Frank continued. "Now, if we were to take the word *priesthood* apart and analyze it, we could gain some additional insights."

Frank had his small whiteboard by the side of the table. He wrote the following on it:

priest   hood

"When a man is called to become a holder of the priesthood, he becomes an officer of that priesthood and is set to minister as a priest in priestly duties. For the sake of discussion, let's assume that the word *priest* refers to the idea of the office.

"Now, if priest refers to the office, what is the hood?"

"It's never entered my mind to take that word apart," Karen said, smiling. "The word *hood* seems to have two meanings to me—and this is my etymology background coming out. As a suffix in a word, it means a state or quality like childhood or manhood. It also means the whole group of something like sisterhood or brotherhood. But perhaps it's the other meaning that gets closer to the direction we seem to be heading, and it reminds me of Little Red Ridinghood. A hood is something that covers the head or shoulders and, depending on its design or color, could be a way of designating or identifying someone."

"That's exactly the direction we want to go, but first let's look at a few scriptures that show that priesthood is light," Frank said. "The first one tells us that the priesthood comes from God himself, and that should automatically alert us to know that it is light."

> **D&C 132**
> 28 I am the Lord thy God, and will give unto thee the **law** of
> *my* Holy **Priesthood**, as was ordained by me and my Father
> before the world was.

"Notice how the Lord calls the priesthood 'my' priesthood," Frank continued. "Then notice that he says in effect, 'I will give unto you the light of my Holy Priesthood.' In another place, he says it this way:

> **D&C 132**
> 44 Then shall you have **power**, by the **power** of my Holy
> Priesthood.

"Or in other words, 'I will give you light by the light of my Holy Priesthood.' We get an increased insight into the meaning of priesthood when we view the next two scriptures. The first is a reference to Bishop Edward Partridge and his work in Missouri. The second is a quote from Isaiah.

> **D&C 85**
> 7 And it shall come to pass that I, the Lord God, will send
> one mighty and strong, holding the scepter of **power** in his
> hand, *clothed with* **light** *for a covering*, whose mouth shall ut-
> ter **words**, eternal **words**; while his bowels shall be a fountain
> of **truth**, to set in order the house of God.
> **Isaiah 30**
> 1 Woe to the rebellious children, saith the LORD, that take
> counsel, but not of me; and that *cover with a covering, but
> not of my* **spirit**, that they may add sin to sin:

"So, we ask again, if priest is the office, what is the hood or covering?"

"I can see that it is light," Steve replied. "Now I understand what it means to magnify the office of the priesthood (see Romans 11:13; Jacob 1:19; D&C 24:9; 66:11). The office is conferred, but it is the responsibility of the individual to so live that the light is present and is increased and magnified in his office. Light is the power in the office, and it seems that once a man has the office, it is up to him how much light he has in it. He can have a little or a lot depending on his faithfulness."

"Speaking of that, let's look at this verse," Frank said.

D&C 121

36 That the rights of the **priesthood** are inseparably connected with the **powers** of **heaven**, and that the **powers** of **heaven** cannot be controlled nor handled only upon the principles of righteousness.

37 That they may be conferred upon us, it is true; but when we undertake to cover our sins, or to gratify our pride, our vain ambition, or to exercise control or dominion or compulsion upon the souls of the children of men, in any degree of unrighteousness, behold, the **heavens** withdraw themselves; the **Spirit** of the Lord is grieved; and when **it** is withdrawn, Amen to the **priesthood** or the **authority** of that man.

D&C 121

36 That the rights of the **office of light** are inseparably connected with the **light** of **heaven**, and that the **light** of **heaven** cannot be controlled nor handled only upon the principles of righteousness.

37 That they (the rights, or the office) may be conferred upon us, it is true; but when we undertake to cover our sins, or to gratify our pride, our vain ambition, or to exercise control or dominion or compulsion upon the souls of the children of men, in any degree of unrighteousness, behold, the **lights** withdraw themselves; the **Light** of the Lord is grieved; and when **it** is withdrawn, Amen to the **office of light** . . . of that man.

"I didn't realize that you men had such awesome responsibility," Joan said. "When I think that priesthood is an office of light, it makes me want to do all in my power to support it and live worthy of its blessings."

"I remember reading something that President Kimball said," Steve replied.

> *There is no limit to the power of the priesthood which you hold.* The limit comes in you if you do not live in harmony with the Spirit of the Lord and you limit yourselves in the power you exert. (James E. Faust, *Finding Light in a Dark World* [Salt Lake City: Deseret Book, 2004], 123; emphasis added)

"As a further witness to these things, look at this verse and tell me what you see," Frank said.

2 Nephi 26

29 He commandeth that there shall be no *priestcrafts*; for, behold, *priestcrafts* are that men preach and set themselves up for a **light** unto the world, that they may get gain and praise of the world; but they seek not the welfare of Zion.

"It teaches me that priestcraft is the opposite of priesthood," Karen said. "The worker of priestcraft sets himself up for a light instead of having the light of God. That's somewhat like the word *X-mas*. It effectively takes Christ out of Christmas. Priestcraft effectively takes light out of priesthood."

"That's insightful," Frank said. "I appreciate what the scriptures are doing to us. This has really been an enjoyable experience. The Prophet Joseph Smith gave us another insight into our study of priesthood. He said:"

D&C 128

11 Now the great and grand secret of the whole matter, and the summum bonum of the whole subject that is lying before us, consists in obtaining the **powers** of the Holy **Priesthood**.

"That suggests two things to me," Joan interjected. "The first is the idea of obtaining light in the office of light until one has a fulness of the light in which there is no darkness at all. Secondly, it suggests that light enables the priesthood holder to function at whatever level in the kingdom he is needed and gives him the power to speak and act in behalf of God. The light is the assurance that the mind of God is present and that the will of God will be done." (See D&C 68:3–4.)

"It is really the process of becoming like God," Steve added, "and is the fundamental principle of the oath and covenant of the priesthood."

"Can you help us understand that, Steve?" Karen asked.

"The oath and covenant of the priesthood is based on the principle of men receiving the power of God into their lives and is itself an outline of the steps for doing so. In fact, receiving light or power in the priesthood is the only avenue to receiving a fulness of the glory of God. These verses from section 84 show that outline:"

D&C 84

35 And also all they who receive this priesthood receive me, saith the Lord;

36 For he that receiveth my servants receiveth me;

37 And he that receiveth me receiveth my Father;

38 And he that receiveth my Father receiveth my Father's kingdom; therefore all that my Father hath shall be given unto him.

39 And this is according to the oath and covenant which belongeth to the priesthood.

"The Savior first teaches that those who receive the priesthood are in effect receiving him. He then outlines how the receiving process works. One way to understand this is to put it in the perspective of the light of God. If we were to assume for a moment that one of the greatest gifts the Lord could give to any man is the light that comes directly from him, then let's put that in the process and see how it reads. The Savior says, for example:"

> All they who receive this priesthood receive light from me.
> For (because) he that receives the light that is in my servants is receiving the light that is in me.
> And he that receives the light that is in me is receiving the light that is in my Father.
> And he that receives the light that is in my Father receives my Father's kingdom.
> Therefore, all the light that my Father has shall be given unto him.
> And this is according to the oath and covenant which belongs to the priesthood.

"Thank you," Karen said. "That gives me a deeper appreciation than I had before."

"Before we end," Frank remarked, "I would just like to share one more bit of information from the book of Abraham that relates to what we are talking about.

"In Facsimile Number Two, Figure Three in the book of Abraham, we are shown a representation of God sitting on his throne. The explanation by the Prophet says it represents God with 'a crown of eternal light upon his head.' I have placed a clipping of that figure here on the page, and to its right is a picture of the same figure found in another place. (See Richard Patrick, *All Color Book of Egyptian Mythology* [London: Octopus Books, 1972], 30) As you study these representations, Joan, what in them seems to represent the crown?"

"Is it the circle over the head?"

"Yes. What do you think that circle is?"

"I don't really know. It could be the sun."

"Why do you say that?"

"Well, it's round, and if you were going to show that the mind and the glory and the power of God are light, you would probably draw a picture of the sun to represent it. In an ancient culture there would be very few symbols other than the sun or the moon or a star or maybe fire that could represent light. The sun, though, is the greatest light of all, and they were speaking about God."

"Thank you very much, Joan. The pharaohs of Egypt," Frank continued, "wore a crown on their heads that derived directly from this circular crown of God. They devised a wearable disk-crown in a practical way by placing it flat on the head like a round cap. If you look at the two pictures to the right, you can see the direct relationship of the circular crown of God to the crown of Pharaoh (including the serpent—a 'spitting adder,' which represented the awful force and power of the light of God. We will talk of this later.) Sometimes the crown of the Pharaoh was shown with an appendage made of stiffened rope or cord that extended upward from the top of the crown ending in a tight coil at its tip. This appendage had great significance in understanding the meaning of the crown.[2]

"It was a spiral, and since the beginning of time, the spiral has suggested to the mind of man the idea that things, phenomena, and beings are in a dynamic state of change and that life is a process. Within that process

Fig 3. Is made to represent God, sitting upon his throne, clothed with power and authority; with a crown of eternal light upon his head . . .

Ra on his throne

Tutankhamun with
his crown

The crown is sometimes shown with
appendages.

Courtesy of Jenny Carrington. www.geocities.com/SoHo/Nook/7916/ArtWorks.html

124

The realm of God

The flow of power from God to the office of Kingship

The realm of Kingship

Nuh—rope, or actions with rope or cord, to tie, to bind, to tie on, to fasten, and so forth.
(Gardiner, *Egyptian Grammar*, Budge, Hieroglyphic Dictionary, vol. 1, 335a, 521)

the universe is constructed on a plan of polarity, beginning and end, male and female, expansion and contraction, ascent and descent, life and death. Processes occur as movement between those poles of the universe. A terminology most appropriate for these processes is the ancient Chinese yang and yin. The idea of yang is a condition of concentration and compactness with its parts tight around a center of heavy density. The idea of yin is the opposite, where the parts are widely diffused and loosely distributed. Movement away from the center of density expresses the yin tendency and movement toward the center, yang. (See Nahum Stiskin, *The Looking-Glass God* [New York: Weatherhill, 1972], 21–22) The very presence of the elongated spiral on the Egyptian crown suggests that it was connected to something above it. And what was above the king? God only!

"It represented the conveyance of light from its greater concentration (God) to its lesser concentration (the king), showing that both God and the king possessed the same light but in varying degrees and that kingship was inseparably connected with Godhood—hence the disk on the head of both God and king. The rope-coil itself is the Egyptian hieroglyphic sign for the idea of tying or knotting, or as we might say sealing or binding— showing that the light of the mind of the king was bound or fastened to the light or the mind of God."

"So the king's crown might have represented to the Egyptians what the 'hood' idea of priesthood represents to us here," Steve said, "the light from God to minister in the office."

"Yes," Frank responded, "and it also demonstrated that the fulness of that light was available to the king at some future time and was in fact the only pathway to it."

"If I might be permitted to say so," Joan interjected, "I see temple relationships in this information. The book of Revelation says that faithful men can become 'kings and priests unto God' (see Revelation 1:6, 5:10). Am I off base?"

"No, Joan, you are not off base. Abraham in his writings tells us that what the Egyptian pharaohs were doing when they practiced their theology was an 'earnest imitation of the true and ancient order,' or in other words, the priesthood and its temple ordinances (see Abraham 1:26). It is significant that the pharaoh was crowned with this crown of light, not in the palace but in the temple, and we know that in the true order of things, the fulness of the priesthood can only be found through temple ordinances.

D&C 124

27 And with iron, with copper, and with brass, and with zinc, and with all your precious things of the earth; and *build a house to my name*, for the Most High to dwell therein.
28 For there is not a *place* found on earth that he may come to and restore again that which was lost unto you, or which he hath taken away, even *the fulness of the* **priesthood**.

"Joseph Smith also said, 'If a man gets a fulness of the priesthood of God he has to get it in the same way that Jesus Christ obtained it, and that was by keeping all the commandments and obeying all the ordinances *of the house of the Lord.*'" (*Teachings of the Prophet Joseph Smith*, 308)

"I read a scripture the other day that puts all this in perspective for me," Karen said. "I didn't understand it then, but our discussion has opened its meaning to me. It was given through the Prophet to Warren Cowdery, who was called to be a presiding high priest over a branch of the Church in New York.

D&C 106

8 And I will give him **grace** *and* **assurance** wherewith he may stand; and if he *continue* to be a faithful witness and a **light** unto the **church** I have prepared a **crown** for him in the mansions of my Father. Even so. Amen.

"The Lord says that he will give him light + light, and by this he will be able to stand. If he continues to be a light to the church, he will be given a crown of light in the kingdom of God. To me this is all about priesthood—magnifying the office of light by receiving and continuing in light, and in time receiving the crowning light in the light of the Father."

As the sun went down and night surrounded the little group, they began to disband and make preparations to retire.

"Again, this has been a superb evening of enlightenment," Steve said. "I'm sad that it's over. It will be hard to get back into our regular routine, but I guess the gospel is as much living as learning."

"Thanks for inviting us here and sharing with us," Joan said. "I truly hope we can do something like this again."

The next morning, the foursome left the resort, and as Steve and Joan drove away, Joan said, "You remember in the beginning all we wanted was a brief understanding of the idea of light in the scriptures. Did you ever imagine that there would be so much to learn about it?"

"No," Steve replied, "but I do know one thing: if God is light, then we haven't even begun."

Notes

1. It may be argued that perfection is an absolute, that there is no such thing as being more and more perfect. Yet that is not so in gospel thinking. We quote the following:

To the Saints in Utah, September 14, 1854 (Letter from the First Presidency)
From these facts it appears strange upon reflection, that any person could be induced to do wrong, though at the same time it requires the most vigilant effort to do right, owing to human infirmity operated on by the spirit of evil; hence the human family require "line upon line, precept upon precept," that by practicing thoroughly upon what they receive they may go on from *perfection to perfection*, or in other words, each walk perfectly in his own sphere.

As these ideas are advanced for your reflection, and action, the counsel is made brief, that you may not overlook it, nor your minds be wearied, or confused while reading. BRIGHAM YOUNG, HEBER C. KIMBALL, JEDEDIAH M. GRANT.
(James R. Clark, comp., *Messages of the First Presidency of The Church of Jesus Christ of Latter-day Saints* [Salt Lake City: Bookcraft, 1965-75], vol. 2, 149)

Discourse By President Brigham Young
The inhabitants of heaven live as a family, . . . their faith, interests and pursuits have one end in view—the glory of God and their own salvation, and that they may receive more and more—*go on from perfection to perfection*, receiving, and then dispensing to others; they are ready to go, and ready to come, and willing to do whatever is required of them and to work for the interest of the whole community, for the good of all. (*Journal of Discourses*, 17:118; emphasis added)
Remarks By Apostle George Teasdale (Delivered at the Quarterly Conference, Logan, Sunday Morning, November 4, 1883)
We are to be educated, we are to receive line upon line, precept upon precept, here a little and there a little, until we shall become perfect in Christ

Jesus. This to me is a glorious philosophy, that we can advance from one degree of perfection to another, until we shall obtain a fulness of truth. (*Journal of Discourses* 24:323)

Discourse By Elder Daniel H. Wells (Second Counselor to Brigham Young in First Presidency)

We should, therefore, be the more careful of our course and conduct in life, and hold fast to that which is given unto us, *and progress and go on from perfection to perfection*, and try to become as godly in our lives as it is possible for us to be in this probation. (*Journal of Discourses* 23:309–10; emphasis added)

2. It has also been suggested that this spiral on the crown represents the antennae of a bee. (See Hugh Nibley, *Lehi in the Desert/The World of the Jaredites/There Were Jaredites* [Salt Lake City: Deseret Book, 1988], 191.) Part of the reason for this suggestion stems from the name of the crown itself. It was the crown of Lower Egypt and was called "dsrt." Because the Egyptians wrote no vowels in their words, we are able to pronounce them only by inserting an "e" or occasionally an "a" between the consonants. We can see immediately when we try to speak the word "dsrt," that it has a relationship to the bee. It is "deseret" (see Ether 2:3). Dr. Nibley links the Egyptian usage of the concept of "deseret" to a parallel use of it by the Jaredites, both having their roots in the same place at the same time—the tower of Babel. The "dsrt" crown was the crown of the kingship of a migrating people. (See Hugh Nibley, *Abraham in Egypt* [Salt Lake City: Deseret Book, 1981], 225–245) Now, what does all this have to do with our current studies? First of all, we have to ask why the Jaredites (and in all probability the Egyptians) took bees with them as they left the tower for the Promised Land. Was it simply because they liked honey? You will remember that the Promised Land had not been peopled since the flood. The Jaredites were to open a new uninhabited land. Remember that they were commanded to take with them seeds of every kind, and even animals and fish. The land was empty. Well, when they planted all those seeds, what would become of them if there were no bees? No bees, no garden! So what did the bee come to represent? It was the idea of transmission of life—the taking of life from the old garden and pollinating from it life in the new—life in the new world patterned after life in the old world. In a kingship sense, then, the bee represented the bringing of the light or life from the heavenly garden down to the earthly garden, where with its pollination, life on the earth could become patterned or generated in the exact image of things as they exist in the heavenly worlds. That is what real kingship is, and that is what real priesthood is. The Egyptian crown—an imitation of the real—was made to convey that message—to receive light from the mind of God and re-create on earth things as they are in heaven. Is it any wonder that on the pulpit of the Tabernacle and of the new Conference Center of the only true Church on the face of the earth, where the voices of its prophets declare its mission to create on earth the kingdom of God in the likeness of things as they are in heaven, and where the eyes of all the faithful in the whole world are centered at every conference, there are three beehives. When will we get the message?

The Light that Is Love and the Light that Is Good

A few days after the delightful getaway at the resort, Steve and Joan were reminiscing about the things they had learned.

"I feel so much warmth and love when I think back on our time with Karen and Frank," Joan said.

"Are you listening to what you just said?" Steve replied.

"What do you mean?" Joan said.

"Warmth and love. That echoes to me that, like so many other words, love is light."

"I guess that just sort of slipped out because that's what I've been studying since we got home," Joan said. "We did discuss earlier that God is light and that he is also love (see 1 John 4:8, 16), and that makes them identical—love is really a manifestation of the light of God."

"Tell me what you've learned," Steve said.

"Well, President Joseph F. Smith in his vision of the Redemption of the Dead spoke of . . .

D&C 138
3 . . . the great and wonderful **love** made *manifest* by the Father and the Son in the coming of the Redeemer into the world.

"Paul says that whatsoever is *manifest* by God is light.

EPHESIANS 5
13 Whatsoever doth make *manifest* is **light**.

"Therefore, the love that is manifested by the Father and the Son in the coming of Christ is light. What this means, as we have seen time and time again, is that everything we know about light can be applied to love and vice versa. For example:

D&C 95

12 If you keep not my commandments, the **love** of the Father shall not *continue* with you, therefore you shall walk in **darkness**.

"The world might not know the relationship between darkness and the withdrawal of the love of God, but here we can plainly see it. This next verse is yet another way of saying that light overcomes darkness:

MORONI 8

16 *Perfect* **love** casteth out all *fear*.

"These next two verses are unique in applying the dispersing properties of light to love:

ROMANS 5

5 The **love** of God is *shed* abroad in our hearts by the Holy Ghost which is given unto us.

1 Nephi 11

22 Yea, it is the love of God, which *sheddeth* itself abroad in the hearts of the children of men . . .

"Other verses show that love can grow brighter and brighter toward a fulness, giving it again the properties of light in D&C 50:24—growing brighter and brighter until the perfect day:"

PHILIPPIANS 1

9 And this I pray, that your **love** may *abound yet more and more* in **knowledge** and in *all* **judgment**;

1 THESSALONIANS 3

12 And the Lord make you to *increase* and *abound* in **love** one toward another . . .

JUDE 1

2 **Mercy** unto you, and **peace**, and **love**, be *multiplied*.

"You've really done some study on this!" Steve exclaimed as he looked at all of Joan's papers.

"But there's more," Joan said. "I found out something about love that I would never have understood if I hadn't learned that it is light."

"What is that?" Steve asked.

"Look carefully at these verses and see if you can tell me why the Lord loves and at the same time chastens us."

D&C 95

1 Verily, thus saith the Lord unto you whom I **love**, and whom I **love** I also *chasten* that their sins may be forgiven . . . and I have **loved** you—

REVELATION 3

19 As many as I **love**, I *rebuke* and *chasten*.

"It seems that he wants the best for us and urges us on to do better," Steve said.

"Yes, but there is a law in place here," Joan said. "You remember our former discussion about the glory of God being light + light. What does light + light do?"

D&C 93

36 The **glory** of God is intelligence, or, in other words, **light** *and* **truth**.

37 **Light** *and* **truth** forsake that **evil one**.

"It forsakes evil," Steve said.

"When the light of God comes into us, it paves the way for more light. The only way that more light can come is for the darkness to give way. That is a law. It is impossible for light to come into us and not demand that darkness shrinks. That is what happens when you turn on a light in a dark room—the darkness is 'rebuked'—light cannot do anything less, and, if you increase the intensity of the light, more darkness has to give way."

"I see," Steve said, "and eventually you get light in which there is no darkness at all."

"Exactly," Joan replied.

"I remember back to the scripture we studied some time ago," Steve replied, "that every man whose spirit receives not the light is under condemnation" (see D&C 93:32).

"That's very important because it shows that we have the agency to accept or reject light," Joan said, "but once we begin to accept light, then comes the other part of the story. Look at these verses."

JOHN 15
1 I am the **true** vine, and my Father is the husbandman.
2 Every **branch** in me that beareth not **fruit** he taketh away: and every **branch** that beareth **fruit**, he *purgeth* it, that it may bring forth more **fruit**.
PROVERBS 16
6 By **mercy** *and* **truth** *iniquity* is *purged*: and by the **fear** of the LORD men depart from *evil*.

"I'm beginning to see what you mean," Steve observed. "The verse in Proverbs says exactly what verse 37 in Section 93 says—light + light forsakes darkness. I have an idea what the word *purge* means, but I don't know exactly. Let me look it up."

Steve took down volume two of the Oxford English Dictionary off the bookshelf and thumbed through the pages.

"To purge, in its 'vineyard' sense, is to prune," he said, "but in its more applicable sense, it means to get rid of objectionable or hostile elements, or, in the line of what we're talking about here, to clear out darkness and evil. So, Jesus is the 'light' vine, and *every* branch on the vine that bears light, the Father chastens, that it might bring forth more light."

Almost to himself, Steve repeated the words, "Whom I light, I chasten . . . that I can give them more light."

Then all at once he said aloud, "If we don't accept chastening, we are not receiving light. That puts a whole new spin on things, doesn't it?"

"It does," Joan said. "I see here in the dictionary that another meaning of the word *purge* is to discipline. Jesus calls his followers disciples. Let me look up that word."

There was a pause while Joan turned the pages.

"A disciple is one who is learning or being taught," Joan said, "or I suppose we could say one who is being 'disciplined' or 'purged.' Do you remember this verse?"

JOHN 8
31 If ye *continue* in my **word**, then are ye my *disciples* indeed;
32 And ye shall *know* the **truth**, and the **truth** shall *make* you **free**.

"So this law in its simplest form," Steve said, "is that when light comes, it compels us to change."

"Yes," Joan added. "It has to, and it is stated so often in the scriptures. Look at this one:"

---

2 TIMOTHY 3
16 All **scripture** is given by inspiration of God, and is profitable for doctrine, for *reproof*, for *correction*, for instruction in righteousness.

"Chastening can sometimes be discouraging, but it is not necessarily negative," Steve stated.

"Not if our hearts are right," Joan replied.

JOB 5
17 Behold, happy is the man whom God correcteth: therefore despise not thou the *chastening* of the Almighty.

"And if our hearts are right, we will be compelled more and more until all darkness is gone from us and we obtain a fulness of light."

"I remember reading in one of the sermons of the Prophet Joseph Smith," Steve reflected, "that he told the brethren not to set up stakes with the Lord. That didn't register until now. Let me just find that on the computer."

> I say to all those who are disposed to set up stakes for the Almighty, You will come short of the glory of God. I want to come up into the presence of God, and learn all things; but the creeds set up stakes, and say, "Hitherto shalt thou come, and no further;" which I cannot subscribe to. (Alma P. Burton, *Discourses of the Prophet Joseph Smith* [Salt Lake City: Deseret Book, 1965], 43; HC 6:57)

"What does it mean to 'set up stakes'?" Joan asked.

"It's like driving a stick in the ground and telling the Lord he can't come past that point, or that you won't go past that point toward him. It's resisting the light and not being willing to be chastened. I hope I never get to that point."

D&C 101
5 For all those who will not endure *chastening*, but deny me, cannot be **sanctified**.

There was a pause as Joan and Steve reflected on what they had learned. Joan was shuffling her papers. After a few minutes, she said, "In one of the verses I was reading earlier, I got the impression that the light of God illuminates everything in his kingdom that needs to be corrected."

"How interesting. Where does it say that?" Steve asked.

"We read part of this verse. Let's read it all," Joan replied.

EPHESIANS 5
13 But all things that are reproved are made manifest by the **light**: for whatsoever doth make manifest is **light**.

"Help me understand," Steve said.

"If we put it in our language," Joan said, "it seems to say: 'everything that is in need of correction is shown forth plainly by the light, because light is the only thing that exposes things for what they really are.'"

"That's an absorbing thought," Steve said. "That idea may be one way to look at the oft-quoted verse in the Book of Mormon—by the light of the Holy Ghost we can know the light of all things."

MORONI 10
5 By the **power** of the Holy Ghost ye may know the **truth** of all things.

"It has such crucial implications for our family, our stewardships, and our church assignments," Joan added. "If we have the light of God in us, we can eventually come to know everything that needs to be corrected, but that's a long and intensive process."

"It is," Steve agreed. "But in the final analysis, the action of light upon all things is to eventually purify them, and that is what Christ agreed to do in the first place, and what he will do.

D&C 76
106 . . . the fulness of times, when Christ shall have subdued all enemies under his feet, and shall have *perfected* his **work**.
107 When *he shall deliver up the* **kingdom**, *and present it unto the Father, spotless* . . .

As Steve was about to shut down his computer, he noticed another statement by the Prophet Joseph Smith.

> Some people say I am a fallen Prophet, because I do not bring forth more of the *word* of the Lord. Why did I not do it? Are we able to receive it? No! not one in this room. He then chastened the congregation for their wickedness and unbelief, 'for whom the Lord *loveth* he *chasteneth,* and *scourgeth every* son and daughter whom he receiveth,' and *if we do not receive chastisements then we are bastards and not sons.* (*Discourses of the Prophet Joseph Smith,* 72; emphasis added)

They both reflected further on the implications of all this information and agreed to discuss it later. Just before retiring, Joan said to her husband, "You know, I never did ask you what you have been studying since we got home from our little vacation with Frank and Karen. I have seen you quite involved."

"I have been studying the word *good.* We touched on it in one of our earlier discussions, and it has really intrigued me."

"Will you share it with me?"

"Tomorrow after work."

"I'll be waiting."

The next evening, after dinner was over and the children were in bed, Joan sat next to her husband on the sofa and said, "I've been waiting all day to have you share with me. Is this a suitable time?"

"Yes, it is," Steve said. "Let's set off from where we ended last night. We were speaking about love and light and how we could appreciate love better once we understood that it was light. We can also understand 'good' better once we recognize it as light. Let's begin with this verse:

ALMA 32
35 Whatsoever is **light**, is **good**, because it is discernible.

"Now, what do these next verses add:

MORONI 10
6 And whatsoever thing is **good** is **just** *and* **true**.
25 If there be one among you that doeth good, he shall work by the **power** *and* **gifts** of God.

"They add that 'good' is light + light," Joan said.

"Yes. That is a key point. 'Good' is light + light. What does this next verse teach?"

PSALM 34

8 O taste and see that *the LORD is* **good**.

"That we can experience for ourselves that the Lord is and gives light + light," Joan said.

"With that understanding, let's look at some verses about the creation of the earth," Steve said. "First, God tells us that he created the earth and it was without form and void. Then he says:

MOSES 2

3 And I, God, said: Let there be **light**; and there was **light**.
4 And I, God, saw the **light**; and that **light** was **good**. And I, God, divided the **light** from the darkness.

"What do you see here?"

"God brought forth the light, and he saw that it was not just light, but light + light,'" Joan said. "To me it suggests that the light was capable of being added to and could be continually."

"That's how it struck me," Steve said. "The Lord then tells of additional steps in creation. He created the dry land, the sea, grass and herbs, trees, the sun and moon, life in the sea, fowl in the air, beasts, and cattle. When these were finished, he said:

MOSES 2

25 And I, God, *saw that all these things were* **good**.
31 And I, God, saw everything that I had made, and, *behold, all things which I had made were very* **good.**

"The Lord affirms that all these things were good by saying:"

MOSES 2

22 And I, God, blessed them, saying: Be **fruitful**, and **multiply**, and **fill** the waters in the sea; and let fowl **multiply** in the earth.

"I'm beginning to see the principle," Joan said.

"Now we come to the part of this that really impresses me. The next act of creation was that of man, but unlike the former creations, only the male species of man was created. After his creation, the Father made this observation to his Son:"

> **MOSES 3**
> 18 And I, the Lord God, said unto mine Only Begotten, that it was *not* **good** that the man should be alone.

"That's impressive," Joan exclaimed. "It affirms that man, who is light, being alone, is not light + light, nor indeed can he ever be."

"I'm not quite sure why the Lord chose to create man in this way," Steve continued, "but perhaps he was trying to emphasize the eternal significance of the light + light principle. At any rate, Adam needed help:

> **GENESIS 2**
> 20 But for Adam there was not found an *help* meet for him.

"But what kind of help?"

"A help that was meet for him," Joan said. "I think meet means sufficient or appropriate. There was no help among all the creations that God had made up to that point that was sufficient or appropriate for him."

"This next verse shows an instance where the word *help* can be understood as *light*.

> **HOSEA 13:4, 9**
> I am the LORD thy God from the land of Egypt, and thou shalt know no god but me: for there is no saviour beside me . . . in me is thine **help**.

"Hence:

> **MOSES 3**
> 18 I will make an **help** meet for him.

"So the Lord made a light that would be sufficient for man that he would become—like all other things in his creation—light + light."

"Commenting on all of this, the Lord says:"

MOSES 2	MOSES 2
26 And I, God, said unto mine Only Begotten . . . Let us make **man** in our image, after our likeness; and it was so. 27 And I, God, created **man** in mine own image . . . **male** *and* **female** created I them. 28 And I, God . . . said unto them: Be *fruitful*, and *multiply*, and *replenish* the earth.	26 And I, God, said unto mine Only Begotten . . . Let us make **light** in our image, after our likeness; and it was so. 27 And I, God, created **light** in mine own image . . . **light** + **light** created I them. 28 And I, God . . . said unto them: Be *fruitful*, and *multiply*, and *replenish* the earth.

"I can see now why there was so much anxiety in the garden when Eve partook of the forbidden fruit," Joan said. "Adam knew that she would be cast out and he would be left alone in the garden—light without light. His agreement to also partake of the fruit provided the way for him and his wife to remain light + light—he partook so that man, or light, could come into the world.

"That's the way I understand it," Steve said. "Paul makes reference to this principle when he was speaking of husbands and wives."

"There is a verse in the Doctrine and Covenants that speaks of this as well," Joan said. "The Lord is speaking of the role of wives:

1 CORINTHIANS 7	1 CORINTHIANS 7
4 The *wife* hath not **power** of her own body, but the *husband*: and likewise also the *husband* hath not **power** of his own body, but the *wife*.	4 The *wife* hath not **light** of her own body, but the *husband*: and likewise also the *husband* hath not **light** of his own body, but the *wife*.

D&C 132
63 They are given unto [their husbands] to *multiply* and *replenish* the earth . . . that they may bear the souls of **men**; for herein is the **work** of my Father *continued*, that he may be **glorified**.

"With that background we can see a deep and profound meaning in some verses that we have seen many times:

D&C 93

29 **Man** was also in the beginning with God. **Intelligence,** or the light of truth, was not created or made, neither indeed can be.

"This tells us that man is intelligence. Now look at this verse again:"

D&C 93
36 The **glory** of God is **intelligence,** or, in other words, **light** *and* **truth**.

D&C 93
36 The **glory** of God is **man,** or, in other words, **man** + **man**.

"That certainly gives depth to the scripture we studied earlier," Joan said, "that God is . . ."

D&C 67
9 . . . the Father of **lights**.

"Speaking of fathers and mothers," Steve said, "here is another verse that is a significant message to every parent:

D&C 50
24 That which is of God is **light**; and he that receiveth **light**, and continueth in God, receiveth more **light**; and that **light** groweth brighter and brighter until the perfect **day**.

D&C 50
24 That which is of God is **man**; and he that receiveth **man**, and continueth in God, receiveth more **man**; and that **man** groweth brighter and brighter until the perfect **man**.

"That is quite intriguing, and you got all this from studying the word *good*," Joan said.

"Well, that and a combination of many other things."

"I hope that we can continue in God with our children," Joan said, "and that they can grow brighter and brighter until they are perfect."

"The gospel holds out such rich promises," Steve said. "I too hope we can endure."

ABRAHAM 3
26 And they who keep their second estate shall have **glory** added upon their heads *for ever and ever.*

"But that isn't all I learned about 'good,'" Steve continued. "I want to share some other things with you. Remembering that 'good' is light + light, I want to show you these verses."

A) JOHN 10
14 I am the **good** shepherd, and know my sheep, and am known of mine.

B) ETHER 4 (See also Ephesians 6:8.)
12 And whatsoever thing persuadeth men to do **good** is of me; for **good** cometh of none save it be of me. I am the same that leadeth men to all **good**.

C) ACTS 10
38 Jesus of Nazareth with the Holy Ghost and with power . . . went about doing **good**.

D) ALMA 37
37 Counsel with the Lord in all thy doings, and he will direct thee for **good**.

E) JAMES 4
17 Therefore to him that knoweth to do **good**, and doeth it not, to him it is sin.

F) MORONI 7
26 Whatsoever thing ye shall ask the Father in my name, which is **good**, in faith . . . behold, it shall be done unto you.

G) 1 Thessalonians 5
21 Prove all things; hold fast that which is **good.**

H) Hebrews 6
5 And have tasted the **good** word of God, and the powers of the world to come.

I) D&C 11
12 Put your trust in that Spirit which leadeth to do **good.**

J) Alma 41
14 My son, see that you . . . do **good** continually; and if ye do all these things . . . ye shall have **good** rewarded unto you again.

K) Alma 13 (Righteous men in pre-earth life)
3 And this is the manner after which they were ordained—being called and *prepared* from the foundation of the world according to the foreknowledge of God, *on account of their exceeding faith and* **good** *works; in the first place being left to choose* **good** *or evil; therefore they having chosen* **good***, and exercising exceedingly great faith, are called with a holy calling,* yea, with that holy calling which was *prepared* with, and according to, a preparatory redemption for such.

L) Abraham 3
22 Now the Lord had shown unto me, Abraham, the *intelligences* that were organized before the world was; and among all these there were many of the noble and great ones;
23 *And God saw these souls that they were* **good***, and he stood in the midst of them, and he said: These I will make my rulers;* for he stood among those that were spirits, and he saw that they were **good**; and he said unto me: Abraham, thou art one of them; thou wast chosen before thou wast born.

M) MOSES 5
11 And Eve, his wife, heard all these things and was glad, saying: Were it not for our transgression we never should have had *seed*, and never should have known **good** and evil, and the joy of our redemption, and the eternal life which God giveth unto all the obedient.

N) D&C 111
11 I will order all things for your **good**, as fast as ye are able to receive them. Amen.

O) JACOB 5 (speaking of the tree of the House of Israel)
36 Nevertheless, I know that the roots are **good**,

P) JACOB 2
19 And after ye have obtained a hope in Christ ye shall obtain riches, if ye seek them; and ye will seek them for the intent to do **good**—to clothe the naked, and to feed the hungry, and to liberate the captive, and administer relief to the sick and the afflicted.

Q) JACOB 5
61 Wherefore, go to, and call servants, that we may labor diligently with our might in the vineyard, that we may *prepare* the way, that I may bring forth again the natural fruit, which natural fruit is **good** and *the most precious* above all other fruit.

R) HELAMAN 12
4 How quick to do iniquity, and how slow to do **good**, are the children of men.

S) MOSES 6
55 They taste the bitter, that they may know to prize the **good**.

T) D&C 122

7 And if thou shouldst be cast into the pit, or into the hands of murderers, and the sentence of death passed upon thee; if thou be cast into the deep; if the billowing surge conspire against thee; if fierce winds become thine enemy; if the heavens gather blackness, and all the elements combine to hedge up the way; and above all, if the very jaws of hell shall gape open the mouth wide after thee, know thou, my son, that all these things shall give thee experience, and shall be for thy **good**.

"What a treasure of information there is in those verses!" Joan said, as she finished reading. "They were a joy to read. Let's make a list of some of the most important points."

"That's a good idea," Steve said as he handed a blank page from his notebook to Joan.

Joan began to write:

- Jesus is the light + light Shepherd; the Shepherd over the light + light process. All light comes from him, and he is the one that leads men to all light. He, himself performed the works of light + light. (Good = light + light) (scriptures A, B, C, D, F, N)
- The scriptures are not just light but 'light + light.' This means that we can increase in light the more we read them, and the Lord can add to them when ever he wishes. (H, I)
- We are to trust in the light that leads us to do light + light. (I)
- If we perform the works of light + light, light + light will be rewarded to us again. (J)
- When Alma speaks of men in the pre-earth life who are preparing themselves to someday have the priesthood when on earth, he is speaking of the same setting that Abraham speaks of when he saw the intelligences in the pre-earth life. These men had chosen light + light there and then have chosen it again here. Abraham was one of them. (K, L)
- Eve said that if it had not been for their transgression, they would never have experienced light + light. (M)
- The roots and the natural fruit of the House of Israel are light + light, which God says is the most *precious* thing of all. This relates to his statement that his very work and glory is to bring to pass the immortality and eternal life of man. Or, in other words, his light + light is to bring to pass the light + light of man. (O, Q)
- Riches are given to men to help them do the works of light + light. Light + light is defined as clothing the naked,

feeding the hungry, liberating the captive, and administering relief to the sick and afflicted. (P)
  • We experience the bitterness of darkness in this life that we might come to *prize* the light + light. (S)
  • We are quick to do evil but slow to do light + light. (R)
  • All the difficult things that we are called to pass through in this life are for our light + light experience. (Come to think of it, so are all the good and pleasurable things.) (T)

"The last verse, D&C 122:7, tells us that Jesus had to descend below all these things in his light + light experience," Joan said. "It's more than we could ever possibly fathom. And another thing that impresses me is that 'good' which is light + light is called the most precious of all things. That reminds me of the words of Alma."

ALMA 32

42 And because of your diligence and your faith and your patience with the **word** in nourishing it, that it may take root in you, behold, by and by ye shall pluck the fruit thereof, *which is most precious, which is* **sweet** *above all that is* **sweet**, *and which is* **white** *above all that is* **white**, *yea, and pure above all that is pure; and ye shall feast upon this fruit even until ye are filled, that ye hunger not, neither shall ye thirst.*

"Thanks for that. I see some other connections there that I've not seen before," Steve said. "I came across a verse yesterday, and I couldn't make sense of it until now. It speaks of the Savior in his mortal life.

ISAIAH 7

15 **Butter** *and* **honey** shall he eat, that he may know to refuse the *evil*, and choose the **good**.

"Butter comes from milk, which is *white*, and honey, 'liquid gold' that is sometimes said to flow from the sun, is *sweet*. These things are the richest and strongest of foods. To eat them together is almost like a force-feed of nourishment. It affirms that Jesus will live by light + light, which will give him the power to refuse darkness and to choose more light + light."

"It just never ends," Joan said. "The insights keep opening up, and it is so thrilling when they do. I remember a statement the Prophet Joseph Smith made:

This is good doctrine. It tastes good. I can taste the principles of eternal life, and so can you. They are given to me by the revelations of Jesus Christ; and I know that when I tell you these words of eternal life as they are given to me, you taste them, and I know that you believe them. You say honey is sweet, and so do I. I can also taste the spirit of eternal life. I know that it is good; and when I tell you of these things which were given me by inspiration of the Holy Spirit, you are bound to receive them as sweet, and rejoice more and more.

(*Discourses of the Prophet Joseph Smith*, 349)

"I enjoy this so much, Joan," Steve said. "I just thought of something else that relates to all of this. Remember how we talked about the priesthood and the light associated with it, and then we talked about 'good' and marriage and the light + light principle associated with them. This scripture ties all these things together."

D&C 131

1 In the celestial **glory** there are three heavens or degrees;
2 And in order to obtain the highest, a man must enter into this order of the **priesthood** [meaning the new and everlasting covenant of **marriage**];
3 And if he does not, he cannot obtain it.
4 He may enter into the other, but that is the end of his **kingdom**; he cannot have an **increase**.

"That's enlightening and also sobering," Joan said. "Isn't there a verse somewhere about remaining separately and singly?"

"It's in the next section."

D&C 132

16 Therefore, when they are out of the world they *neither marry nor are given in marriage*; but are appointed angels in heaven, which angels are ministering servants, *to minister for those who are worthy of a far more, and an exceeding, and an eternal weight of* **glory**. *[Note: "Weight" in this instance can refer to the 'intensity' of the light]*
17 For these angels did not abide my law; therefore, they *cannot be enlarged, but remain separately and singly*, without exaltation, in their saved condition, to all eternity; and from henceforth *are not gods*, but are angels of God forever and ever.

"Well, it's time to turn in. Thanks, Steve, for opening your studies to me. I really love these things and the glorious feast that they are, and I love you. I'm so glad that we are bound together in the priesthood, and I hope we will increase forever. I'll add that point to this list and hang it on the fridge so we can see it every day."

As Steve and Joan retired, they had gained again a new appreciation for each other and for the wonder of the scriptures and the language of the Spirit.

The next afternoon, Joan sat in a soft wing-tipped chair in the study and observed how the beams from the evening sun played on the curtain lace. She was deep in thought and was surprised when the sunlight crossed her eyes and made her blink. She had been thinking about a scripture she had read that morning which stirred in her mind and wouldn't rest.

---

1 JOHN 1

8 If we say that we have no **sin**, we deceive ourselves, and the **truth** is not in us.

It was such a simple verse, yet she felt that there were great implications in it. She repeated it aloud, transposing the words: "If we say we have no darkness, we deceive ourselves, and the light is not in us." Then into her mind came the so-often quoted scripture:

---

1 JOHN 1

5 This then is the message which we have heard of him, and declare unto you, that God is **light**, and in him is **no *darkness*** at all.

Suddenly she exclaimed, "If we say we have no darkness at all, then we are literally saying that we have all the light, or in other words, we are putting ourselves in the place of God. And if that is what we think, we really have no light at all! That," she remembered, "was the definition of priestcraft, to set one's self up as a light.

"The scriptures say," she continued, "that God is in the sun, and the light of the sun, and the power thereof by which it was made, and also the light of the stars and the power thereof by which they were made (see

D&C 88:7–9). If a person says they have no darkness, they are inferring, without knowing it, that they have as much light as God!"

Surely there are some other scriptures that relate to this, she thought.

She began to search for the keywords *light* and *darkness* in Gospel Explorer on her laptop computer.

Matthew 6

23 If thine eye be evil, thy whole body shall be full of darkness. *If therefore the* **light** *that is in thee be* **darkness***, how great is that* **darkness***!*

Just how can the light that is in us be darkness? she wondered. Then it became clear. "If what we have chosen inside to be our light, i.e., our guide or our compass, is really darkness, then how *great* is that darkness, for we have put the darkness for our light and we believe that it is light. Then when the true light comes along, we believe that it is darkness and reject it."

She remembered thinking about this idea some weeks back as she was reading about Enoch in the book of Moses.

Moses 6

37 Enoch went forth in the land, among the people, standing upon the hills and the high places, and cried with a loud voice, testifying against their works; and all men were offended because of him.

38 And they came forth to hear him, upon the high places, saying unto the tent-keepers: Tarry ye here and keep the tents, while we go yonder to behold the seer, for he prophesieth, and there is *a strange thing in the land; a wild man hath come among us.*

As he testified against their darkness, they called him a strange thing and a wild man. Well, *he* was not strange; *they* were. *He* was not a wild man; it was *they* who were wild and had turned against the light. It was a perfect case of darkness calling the light darkness.

---

2 Nephi 15

20 Wo unto them that call *evil* **good**, and **good** *evil*, that put *darkness* for **light**, and **light** for *darkness*, that put *bitter* for **sweet**, and **sweet** for *bitter*!

Joan remembered an experience she had when she was a young girl in the swimming pool in her hometown. She had dived into the deep end and became disoriented when she reached the bottom. She was upside down and didn't know it. She thought that the bottom of the pool was up and was trying to force her way up by really going down. Her head was pressed against the concrete, and of course it wouldn't budge. It was such a frightening experience. She remembered looking for the light and saw, to her horror, that it was below her, not above. She recalled the agony, lungs bursting, as she determined to turn herself upside down and go toward the light in spite of the fact that she could not believe that it was up. When she burst through the crest of the water, she was relieved and knew that she would have drowned if she had hung onto her belief that up was down.

"So much for our own thinking," she said to herself.

It was sobering for her when she remembered that all men . . .

ALMA 12

15 . . . *must come forth and stand before him in his* **glory**, *and in his* **power**, *and in his* **might**, **majesty**, *and* **dominion**, *and acknowledge to our everlasting shame* that all his judgments are just; that he is just in all his works, and that he is merciful unto the children of men, *and that he has all* **power** *to save every man* that believeth on his name and bringeth forth fruit meet for repentance.

How sad for those who believed, either in their ignorance or their arrogance, that there was no greater light than their own.

ROMANS 3

23 For all have ***sinned***, and *come short* of the **glory** of God.

A few days later, Steve sat in his study looking at the screen of his laptop computer. He had been awakened early by the desire to understand something he had read in the scriptures the day before. He now read the verses from Gospel Explorer about Moses who "was caught up into an exceedingly high mountain":

Moses 1
2 And he saw God face to face, and he talked with him, and the **glory** of God was upon Moses; therefore Moses could endure his **presence**.

From previous studies he knew this was speaking of the light of God that had come upon Moses, and that he could endure the light because of the action of the light upon him. The Lord then invited Moses to view the workmanship of his hands but reminded him that no man could behold all his works, except he should behold all of his glory; and no man could behold all of his glory and afterwards remain in the flesh on the earth. Based on D&C 88: 67, Steve reasoned that to comprehend all things, one would require a body filled with light, and that meant being resurrected. The Lord then told Moses:

Moses 1
6 All things are *present* with me, for I know them all.

Steve was intrigued with the word *present* in this verse and wondered how it related to the "presence" of God mentioned in verse 2. He decided to search the word *present* and see if he could learn more. He read many verses with that word in them, and then he came to this one:

D&C 38
2 The same which knoweth all things, for all things are *present* before mine eyes;

There were deep meanings here. One meaning, he thought, is that all things are visible to the Lord's eyes, and another meaning is that all things before his eyes are in the "present," meaning that they are "here and now." He remembered reading a statement by the Prophet Joseph on that. He did a quick search and found that Joseph had said: "The great Jehovah contemplated the whole of the events connected with the earth . . . *the past, the present, and the future were and are, with him, one eternal 'now.'*" (HC 4:597)

What this suggested to his mind was a distance-time contraction— that with God all distance and time are contracted to zero. He remembered other scriptures that seemed to relate to this:

> **D&C 88**
>
> 13 . . . **light** which is . . . even the **power** of God who sitteth upon his throne, who is in the bosom of eternity, who is in the midst of all things.

Here he saw that God is "in the *bosom* of eternity" and "in the *midst* of all things." To be certain of the meaning of the word *bosom*, he looked in the dictionary and found it to mean "the center, core, or heart of someone or something." So he reasoned that by the light which is in him, God dwells at the center, core, or heart, of eternity. That seemed to represent the idea of a state where all eternity past and all eternity future meet or flow into each other and become the present—the "one eternal now," spoken of by Joseph.

The second word, *midst*, seemed almost to represent the same idea of center, core, or heart, but Steve noticed that it related not so much to the big picture of eternity but to the small picture of *each* thing. The first seemed to be global or macro in nature, and the second seemed to be micro in nature. By his light, God penetrates into the heart or core of every *single* thing.

> **D&C 88**
>
> 41 He comprehendeth all things, and all things are before him, and all things are *round* about him; and he is above all things, and in all things, and is through all things, and is *round* about all things; and all things are by him, and of him, even God, forever and ever.

> **1 NEPHI 10**
>
> 19 The course of the Lord is one eternal *round*.

Steve was impressed to understand that all things are "round" about God and that he is "round" about all things. A symbol, he reasoned, that could most effectively express that idea was a sphere—a sphere in which God was not only the center but the circumference as well. Reduced to its simplest form, it would be a circle with a dot in the center. He suddenly remembered from the book of Abraham studies Frank had shared with him that this symbol was the hieroglyphic sign for the sun god, Ra, shown in Figure Three of Facsimile Number Two, and also represented the pupil of his eye.

Sphere

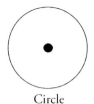

Circle

Rā

(Budge, *Hieroglyphic Dictionary*, 1:418b)

In these illustrations, Steve could see a lot of things coming together—the light, the bosom, the eye, the glory, and the presence of God—all these things being different ways of expressing the same thing.

Looking further in the scriptures, Steve read:

Moses 1

8 And it came to pass that Moses looked, and beheld the world upon which he was created; and *Moses beheld the world and the ends thereof, and all the children of men which are, and which were created*; of the same he greatly marveled and wondered.

9 And the **presence** of God withdrew from Moses, that his **glory** was not upon Moses; and Moses was left unto himself.

He saw that Moses was given to see into the presence or light of God, and while doing so, saw things that are and were created. Then that presence or glory was withdrawn. Moses explains what happened to him:

Moses 1

10 And it came to pass that it was for the space of many hours before Moses did again receive his natural strength like unto man; and he said unto himself: Now, for this cause I know that man is nothing, which thing I never had supposed.

11 But now mine own eyes have beheld God; but not my natural, but my spiritual eyes, for my natural eyes could not have beheld; for I should have withered and died in his presence; but his glory was upon me; and I beheld his face, for I was transfigured before him.

The scriptures then went on to explain about Moses' encounter with Satan, and these insightful verses:

Moses 1

25–26 And calling upon the name of God, he beheld his glory

---

again, for it was upon him; and . . . as the voice was still speaking, Moses cast his eyes and beheld the earth, yea, even all of it; and there was not a particle of it which he did not behold, discerning it by the spirit of God.

28 And he beheld also the inhabitants thereof, and there was not a soul which he beheld not; and he discerned them by the Spirit of God; and their numbers were great, even numberless as the sand upon the sea shore.

31 And behold, the glory of the Lord was upon Moses, so that Moses stood in the presence of God, and talked with him face to face.

Steve thought about this for a long time and pondered the things Moses had said. His mind kept coming back to the idea of a distance–time contraction. Distance with God is reduced to zero because he is in the middle of everything, and time is reduced to zero because the past and the future are all present to him. He wondered how he could visualize a space/time contraction. He began to draw.

Independence, Missouri ———————— Salt Lake City, Utah
1,500 miles

He imagined a person traveling from Salt Lake City to Independence by various means, and tried to think of time and its implications:

Means of Travel	Time
Man on foot	3 months
Man in covered wagon	2 months
Man on horse	20 days
Man in locomotive	4 days
Man in car	3 days
Man in jet	3 hours
Man in super sonic transport	12 minutes

He reasoned that the actual distance for each traveler would be the same, but shorten the time with which they would cover the distance, and you effectively reduce the distance to the time. Hence, if you ask the man on foot how long it takes to get to Independence, he would say three months. If you ask the person riding on the SST, he would say twelve minutes. If you asked the Lord, he would say it is "present" with him.

God, Steve reasoned, can do this, not because he travels at the speed of light but because he *is* light. Understanding this must have been part of the reason for Moses' astonishment when he saw and comprehended the "presence" of God. After all, he had been raised in the *glory* of the Egyptian pharaohs:

MOSES 1
10 Now, for this cause I know that **man** is *nothing*, which thing I never had supposed.

There was another thing that kept rolling around in Steve's mind. He remembered reading in Facsimile Number Two in the book of Abraham about Kolob and some of its characteristics:

EXPLANATION
Fig. 1. Kolob, signifying the first creation, nearest to the celestial, or the residence of God. First in government, the last pertaining to the measurement of time. The measurement according to *celestial time, which celestial time signifies one day to a cubit. One day in Kolob is equal to a thousand years* according to the measurement of this earth.

This certainly described a time-distance relationship. On the planet Kolob, one day (one rotation of the planet on its axis) equals 1000 of our years. This is called celestial time. Additionally, "celestial time" has a space–time contraction in which one day is equal to one cubit. Or said another way, a cubit of space is equal to 1000 years of time. (A cubit is about 18 inches, the distance from the elbow to the tip of the middle finger.)

Distance = one cubit (about 18 inches)
Time = one day (1000 years)

Steve wondered what this could possibly mean. In what way could 1000 years of time relate to a cubit of space? In the celestial light of the Lord, could 1000 years of time be contracted to the space of 18 inches? Or could a 1000 of our years pass by in the time it takes celestial beings to move the distance of one cubit? (Could 1000 of our years be so infinitesimal that they could pass by in the time it takes a celestial being to turn halfway around?) Could 1000 years of time be kept or stored within the space of one cubit of light? Could a cubit of light-space be like a computer chip or storage bank where time is stored? If one cubit of light could hold 1000 years of time, how much time would one cubic-cubit hold? Steve reached for his calculator: 1000 x 1000 x 1000 = one billion years!

Steve thought about Enoch's experience of being admitted into the presence of God:

MOSES 7
3 And it came to pass that I turned and went up on the mount; and as I stood upon the mount, I beheld the heavens open, and I was *clothed* upon with **glory**;
4 And I saw the Lord; and he stood before my face, and he talked with me, even as a man talketh one with another, face to face; and he said unto me: *Look, and I will show unto thee* the world for the *space* of many *generations*.

If being clothed upon with light allowed Enoch to see into the space–time contraction of the light of the Lord, he could have seen 1000 years of future earth-time by looking through only one cubit of space. Viewing through seven cubits of space would have afforded him a look at the entire temporal existence of the world.

The idea of a space–time contraction was at the center of Albert Einstein's theory of relativity. Of this theory he said:

> Out yonder there was this huge world, which exits independently of us human beings and which stands before us like a great, eternal riddle, at least partially accessible to our inspection and thinking. The contemplation of this world beckoned like a liberation. (Albert Einstein, *Autobiographical Notes* [Open Court Publishing, 1979], 5)

Try as he might, there was no way for Einstein to experiment directly with a space–time contraction other than with mathematics, for the scriptures are explicit in saying:

JOB 11
7 Canst thou by searching find out **God**?
1 CORINTHIANS 2
11 The things of God knoweth no man, but the **Spirit** of God.

---

1 Corinthians 2
14 But the natural man receiveth not the things of the **Spirit** of God . . . neither can he know them, because they are **spiritually** discerned.

Many who have entered into the space–time contraction of the Lord have been very explicit in their explanations of *how* they entered.

Moses:

Moses 1
2 The **glory** of God was upon Moses; therefore Moses could endure his **presence**.
14 I could not look upon God, except his **glory** should come upon me, and I were **transfigured** before him.

Abraham:

Abraham 3
12 He put his hand upon mine eyes, and I saw those things which his hands had made, which were many; and they multiplied before mine eyes, and I could not see the end thereof.

Joseph:

D&C 76
12 By the power of the **Spirit** our eyes were opened and our understandings were enlightened, so as to see and understand the things of God
D&C 110
1 The veil was taken from our minds, and the eyes of our understanding were opened.
D&C 67
11 For no man has seen God at any time in the flesh, except **quickened** by the **Spirit** of God.

The word *quicken* rang a bell to Steve. He had seen that word before and now could understand that a man could not see into the space–time contraction of the Lord except he be acted upon by the light. The intensity or velocity of the eternal light speeds up or quickens his understanding so as to be able to enter into the space–time contraction and comprehend for a moment as God comprehends.

The Lord said something very interesting to those who do not keep his commandments:

D&C 29
29 *Where I am* they cannot come, for they have no **power**.

Steve reasoned that if God dwells in the "bosom of eternity" and "in the midst of all things," no man can come *where he is*, unless they have his light, for that is how he is able to dwell in the midst of these things. The wicked will always dwell at a great time and distance from God and therefore can never be "present" with him. Yet to the righteous, he says:

D&C 27
18 Ye shall be **caught** *up*, that *where I am ye shall be also*.

This, of course, will happen because they have the power or light to do so.

CHAPTER 9

The Light + Light Principle

Frank and Steve spotted each other over the top of a row of cars in the parking lot at Costco. They waved and skirted around the in-and-out traffic to get together. It had been a long time since they had talked. They visited briefly, and it was easy to tell they had much to share and to catch up on. They wondered aloud if it was just about time they got together again for another discussion. They decided to set a date for dinner and a scripture discussion in the conference room at Steve's office. They planned it for a Saturday afternoon when the room would be free and they could use the blackboard and have facilities for their computers. They parted with the plan to confirm the date after conferring with their wives.

The day came, and they were excited to be together again. They talked of their children, their families, their work, and their callings. When they had set up all their materials, Steve said, "We've looked forward to getting together again for a long time. Joan and I have been studying regularly, as we know both of you have, and we've had some truly remarkable experiences."

"We've done the same thing," Karen said. "We marvel every day over one insight or another."

"Joan and I have thought a lot lately about the light + light principle in the scriptures," Steve said. "Joan has done some concentrated work in that area, and it has opened up more meaning and appreciation for both of us."

"That sounds intriguing. Would you share it with us, Joan?" Karen said. "We would love to hear what you've discovered."

"I didn't really plan to be first today, but I am excited about our study," Joan began. "We've already discussed the foundation of the light + light principle when we were together earlier—you'll remember Frank used D&C 93:36 to help us discover it. Let's just get that verse in front of us again and review it.

D&C 93

36 The **glory** of God is intelligence, or, in other words, **light** and **truth**.

"This verse has many meanings and layer upon layer of depth, but the core meaning surely must be that the glory of God is light as it is used with truth. Through the central verse that we have used through all our study (see D&C 84:45), we have learned that 'whatsoever is truth is light' and conversely, 'whatsoever is light is truth.' Knowing and believing this, we cannot escape the fact that the glory of God may be referred to as a factor of light used with light, or as we have said so many times, light + light. And of course it would be just as satisfactory to say that it is a factor of truth used with truth, for these things may be interchanged.

"The word *glory* has many meanings. It can refer to the greatness and magnificence of God, or it can refer to that which God glories in—that which is of the most worth to him or gives him the most satisfaction or joy or triumph. The above verse says in effect: The greatness and magnificence of God is light + light, and that is the thing that is of most worth to him and which gives him the most satisfaction, joy, and triumph.

"I have asked myself what that means. In what way is the greatness of God centered in light + light? In what way is light + light the thing that gives God the most satisfaction? The answer that is most satisfying to me is that he, who once was as we are now, obtained light from his Father through the principle of light + light, that he now possesses all light, and that he can, as he chooses, organize, distribute, and administer light after light after light. This refers not only to light as a living moving and vital essence but light as it may be organized into beings (his sons and daughters) and light as it acts upon them to enlarge them and fashion them in his image and exalt them in his presence where they—who have now become as he is—may administer for those who are yet to be (their own children) in the same manner and in the same fashion as they have been administered to. Thus, we see the light working in all things past, present, and future.

"Hence the Lord says, in effect (as we combine thoughts from a series of verses): This is my light + light, to bring to pass the light + light of man—man himself being light—whose light + light is brought to pass through the eternal principle of adding light to light until he is glorified in light and can light all things, in the same manner and to the same degree that God is the light which is in all things." (See Moses 1:39; D&C 93:29,33, 28; D&C 88:6.)

"I reasoned," Joan continued, "that if this is the central idea of what the glory of God is, and in effect the principle of how it works, I wanted to see how many times and in how many different ways it is referred to in the scriptures. I, of course, won't show you all the references, but I want to show you a representation of them in three categories: First, scriptures that relate specifically to God the Father and describe him as possessing and working through the principle of light + light. Second, sriptures that relate specifically to Christ and describe him as possessing and working through the principle of light + light. Third, scriptures that relate specifically to the idea that man, if he is to become like God and Christ, must follow, obtain, and become personages of light + light even as God and Christ have done.

"I will show each of the categories to you in a table format and give each of you copies when we're finished. I have given a short commentary on each verse at the right of the table. Take a few minutes and view the first table."

Table 1: Scriptures that relate specifically to God the Father and describe him as possessing and working through the principle of light + light.

Original (words highlighted)	Transposed	Commentary
D&C 93:36 The **glory** of God is intelligence, or, in other words, **light** *and* **truth.**	**D&C 93:36** The **light** of God is intelligence, or, in other words, **light + light.**	The light of the Father is not light in a singular sense. It is a light of process and action—light + light.

Original (words highlighted)	Transposed	Commentary
D&C 66 12 You shall have a crown of eternal **life** at the right hand of my Father, who is full of **grace** *and* **truth.**	**D&C 66** 12 You shall have a crown of eternal **light** at the right hand of my Father, who is full of **light + light.**	The Savior gives his witness that his Father's light is the light of light + light.

Original (words highlighted)	Transposed	Commentary
EPHESIANS 1 17 That the God of our Lord Jesus Christ, the **Father** of **glory,** may give unto you the **spirit** of **wisdom** and **revelation** in the **knowledge** of him:	EPHESIANS 1 17 That the God of our Lord Jesus Christ, the **Light of light,** may give unto you the **light** of **'light + light'** in the **light** of him:	This is a plea to God, who is the Lighter of all lights, to give men the light of light + light, that they might be in the light that comes from him.

Original (words highlighted)	Transposed	Commentary
MATTHEW 6:9 9 Our Father which art in heaven, Hallowed be thy **name.** 10 Thy **kingdom** come. Thy **will** be done in earth, as it is in heaven. 11 Give us this day our daily **bread.** 12 And forgive us our debts, as we forgive our debtors. 13 And lead us not into temptation, but deliver us from evil: For thine is the **kingdom,** and the **power,** and the **glory,** for ever. Amen.	MATTHEW 6:9 9 Our Father which art in heaven, Hallowed be thy **light.** 10 Thy **light** come. Thy **light** be done in earth, as it is in heaven. 11 Give us this day our daily **light.** 12 And forgive us our debts, as we forgive our debtors. 13 And lead us not into temptation, but deliver us from **evil:** For thine is the **'light, + light, + light',** for ever. Amen.	Again the Savior is giving witness of his Father's light; that it is a light of light + light + light. He pleads that it will come on earth and work its miracle. Verse 13 is a confirmation of D&C 93:37, that light and truth (or in other words light + light) forsakes evil.

Original (words highlighted)	Transposed	Commentary
EPHESIANS 1 3 Blessed be the God and Father of our Lord Jesus Christ, who hath **blessed** us with all **spiritual** blessings in heavenly places in Christ: 8 Wherein he hath abounded toward us in all **wisdom** and **prudence**.	EPHESIANS 1 3 Blessed be the God and Father of our Lord Jesus Christ, who hath **lighted** us with all **lighted** blessings in heavenly places in Christ: 8 Wherein he hath *abounded* toward us in all **light + light**.	The light of God the Father abounds to men coming to them in waves, swelling light after light after light.

Original (words highlighted)	Transposed	Commentary
ROMANS 14 17 For the **kingdom** of **God** is not meat and drink; but **righteousness**, and **peace**, and **joy** in the **Holy Ghost**.	ROMANS 14 17 For the **light of God** is not meat + drink; but **light, + light, + light** in the **light**.	The light of God is not darkness + darkness, but 'light + light + light' in the light.

Original (words highlighted)	Transposed	Commentary
2 CORINTHIANS 13 11 Finally, brethren, farewell . . . be of one **mind**, live in **peace**; and the **God** of **love** and **peace** shall be with you.	2 CORINTHIANS 13 11 Finally, brethren, farewell . . . be of one **light**, live in **light**; and the **God** of **light + light** shall be with you.	If men are of one light, and live in light, the God of light + light will be with them and they will increase continually in the light together.

Original (words highlighted)	Transposed	Commentary
JAMES 1 17 Every good **gift** and every perfect **gift** is from above, and cometh down from the **Father** of **lights**, with whom is no variableness, neither shadow of turning. 18 Of his own **will be-gat** he us with the **word** of **truth**, that we should be a kind of firstfruits of his creatures.	JAMES 1 17 Every good **light** and every perfect **light** is from above, and cometh down from the **Father** of **lights**, with whom is no variableness, neither shadow of turning. 18 Of his own **light lighted** he us with the '**light of light**', that we should be a kind of first-fruits of his creatures.	From his own good and perfect light, the Father has lighted men and he desires to give them light + light, continually.

After the group had read and studied the table, Frank and Karen commented that it certainly confirmed that the light + light principle comes from God the Father. They thanked Joan for the information.

"I like the way you have prepared and presented this material," Karen said. "We miss many things in the scriptures because we don't stop to think about what they are saying. Your table methodology shows me that we can find innovative ways to study if we really try."

"The next table," Joan said, "is similar to the first and shows scriptures that relate specifically to Christ and describe him as possessing and working through the principle of light + light."

Table 2. Scriptures that relate specifically to Christ and describe him as possessing and working through the principle of light + light

Original (words highlighted)	Transposed	Commentary
COLOSSIANS 2 9 For in him [Christ] dwelleth all the fulness of the **Godhead** bodily. 10 And ye are **complete** in him, which is the head of all **principality** and **power**.	COLOSSIANS 2 9 For in him [Christ] dwelleth all the fulness of the **Godhead** bodily. 10 And ye are **complete** in him, which is the head of all **light + light.**	In Christ, all the fulness of the Father, the Son and the Holy Ghost dwell. We can be lighted in him who is the head or director of all light + light.

162

Original (words highlighted)	Transposed	Commentary
HEBREWS 2 9 But we see **Jesus**, who was made a little lower than the angels for the suffering of death, **crowned** with **glory** and **honour**; that he by the **grace** of **God** should taste death for every man.	**HEBREWS 2** 9 But we see **Jesus**, who was made a little lower than the angels for the suffering of death, **lighted** with **light + light**; that he by the **light of Light** should taste *death* for every man	Jesus, lighted with the light of his Father experienced death that he might comprehend them and overcome them and free every man from their effects.

Original (words highlighted)	Transposed	Commentary
JOHN 5 26 For as the Father hath **life** in himself; so hath he given to the Son to have **life** in himself.	**JOHN 5** 26 For as the Father hath **light** in himself; so hath he given to the Son to have **light** in himself.	The Father who possesses a fulness of light has given to the Son also to possess a fulness of his light.

Original (words highlighted)	Transposed	Commentary
HEBREWS 1 1-3 **God** . . . hath spoken unto us by his **Son** . . . being the **brightness** of his **glory**, and the express image of his person, and upholding all things by the **word** of his **power**, 4 Being made so much better than the angels, as he hath by inheritance obtained a more excellent **name** than they. 8 Unto the **Son** he saith, Thy **throne**, O God, is for ever and ever: a **sceptre** of **righteousness** is the **sceptre** of thy **kingdom**. 9 Thou hast loved righteousness, and hated iniquity; therefore God, even thy God, hath anointed thee with the oil of gladness above thy fellows.	**HEBREWS 1** 1-3 **God** . . . hath spoken unto us by his **Light** . . . being the **light** of his **light**, and the express image of his person, and upholding all things by the **light** of his **light**, 4 Being made so much better than the angels, as he hath by inheritance obtained a more excellent **light** than they. 8 Unto the **Light** he saith, Thy **light**, O God, is for ever and ever: a **light of light** is the **light** of thy **Light**. 9 Thou hast loved **light**, and hated **iniquity**; therefore **Light**, even thy **Light**, hath **lighted** thee with the **light of light** above thy fellows.	God has given his light to the Son by which he does all that he does. He has even obtained the a more excellent light than the angels. God has said to the Son that the light he has given to him is a light of light + light for ever. He has been lighted with the light of light above all the other children (lights) of God.

Original (words highlighted)	Transposed	Commentary
1 Timothy 1 14 And the **grace** of our **Lord** was exceeding abundant with **faith** and **love** which is in **Christ Jesus**.	**1 Timothy 1** 14 And the **light** of our **Lord** was exceeding *abundant* with **light + light** which is in **Christ Jesus**.	The light of the Father which is light + light, is exceedingly abundant in Christ.

Original (words highlighted)	Transposed	Commentary
2 Timothy 1 10 . . . our **Saviour Jesus Christ**, who . . . hath brought **life** and **immortality** to **light** through the **gospel**.	**2 Timothy 1** 10 . . . our **Saviour Jesus Christ**, who . . . hath brought **light + light** to **light** through the **light**.	The Savior though the light has brought the principle of light + light into the light for all to see and comprehend, if they will.

Original (words highlighted)	Transposed	Commentary
2 Peter 1 2 **Grace** and **peace** be multiplied unto you through the **knowledge** of **God**, and of **Jesus** our Lord, 3 According as his divine **power** hath given unto us all things that pertain unto **life** and **godliness**, through the **knowledge** of him that hath **called** us to **glory** and **virtue**.	**2 Peter 1** 2 **light + light** be multiplied unto you through the **light of God**, and of **Jesus** our Lord, 3 According as his divine **light** hath given unto us all things that pertain unto **light + light**, through the **light** of him that hath **lighted** us to **light + light**.	Peter is asking that light + light be given to the Saints through the light of the Father and the Son, whose light, he says, has given to them all things that pertain to light + light.

Original (words highlighted)	Transposed	Commentary
2 PETER 1 17 For he received from God the **Father** hon-our and **glory**, when there came such a voice to him from the excellent **glory**, This is my beloved **Son**, in whom I am well **pleased**.	2 PETER 1 17 For he received from God the **Father light + light**, when there came such a voice to him from the excellent **light**, This is my beloved **Son**, in whom I am well **lighted**.	Jesus received light + light from the Father when he spoke to him from his excellent light, saying - This is my beloved 'Light" in whom I am well 'lighted'. In other words, Jesus is lighting well the light of the Father in the world.

Original (words highlighted)	Transposed	Commentary
COLOSSIANS 2 2 That their hearts might be comforted, being knit together in **love**, and unto all riches of the full **assurance** of **understanding**, to the acknowledgement of the **mystery** of God . . . the **Father**, and of **Christ**; 3 In whom are hid all the **treasures** of **wisdom** and **knowledge**.	COLOSSIANS 2 2 That their hearts might be comforted, being knit together in **light**, and unto all riches of the full **light of light**, to the acknowledgement of the **light** of God . . . the **Father**, and of **Christ**; 3 In whom are hid all the **lights** of **light + light**.	Paul is asking that the Saint's hearts be knit together in light that they might be able to obtain all the riches of the fulness of light + light, And acknowledge God and Christ in whom are hidden all the lights of light + light, i.e., they know all the principles and practices of the light + light process.

Original (words highlighted)	Transposed	Commentary
REVELATION 19 11 And I saw heaven opened, and behold a white horse; and he that sat upon him was called **Faithful** and **True**, 13 And he was clothed with a vesture dipped in blood: and his name is called The **Word** of **God**.	REVELATION 19 11 And I saw heaven opened, and behold a white horse; and he that sat upon him was called **light + light**, 13 And he was clothed with a vesture dipped in blood: and his name is called The **Light of Light**.	Here the Savior's very names are light + light, and 'The Light of Light'. (Notice how these names are capitalized in the original text.)

"The language of light certainly opens the meaning, doesn't it?" Karen said. "It adds so much depth; and your comments are helpful—tying things together. I'm glad you are giving us copies so I can study it in more detail."

"There's one other verse that relates to the Savior as dispenser of light + light that we ought not to miss," Steve said. "Joan and I discussed it the other day. Jesus, of himself said:

JOHN 10
14 I am the **good** shepherd.

"We learned from the words of Moroni that 'good' is light + light."

MORONI 10
6 And whatsoever thing is **good** is **just** *and* **true** . . .
MORONI 10
25 If there be one among you that doeth **good**, he shall work by the **power** *and* **gifts** of God.

"What this taught us is that Jesus is the light + light shepherd—the shepherd over the light + light process."

"That is simply marvelous," Karen said. "There is such peace and power in that concept. It contains everything. It is worth all the effort it has taken to discover it."

"Thanks, you guys," Joan said. "The last table shows scriptures that speak of man and confirm that he must follow the light + light principle in order to be saved."

Table 3: Scriptures that relate specifically to the idea that man, if he is to become like God and Christ, must follow, obtain, and become personages of light + light even as God and Christ have done.

Original (words highlighted)	Transposed	Commentary
1 THESSALONIANS 2 12 That ye would walk worthy of **God**, who hath called you unto his **kingdom** *and* **glory**.	1 THESSALONIANS 2 12 That ye would walk worthy of **God**, who hath called you unto his **light + light.**	God is calling each of us into the processes of his light + light. It requires diligent effort to add light to the light we already have.

Original (words highlighted)	Transposed	Commentary
1 THESSALONIANS 2 12 That ye would walk worthy of **God**, who hath called you unto his **kingdom** *and* **glory**.	1 THESSALONIANS 2 12 That ye would walk worthy of **God**, who hath called you unto his **light + light**.	God is calling each of us into the processes of his light + light. It requires diligent effort to add light to the light we already have.

Original (words highlighted)	Transposed	Commentary
ROMANS 15 13 Now the **God** of **hope** fill you with all **joy** and **peace** in believing, that ye may abound in **hope**, through the **power** of the **Holy Ghost**.	ROMANS 15 13 Now the **God** of **light** fill you with all **light + light** in believing, that ye may *abound* in **light**, through the **light** of the **Holy Ghost**.	Paul is promising that God will fill the Saints with light + light so that they might abound in light through the Holy Ghost.

Original (words highlighted)	Transposed	Commentary
1 PETER 1 7 That the trial of your **faith**, being much more precious than of gold that perisheth, though it be tried with fire, might be found unto **praise** and **honour** and **glory** at the appearing of **Jesus Christ**: 21 Who by him do believe in **God**, that raised him up from the dead, and gave him **glory**; that your **faith** and **hope** might be in **God**.	1 PETER 1 7 That the trial of your **light**, being much more precious than of gold that perisheth, though it be tried with fire, might be found unto '**light + light + light**' at the appearing of **Jesus Christ**: 21 Who by him do believe in God, that raised him up from the dead, and gave him **light**; that your **light + light** might be in **God**.	The trial of the light that is in you, is more precious than gold, and great it will be if that light is found to be light + light when the Savior appears, for he it is that is the giver of the light of light + light.

Original (words highlighted)	Transposed	Commentary
1 TIMOTHY 6 [JST] 15 Which in his times he shall show, who is the blessed and only Potentate, the King of kings, and Lord of lords, to whom be **honor** and **power** everlasting; 16 Whom no man hath seen, nor can see, unto whom no man can approach, only he who hath the **light** and the **hope** of **immortality** dwelling in him.	**1 TIMOTHY 6 [JST]** 15 Which in his times he shall show, who is the blessed and only Potentate, the King of kings, and Lord of lords, to whom be **light + light** everlasting; 16 Whom no man hath seen, nor can see, unto whom no man can approach, only he who hath the **light** and the **light of light** dwelling in him.	Light + light will be given unto the Savior for ever. No man can see or approach him unless he has the light of light + light dwelling in him.

Original (words highlighted)	Transposed	Commentary
1 PETER 4 14 If ye be reproached for the **name** of **Christ**, happy are ye; for the **spirit** of **glory** and of **God** resteth upon you:	**1 PETER 4** 14 If ye be reproached for the **light** of **Christ**, happy are ye; for the **light** of **light + light** resteth upon you:	If we are persecuted for the light of Christ, we should be happy, for it is proof that we are not unfaithful, but are following the principle of light + light.

Original (words highlighted)	Transposed	Commentary
2 TIMOTHY 1 7 For **God** hath not given us the **spirit** of *fear*; but of **power**, and of **love**, and of a sound **mind**.	**2 TIMOTHY 1** 7 For **God** hath not given us the **spirit** of *fear*; but of **light + light + light**.	God has not given us a light that leads to darkness, but a light of 'light + light + light'.

Original (words highlighted)	Transposed	Commentary
ROMANS 8 6 For to be carnally minded is death; but to be **spiritually** minded is **life** and **peace**.	ROMANS 8 6 For to be **carnally** minded is **death**; but to be **light** minded is **light + light**.	Carnal mindedness leads to darkness and death, while light mindedness leads to light + light.

Original (words highlighted)	Transposed	Commentary
PHILIPPIANS 1 9 And this I pray, that your **love** may abound yet more and more in **knowledge** and in all **judgment**;	PHILIPPIANS 1 9 And this I pray, that your **light** may abound yet more and more in **light + light**;	Paul prays that the light of the Saints may increase more and more in light + light.

Original (words highlighted)	Transposed	Commentary
1 THESSALONIANS 5 8 But let us, who are of the **day**, be sober, putting on the breastplate of **faith** and **love**; and for an helmet, the **hope** of **salvation**.	1 THESSALONIANS 5 8 But let us, who are of the **light**, be sober, putting on the breastplate of **light + light**; and for an helmet, the **light of light**.	We who are of the light should put on the breastplate of light + light, and the helmet of the light of light.

Original (words highlighted)	Transposed	Commentary
1 TIMOTHY 3 15 . . . **house** of **God**, which is the **church** of the living **God**, the **pillar** and **ground** of the **truth**.	1 TIMOTHY 3 15 . . . **house** of **God**, which is the **light** of the living **God**, the **light + light** of the **light**.	The house or church of God is the light of the living Light and the light + light of the light of God.

Original (words highlighted)	Transposed	Commentary
JAMES 2 26 For as the body without the **spirit** is **dead**, so **faith** without **works** is **dead** also.	JAMES 2 26 For as the body without the **light** is **dead**, so **light** without **light** is dead also.	As the body without light is dead, so is our light if we do not add more light to it. (See also 2 Nephi 2:11.)

Original (words highlighted)	Transposed	Commentary
1 JOHN 4 12 If we **love** one another, **God** dwelleth in us, and his **love** is **perfected** in us.	1 JOHN 4 12 If we **light** one another, **God** dwelleth in us, and his **light** is **lighted** in us.	If we light one another, it is because God is in us and it is his light that is lighting us.

Original (words highlighted)	Transposed	Commentary
JUDE 1 2 **Mercy** unto you, and **peace**, and **love**, be multiplied.	JUDE 1 2 **Light** unto you, and **light + light**, be multiplied.	Jude commends the light to us and asks that the light + light of that light be multiplied on us.

Original (words highlighted)	Transposed	Commentary
1 THESSALONIANS 4 4 That every one of you should know how to **possess** his **vessel** in **sanctification** and **honour**;	1 THESSALONIANS 4 4 That every one of you should know how to **light** his **light** in **light + light**;	Every one of us should know how to light the light that is in us with the light + light of Christ.

Original (words highlighted)	Transposed	Commentary
2 JOHN 1 9 Whosoever transgresseth, and abideth not in the **doctrine** of **Christ**, hath not **God**. He that abideth in the **doctrine** of **Christ**, he hath both the **Father** and the **Son**.	**2 JOHN 1** 9 Whosoever transgresseth, and abideth not in the **light** of **Christ**, hath not **God**. He that abideth in the **light** of **Christ**, he hath both the **Father** and the **Son**.	He that is not true to the light of Christ has no light. He that abides in the light of Christ has access both to the Father and to the Son.

Original (words highlighted)	Transposed	Commentary
EPHESIANS 4 24 And that ye put on the new man, which after **God** is created in **righteousness** and **true holiness**.	**EPHESIANS 4** 24 And that ye put on the new man, which after **God** is created in **light + light**.	When we put on the new man, we, through the principle of light + light may become as God.

Original (words highlighted)	Transposed	Commentary
EPHESIANS 4 7 But unto every one of us is given **grace** according to the **measure** of the **gift** of **Christ**.	**EPHESIANS 4** 7 But unto every one of us is given **light** according to the **lighting** of the **light** of **Christ**.	Every one of us is given light according to the discretion of the light of Christ. (See Moses 6:61)

Original (words highlighted)	Transposed	Commentary
EPHESIANS 5 8 For ye were sometimes **darkness**, but now are ye **light** in the **Lord**: walk as **children** of **light**: 9 (For the **fruit** of the **Spirit** is in all **goodness** and **righteousness** and **truth**;)	EPHESIANS 5 8 For ye were sometimes **darkness**, but now are ye **light** in the **Lord**: walk as **children** of **light**: 9 (For the light of the light is in all **'light + light + light'** ;)	Whereas some have been in darkness, they are now light in the Lord. We must now walk as lights of the light, and that light is 'light + light + light.

Original (words highlighted)	Transposed	Commentary
D&C 121 46 The **Holy Ghost** shall be thy constant companion, and thy **scepter** an unchanging scepter of **righteousness** and **truth**; and thy **dominion** shall be an everlasting **dominion**, and without compulsory means **it** shall flow unto thee forever and ever.	D&C 121 46 The **Holy Ghost** shall be thy constant companion, and thy **light** an unchanging **light** of **light + light**; and thy **light** shall be an everlasting **light**, and without compulsory means **light** shall flow unto thee forever and ever.	This is perhaps one of the greatest verses in all scripture about the promise of light + light to the faithful in the eternal worlds

Original (words highlighted)	Transposed	Commentary
REVELATION 1 6 And hath **made** us **kings** and **priests** unto **God** and his **Father**; to him be **glory** and **dominion** for ever and ever.	REVELATION 1 6 And hath (anointed) **lighted** us **'lights + lights'** unto **God** and his **Father**; to **him** be **light + light** for ever and ever.	God has anointed us or lighted us to be 'lights + lights' unto 'Christ' and to his 'Father'. Hence, we will give to him light + light for ever and ever.

172

"After I had completed these tables," Joan continued, "I found a chapter in the Book of Mormon that ties all these things together. To me it's the bottom-line scripture about the light + light of God. Let me put it up on the screen. I would like you to just read it through and become familiar with it, and then let's discuss it."

---

2 Nephi 2

6 Wherefore, redemption cometh in and through the Holy Messiah; for he is full of **grace** and **truth**.

7 Behold, he offereth himself a sacrifice for sin, to answer the ends of the **law**, unto all those who have a broken heart and a contrite spirit; and unto none else can the ends of the **law** be answered.

8 Wherefore, how great the importance to make these things known unto the inhabitants of the earth, that they may know that there is no flesh that can dwell in the **presence** of **God**, save it be through the **merits**, and **mercy**, and **grace** of the **Holy Messiah**, who layeth down his life according to the flesh, and taketh it again by the **power** of the **Spirit**, that he may bring to pass the resurrection of the dead, being the first that should rise.

9 Wherefore, he is the firstfruits unto God, inasmuch as he shall make intercession for all the children of men; and they that believe in him shall be saved.

10 And because of the intercession for all, all men come unto **God**; wherefore, they stand in the **presence** of him, to be **judged** of him according to the **truth** and **holiness** which is in him. Wherefore, the ends of the **law** which the Holy One hath given, unto the inflicting of the *punishment* which is affixed, which *punishment* that is affixed is in *opposition* to that of the **happiness** which is affixed, to answer the **ends** of the atonement—

11 For it must needs be, that there is an *opposition* in all things. If not so, my first-born in the wilderness, **righteousness** could not be brought to pass, neither *wickedness*, neither **holiness** nor *misery*, neither **good** nor **bad**. Wherefore, all **things** must needs be a compound in one; wherefore, if **it** should be one body **it** must needs remain as *dead*, having no **life** neither *death*, nor *corruption* nor **incorruption**, **happiness** nor *misery*, neither **sense** nor *insensibility*.

12 Wherefore, **it** must needs have been created for a thing of naught; wherefore there would have been no purpose in the end of **its** creation. Wherefore, this thing must needs

destroy the **wisdom** of **God** and his eternal **purposes**, and also the **power**, and the **mercy**, and the **justice** of **God**.

"Now let's just take this concept by concept," Joan said.

6 Redemption cometh in and through the Holy Messiah; for he is full of **grace** *and* **truth**.

"In the spirit of what we have been talking about, what does this tell us about Jesus Christ?"

"It tells us that he is full of light + light," Karen answered.

7 Behold, he offereth himself a sacrifice for sin, to answer the *ends of the* **law**, unto all those who have a broken heart and a contrite spirit; and unto none else can the *ends of the* **law** be answered.

"This next verse says that Jesus, who is full of light + light, will offer himself to answer the ends of the law. Verse 10 explains what the 'ends of the law' are. Could you please explain that, Steve?"

10 The ends of the **law** . . . (are the) . . . inflicting of the punishment which is affixed, which punishment that is affixed is in *opposition* to that of the happiness which is affixed, to answer the ends of the atonement.

"It seems to me that there are two ends," Steve said. "The one is to end up with more light; the other is to end up with less or no light. It terms these ends happiness or punishment. The two are opposites.

"This next verse tells us of the sacrifice and role of the Savior," Joan said.

8 There is no flesh that can dwell in the **presence** of **God**, save it be through the **merits**, and **mercy**, and **grace** of the **Holy Messiah**, who layeth down his life according to the flesh, and taketh it again by the **power** of the **Spirit**, that he may bring to pass the resurrection of the dead, being the first that should rise.

"What does this add?" Joan asked.

"It says that the only way flesh can dwell in the light of God is through the light + light + light of Christ," Frank responded.

"The next verse tells of the judgment," Joan said. "Will you explain it, Karen?"

---

10 And because of the intercession for all, all men come unto God; wherefore, they stand in the **presence** of him, to be **judged** of him according to the **truth** and **holiness** which is in him. Wherefore, the ends of the **law** which the Holy One hath given, unto the inflicting of the *punishment* which is affixed, which **punishment** that is affixed is in *opposition* to that of the **happiness** which is affixed, . . . answer the ends of the atonement.

"Because of the light + light of Christ, all men come to God (the Light), and they will stand in his light to be lighted-up of him according to the light + light which is in him. That probably means that they will be revealed for what they really are. It then says that the ends of the light will then be handed out to each person. One of the ends is punishment or darkness. The other end is light, or happiness. It then says that these ends were made possible by the atonement."

"Now we come to the core statement," Joan said.

---

11 For it must needs be, that there is an *opposition* in all **things**. If not so . . . **righteousness** could not be brought to pass, neither **wickedness**, neither **holiness** nor **misery**, neither **good** nor **bad**. Wherefore, all **things** must needs be a compound in one; wherefore, if **it** should be one body **it** must needs remain as dead, having no **life** neither **death**, nor **corruption** nor **incorruption**, **happiness** nor **misery**, neither **sense** nor **insensibility**.

12 Wherefore, **it** must needs have been created for a thing of naught; wherefore there would have been no purpose in the end of **its** creation. Wherefore, this thing must needs destroy the **wisdom** of God and his eternal **purposes**, and also the **power**, and the **mercy**, and the **justice** of **God**.

"In the giving of light to us by God, there has to be an opposition," Joan summarized. "If this were not so, there could be no agency to choose righteousness or holiness or good—which things we know are light + light. Neither could there be a choice for darkness. If there were no opposition, all light would be a compound in one. Or in other words, it would just be light—a single dimension—with no opportunity for light + light. It would be dead. And if light were like that, it would have been created for nothing—there would have been no purpose in its creation. If that were to have been the case, it would have destroyed the light + light of God—for remember, the glory of God is intelligence, or in other words, light + light. The Garden of Eden, as you recall, was a place of light, with no opportunity for increase until opposition was introduced and opted for. The Fall brought the opportunity for light + light.

---

2 NEPHI 2

22 And now, behold, if Adam had not transgressed he would not have fallen, but he would have remained in the garden of Eden. And *all* **things** *which were created must have remained in the same state in which they were after they were created; and they must have remained forever, and had no end.*

23 And they would have had no children; wherefore they would have remained in a state of innocence, having no **joy**, for they knew no **misery**; doing no **good**, for they knew no **sin**.

25 Adam fell that **men** might be; and **men** are, that they might have **joy**.

"The Lord, speaking directly to Adam, emphasized what the Fall had done:

MOSES 6

55 And the Lord spake unto Adam, saying: . . . thy children . . . taste the **bitter**, that they may know to prize the **good**.

56 And it is given unto them to know **good** from **evil**; wherefore they are *agents* unto themselves, and I have given unto you another **law** *and* **commandment**.

"The Fall gave Adam, and later his children, an opportunity to choose light + light and afforded the Lord an opportunity to give it to them, whereas, there had been no opportunity before. Incidentally, don't miss the last statement in this verse. The Lord says to Adam—and you can almost hear the satisfaction in his voice—that the information he has just given to him is another light added to the light he already has (light +

light). Because of the Fall, the Lord was now free to give to his righteous children all the light they truly desire and qualify for."

"The scriptures you have presented to us are thrilling," Frank said. "Their organization is commendable, Joan. What you have presented reminds me of a study I did once on the law of Moses. The law of Moses was given to the house of Israel as a replacement of the higher law that they had failed to obey. (See Bible Dictionary, 722) Essentially it created a condition much like things were in the Garden of Eden. The scriptures say this about it:

EZEKIEL 20
13 But the house of Israel rebelled against me in the wilderness: they walked not in my **statutes**, and they despised my **judgments**, which if a man do, he shall even **live** in them . . .
25 Wherefore I gave them also **statutes** that were *not* **good**, and **judgments** whereby they should *not* **live**;
HEBREWS 10
1 For the **law** having a shadow of **good** things to come, and not the very image of the things, can never with those sacrifices which they offered year by year continually make the comers thereunto perfect.
ROMANS 7
6 But now we are delivered from the **law**, that being dead wherein we were held; that we should serve in newness of **spirit**, and not in the oldness of the letter.
HEBREWS 7
19 For the **law** made nothing perfect, but the bringing in of a better **hope** did; by the which we draw nigh unto God.
JOHN 1
17 For the **law** was given by Moses, but **grace** *and* **truth** came by **Jesus Christ**.

"As you can see, the Lord gave a light to ancient Israel that was not light + light. It was only a shadow of it and was fundamentally dead, making nothing perfect. Thankfully, the last verse confirms that while the light was given by Moses, light + light came by Jesus Christ."

"Speaking of light + light," Karen said, "I have done a little study in section 132 of the Doctrine and Covenants. This section is full of plural words and words that signify increase and expansion. In relationship to all that has been presented here today, it is another witness to the glory of God being light + light. As I have concentrated on this section, a definition of God seems to emerge that is synonymous with 'enlargement.' As I was doing this study, I suddenly remembered that the very name of God—Elohim—is plural. It signifies to me not only a plurality of Gods but the plurality or continuation of lives and light and power. Not only did he achieve his light by the principle of light + light, but he also manifests light to his children upon the same principle. Let me put this up on the screen so we can view it."

Verses in D&C Section 132 that relate to the light + light nature of the things of God

D&C 132

16 . . . a far **more**, and an **exceeding**, and an eternal **weight** of glory.

17 They cannot be **enlarged**, but remain separately and singly, without exaltation, in their saved condition, to all eternity; and from henceforth are not **gods**,

19 . . . shall inherit **thrones, kingdoms, principalities, and powers, dominions, all heights and depths**— . . . which glory shall be a fulness and a **continuation of the seeds forever and ever.**

20 Then shall **they be gods, because they have no end**; therefore **shall they be from everlasting to everlasting, because they continue**;

22 . . . narrow the way that leadeth unto the exaltation and **continuation of the lives**,

29 Abraham received all things, whatsoever he received, by **revelation** *and* **commandment**, by my **word**,

30 Abraham received promises concerning his seed—which were to **continue so long as they were in the world; and as touching Abraham and his seed, out of the world they should continue; both in the world and out of the world should they continue as innumerable as the stars; or, if ye were to count the sand upon the seashore ye could not number them.**

31 . . . by this law is the **continuation** of the **works** of my Father, wherein he **glorifieth** himself.

55 And I will bless him and **multiply him and give unto him an hundredfold in this world, of fathers and mothers, brothers and sisters, houses and lands, wives and children, and crowns of eternal lives in the eternal worlds.** (Note: these are all plural words)

56 I, the Lord thy God, will **bless her, and multiply her,**

63 . . . are given unto him to **multiply and replenish the earth**, . . . that they may bear the souls of men; for herein is the work of my Father **continued**, that he may be **glorified**.

64 for I will **magnify my name upon all those who receive and abide in my law.**
66 **I will reveal** *more* **unto you, hereafter**;

A feeling of reverence and awe spread through the four studiers as they again took in the feast that was projected before them. They asked questions and pointed out to each other things that impressed them. Karen then said, "I became so passionate about words that signify increase that I decided to compose a list from the Topical Guide, footnotes, and cross-references of all those kinds of words in the scriptures I could find. Then I searched in the scripture program on the computer to find the number of times they appear in the scriptures. This next slide is that list.

A list of scriptural words that relate to the idea of "increase," as suggested by the principle of light + light, and the number of times they occur

(Note: Various forms of some words are included in the number. This list is by no means exhaustive.)

Abound................37	Forward................85	Regeneration...........2
Add.....................34	Fruitful................40	Renew...................20
Awake...................53	Glorify.................30	Replenish..............12
Blessings...............77	Grow...................117	Restoring................5
Bountifully.............6	Increase...............170	Rising...................48
Brighter & brighter.....2	Lengthen.................9	Spread................132
Bring forth..........189	More & more.....1271	Springing................6
Buildeth.............14	Multiplicity.............9	Sprout.....................4
Continue............172	Multiply..............132	Sprung....................9
Edify.....................15	Never cease.............8	Stir......................112
Endless.................30	Overflowing..........32	Stretch................169
Endure.................134	Perfecting.................3	Stronger & stronger...24
Enlarge.................15	Perpetual..............31	Swell.....................22
Enlighten..............21	Plenteous...............36	Unceasingly............1
Enliven...................1	Propagating............1	Wax.....................118
Eternally.................8	Prosper................172	Wellspring...............2
Evermore..............27	Purifying..............12	Without end.........15
Exceeding abundant.1	Quicken...............41	Workings................6
Exercise.................36	Reaching................3	Wrought..............141
Expand...................2	Reaping................74	
Flourish................26	Receiving..............22	Words: 64
For ever & ever.....427	Redound................2	Total: 4475

"Thank you, Karen, for this information," Steve said. "It's astonishing how the use of the computer can enhance our study. Searches that used to take days or even months can now be done in a very short time."

"That is true, Joan said, "but the issue is not so much how fast it is, as what you search for and how you interpret the information you find."

"That makes sense," Karen said. "And it's the making sense that really matters. I want to share one more slide with you. It shows again the Lord's use of plural words and emphasizes the light + light principle."

D&C 97
5 And I will **bless** him with a *multiplicity* of **blessings**. (See also D&C 124:13,90.)
D&C 97
28 And I will **bless** her with **blessings**, and *multiply a multiplicity* of **blessings** upon her, and upon her generations *forever and ever*, saith the Lord your God. Amen.
D&C 104
2 Inasmuch as those whom I commanded were faithful they should be **blessed** with a *multiplicity of* **blessings**;
D&C 104
33 I will *multiply* **blessings** upon them and their seed after them, even a *multiplicity* of **blessings**.
D&C 104
38 I will *multiply a multiplicity* of **blessings** upon him.
D&C 104
42 I will *multiply* **blessings** upon him and his seed after him, even a *multiplicity* of **blessings**.
46 And I will *multiply* **blessings** upon the house of my servant Joseph Smith, Jun., inasmuch as he is faithful, even a *multiplicity* of **blessings**.

"With all this talk about expansion," Frank said, "I can't help but reflect on a statement that Dr. Hugh Nibley made on the subject. I have it here in my briefcase. Let me share it with you."

It is . . . light that imposes form and order on all else; . . . it is . . . light that purifies contaminated substances, and the light that enables dead matter to live. Reduced to its simplest form, creation is the action of light upon matter; matter of itself has no power, being burnt-out energy, but light reactivates it; matter is incapable of changing itself—it has no desire to, and so light forces it into the recycling process where it can again work upon it—for light is the organizing principle. . . . As light emanates out into space in all directions it does not weaken but mysteriously increases more and more, not stopping as long as there is a space to fill. In each world is a gathering of light ("synergy"?), and as each is the product of a drive toward expansion, each becomes a source of new expansion, "having its part in the expansion of the universe." (Hugh Nibley, *Old Testament and Related Studies* [Salt Lake City: Deseret Book, 1988], 183–4)

"We are so turned-in as humans and even as Latter-day Saints," Joan said. "We have so little idea what the work of God really is and the level on which he is operating. We are so slow to make necessary changes and so resistant to the stretch marks of growth, yet those are the very principles that motivate God."

ISAIAH 9
7 Of the increase of his **government** *and* **peace** there shall be no end,

---

"All of us have shared our thoughts except you, Steve. I know you must have something to share with us," Frank said.

"I do," Steve responded. "I'd like to show you some unique verses that take on exceptional meaning when transposed into the language of light. Joan has shown you some that relate specifically to the Father and the Son. The ones I will show you relate to other things in the scriptures. Some of them are quite surprising in their revelations."

---

2 NEPHI 25
23 We know that it is by **grace** that we are **saved**, after all we can do.
ETHER 12:27
27 My **grace** is sufficient for all men that humble themselves before me.
MORMON 2
15 I saw that the **day** *of* **grace** was passed with them,
D&C 101
3 They shall be mine in that day when I shall come to make up my **jewels**.
ALMA 28
12 Dwell at the right hand of God, in a state of never-ending **happiness**.

ALMA 42
16 . . . the **plan of happiness**, which was as eternal also as the **life** of the soul
D&C 29
34 All things unto me are **spiritual**.
2 Corinthians 13
1 In the mouth of *two or three* **witnesses** shall every **word** be **established**.
D&C 82
3 For of him unto whom **much** is given **much** is required; and he who sins against the greater **light** shall receive the greater condemnation.
D&C 132
18 For my **house** is a **house** *of* **order**, saith the Lord God.
LUKE 22
32 When thou art **converted**, **strengthen** thy brethren.
LUKE 2
49 Wist ye not that I must be about my **Father's business**?
MARK 4
3 Behold, there went out a **sower** to **sow**:
14 The **sower soweth** the **word**.
26 The **kingdom** *of* **God**, as if a man should cast *seed* into the ground;
PSALM 97
11 **Light** is **sown** for the **righteous**, and **gladness** for the **upright** in heart.
GENESIS 3
20 Adam called his wife's name Eve; because she was the **mother** of all **living**.
PSALM 36
9 With thee is the **fountain** *of* **life**: in thy **light** shall we see **light**.
D&C 5
10 But this generation shall have my **word** through **you** (speaking of Joseph Smith);
3 NEPHI 12
6 And blessed are all they who do hunger and thirst after **righteousness**, for they shall be **filled** with the **Holy Ghost**.
HEBREWS 5
4 No man taketh this **honour** unto himself, but he that is **called** of God, as was Aaron.
PSALM 89
24 But my **faithfulness** *and* my **mercy** shall be with him: and in my **name** shall his **horn** be **exalted**.

2 SAMUEL 14

4 And, ye fathers, provoke not your children to wrath: but bring them up in the **nurture** *and* **admonition** of the Lord. (See this in relationship to D&C 93: 40,42.)

1 JOHN 3

8 The devil sinneth from the beginning. For this purpose the **Son of God** was **manifested**, that he might destroy the **works** of the **devil**.

PSALM 145

16 Thou openest thine **hand**, and satisfiest the desire of every **living** thing.

PSALM 95

7 For he is our **God**; and we are the **people** *of* his **pasture**, and the **sheep** *of* his **hand**.

PSALM 119

121 I have done **judgment** *and* **justice**: leave me not to mine oppressors.

PSALM 85

10 **Mercy** *and* **truth** are met together; **righteousness** *and* **peace** have **kissed** each other. (See this in relationship to D&C 88:40.)

PSALM 23

6 Surely **goodness** *and* **mercy** shall follow me all the days of my life: and I will dwell in the **house** *of* the **Lord** for ever.

PSALM 25

21 Let **integrity** *and* **uprightness** preserve me; for I wait on thee.

HEBREW 12

2 Looking unto **Jesus** the **author** *and* **finisher** of our **faith**;

JACOB 6

11 Enter in at the **strait gate**, and *continue* in the **way** which is **narrow**, until ye shall obtain eternal **life**.

2 NEPHI 31

18 Then are ye in this **strait** *and* **narrow path** which leads to eternal **life** . . . unto the fulfilling of the promise which he hath made, that if ye entered in by the **way** ye should receive.

19–20 After ye have gotten into this **strait** *and* **narrow** path, I would ask if all is done? Behold, I say unto you, Nay; for . . . ye shall *press forward, feasting* upon the **word** *of* **Christ**, and *endure to the end*, behold, thus saith the Father: Ye shall have eternal **life**.

21 And now, behold, my beloved brethren, this is the **way**; and there is none other **way** nor **name** given under heaven whereby man can be **saved** in the **kingdom** *of* **God**.

> **D&C 1**
>
> 37 Search these **commandments**, for they are **true** *and* **faithful**, and the **prophecies** *and* **promises** which are in them shall all be **fulfilled**.
>
> **D&C 84**
>
> 33 For whoso is faithful unto the obtaining these two **priesthoods** of which I have spoken, and the **magnifying** their **calling**, are **sanctified** by the **Spirit** unto the **renewing** of their **bodies**. (Remember that that body which is filled with light comprehendeth all things [D&C 88:67].)
>
> 34 They become the **sons** of Moses and of Aaron and the **seed** of Abraham, and the **church** *and* **kingdom**, and the **elect** of **God**.
>
> 35 And also all they who receive this **priesthood** receive **me**, saith the Lord;
>
> 37 And he that receiveth **me** receiveth my **Father**;
>
> 38 And he that receiveth my **Father** receiveth my **Father's kingdom**; therefore *all* that my **Father** hath shall be given unto him.
>
> 39 And this is according to the **oath** *and* **covenant** which belongeth to the **priesthood**.
>
> **D&C 1**
>
> 30 And also those to whom these **commandments** were given, might have **power** to lay the **foundation** of this **church**, and to bring it forth out of obscurity and out of darkness, the only **true** *and* **living church** upon the face of the whole earth,
>
> **JST John 8**
>
> 54 Jesus answered, If I **honor** myself, my **honor** is nothing; it is my father that **honoreth** me; of whom ye say, that he is your God.

"What an enlightening selection of scriptures," Karen said. "I was particularly impressed with the idea that we are lighted by light after all we can do and that for some the light of light has past. I also like the one that says we will dwell with God in a never-ending state of light. However, the one that struck me the most was the last one where Jesus says, 'If I light myself, my light is nothing; it is my father that lighteth me; of whom ye say, that he is your God.'"

"I couldn't help but be impressed with verse 18 of section 132," Frank said. "My light is a light of light, and I also loved the idea of the sower or lighter—lighting the light. I also was touched by D&C 1:30—the only light (church) on the face of the whole earth that is light + light. Mining the scriptures and discovering the language of light is such a rich experience. All of you have contributed such a great deal today. I thank you for what you have done."

"I also wanted to share with you an insight into the Book of Mormon," Steve said, "that Joan and I worked on a few weeks ago. The verses show the relationship of the Book of Mormon to light and how the Lord views it. Let me just project it onto the screen and let you look at it."

Light and the Book of Mormon

MORMON 8

14 And I am the same who hideth up this **record** unto the Lord; the plates thereof are of no worth . . . but the **record** thereof is of great worth; and whoso shall bring it to **light**, him will the Lord bless.

15 For none can have **power** to bring it to **light** save it be given him of **God**; for **God** wills that it shall be done with an **eye** single to his **glory** [this is an unmistakable reference to the Urim and Thummim—an eye or light single to his light],

16 And blessed be he that shall bring this thing to **light**; for it shall be brought out of *darkness* unto **light**, according to the **word** of **God**; yea, it shall be brought out of the earth, and it shall **shine** forth out of *darkness*, and come unto the knowledge of the people; and it shall be done by the **power** of **God**.

MORONI 10

4 And when ye shall receive these things, I would exhort you that ye would ask God, the Eternal Father, in the name of Christ, if these things are not **true**; and if ye shall ask with a sincere heart, with real intent, having faith in Christ, he will manifest the **truth** of it unto you, by the **power** of the Holy Ghost.

D&C 1

29 And after having received the **record** of the Nephites, yea, even my servant Joseph Smith, Jun., might have **power** to **translate** through the **mercy** of **God**, by the **power** of **God**, the **Book of Mormon**.

D&C 6

27 If you [Oliver Cowdery] have **good** desires—then shall you assist in bringing to **light**, with your gift, those parts of my **scriptures** which have been hidden because of **iniquity**.

28 And now, behold, I give unto you, and also unto my servant Joseph, the *keys of this* **gift**, which shall bring to **light** this ministry;

D&C 20

8 And gave him **power** from on high, by **means** (another

reference to the Urim and Thummim) which were before **prepared** to **translate** the Book of Mormon;
D&C 10
60 And I will **show** unto this people that I had other sheep, and that they were a branch of the house of Jacob;
61 And I will bring to **light** their marvelous **works**, which they did in my **name**;
62 Yea, and I will also bring to **light** my **gospel** which was **ministered** unto them, and, behold, they shall not deny that which you have received, but they shall **build** it up, and shall bring to **light** the **true points** of my **doctrine**, yea, and the only **doctrine** which is in me.
D&C 17
6 And he has **translated** the **book**, even that part which I have **commanded** him, and as your **Lord** and your **God liveth** it is **true**.

Silence filled the room as the magnitude of the words sank into their hearts. In the last verse, particularly, the Lord was giving the greatest witness of the Book of Mormon that it was possible for him to give—that it is light—even as he is light.

It had been another fulfilling experience for the four of them. They exchanged handouts, and Karen remarked that it was surely going to be fun reviewing and comparing all those specially marked verses.

Light—The Record of Heaven

Knowing that there was still some time left, Frank asked if there were any questions before they ended the day.

"I have one," Joan said. "As we looked at that last slide with verses about the Book of Mormon, I saw references to the word *record*. That's what Mormon calls his writings. It reminded me of a question I had a couple of weeks ago when I was reading from Moses chapter 6. Verse 61 makes reference to the 'record of heaven.' There's obviously a connection between the record of heaven and the Holy Ghost, but I'm not sure what it is. Has anyone ever studied that?"

"I remember doing some work on that," Frank said. "Steve, could we could use your laptop, since it's already projecting onto the screen?"

"That would be fine," Steve said.

Frank sat down, opened Gospel Explorer, typed in the words *record* and *heaven*, and designated that the program find occurrences of those words used together in any verse of scripture. Having found that there were twenty occurrences, he clicked the view button, and those twenty verses appeared on the screen. As the four of them perused the verses, they found that some were not applicable or seemed not to be applicable at all to their study. For example:

Moses 7

28 And it came to pass that the God of *heaven* looked upon the residue of the people, and he wept; and Enoch bore *record* of it, saying: How is it that the heavens

weep, and shed forth their tears as the rain upon the
mountains?

This verse contained both of the desired words, but as far as they
could tell, it didn't enlighten them specifically about the 'record of heav-
en.' However, they found other verses that excited them a great deal:

MOSES 6
61 Therefore it is given to abide in you; the *record* of *heaven*;
the Comforter; the peaceable things of immortal glory; the
truth of all things; that which quickeneth all things, which
maketh alive all things; that which knoweth all things, and
hath all power according to wisdom, mercy, truth, justice,
and judgment.

MOSES 6
66 And he heard a voice out of *heaven*, saying: Thou art baptized with fire, and with the Holy Ghost. This is the *record* of
the Father, and the Son, from henceforth and forever.

---

1 JOHN 5
7 For there are three that bear *record* in *heaven*, the Father,
the Word, and the Holy Ghost: and these three are one.

MOSES 1
24 And it came to pass that when Satan had departed from
the presence of Moses, that Moses lifted up his eyes unto
heaven, being filled with the Holy Ghost, which beareth *record* of the Father and the Son.

D&C 128
7 The book of life is the *record* which is kept in *heaven*.

"The first reference is the one I was referring to," Joan pointed out.

"It says that the record of heaven is the Comforter—'Comforter' is capitalized, so I assumed it was referring to the Holy Ghost (see John 14:26; D&C 35:19)."

"Moses 6:66 confirms that the record is the Holy Ghost," Steve said. "And look at the added insight it offers. It tells us that the Holy Ghost is 'the record of the Father, and the Son, from henceforth and forever.'"

"I understand that the Holy Ghost bears record of the Father and the Son," Joan said, "but this verse says that he *is* the 'record.' What could that mean?"

"I think I can add an insight here," Karen said. "Joan, you and I had a discussion a few months back about the mind of God. You remember we discovered that the word, the truth, the light, and the spirit of God all originate and flow out from his mind."

"Yes, I remember," Joan said.

"Remembering that, look again at the scripture you just quoted," Karen continued.

D&C 42
17 For, behold, the Comforter knoweth all things, and beareth **record** of the Father and of the Son.

"I don't see how that answers the question," Joan said.

"What in this verse equates to the mind of God?" Karen asked.

"Well, the Comforter does, and the fact that he knows all things," Joan said.

"Yes, but there is something else in there," Karen said.

"Are you referring to the word *record*?" Joan asked.

"Read it that way and see," Karen said.

"The comforter knoweth all things and beareth mind of the Father and of the Son," Joan said out loud. "I'm still not getting it."

"The word *bear* in this instance has many insightful meanings," Karen observed. "It means to possess, to hold, or to carry. It also means to transmit, to reveal, or to convey."

"Oh, I see!" Joan said. "The Holy Ghost possesses or carries the mind of the Father and the Son! I had no idea that scripture meant any more than that the Holy Ghost gives testimony of the Father and the Son."[1]

"He certainly does that," Karen said. "But he is only able to give that testimony because he possesses the same mind with the Father and the

189

Son and can reveal to man whatever portion of that mind he sees fit."

"So the record is really the mind or the light of God as carried by the Holy Ghost," Joan observed.

"There are some remarkable scriptures that teach these things," Frank said. "Let me just share a couple of them with you. Let's go back to the first scripture we found in our search. It is speaking of Adam receiving the Holy Ghost after his baptism and says:

MOSES 6

61 Therefore it is given to abide in you; the **record** of heaven.

"Knowing, as Joan has just pointed out, that the record of heaven is the mind or the light of God as carried by the Holy Ghost, we get an insight, through the teachings of the Savior to the Nephites, into how that 'record' can come to abide in us."

---

3 NEPHI 11

31 Behold, verily, verily, I say unto you, I will declare unto you my **doctrine**.

Here, Jesus says, in effect, I will teach you about my doctrine, or in other words my mind or my light.

---

32 And this is my **doctrine**, and it is the **doctrine** which the Father hath given unto me; and I bear record of the Father, and the Father beareth **record** of me, and the Holy Ghost beareth record of the Father and me; and I bear **record** that the Father commandeth all men, everywhere, to repent and believe in me.

And this is my **light**, and it is the **light** which the Father has given to me, and I carry the **light** of the Father, and the Father carries my **light**, and the Holy Ghost carries the **light** of the Father and me, and the **light** that I carry is that the Father commands all men everywhere to repent and believe in me.

---

33 And whoso believeth in me, and is baptized, the same shall be **saved**; and they are they who shall inherit the **kingdom of God**.
34 And whoso believeth not in me, and is not baptized, shall be *damned*.

And those who believe in me and are baptized, shall be saved; and they are the ones who shall inherit the **Light of God** (the Light of the Father and me.)
And those that do not believe in me, and are not baptized shall be damned from the **Light of God**.

---

35 Verily, verily, I say unto you, that this is my **doctrine**, and I bear **record** of **it** from the Father; and whoso believeth in me believeth in the Father also; and *unto him will the Father bear* **record** *of me, for he will* **visit** *him with* **fire** *and with the Holy Ghost.*

This is my **light**. And I carry the **light** of this **light** from the Father, and those who believe in me believe in the Father also, and unto him will the Father carry my **light**, for he will **visit** him with **light** and with the Holy Ghost.

---

36 And thus will the Father bear **record** of me, and the Holy Ghost will bear **record** unto him of the Father and me; for the Father, and I, and the Holy Ghost are one.

This is the way that the Father will carry my **light** to him—the Holy Ghost will carry the **light** unto him of the Father and me; for the Father and I, and the Holy Ghost are one.

"I didn't realize all that was happening when we are baptized and receive the gift of the Holy Ghost," Joan said.

"None of us are really ready for what the Holy Ghost could give us," Frank said. "But look at what happened to Jesus, who certainly was ready when he was baptized."

D&C 93

15 And I, John, bear record, and lo, the heavens were opened, and the **Holy Ghost** descended upon him in the form of a dove, and sat upon him, and there came a voice out of heaven saying: This is my beloved Son.

16 And I, John, bear record that *he received a fulness of the* **glory** *of the Father*;

17 *And he received all* **power**, *both in heaven and on earth, and the* **glory** *of the Father was with him, for he dwelt in him.*

"If I understand correctly, Jesus had a fulness of the glory of the Father in his pre-earth life," Joan said, "but did not have that in his mortal life until he was baptized. He then received a fulness of the light of the Father and that came to him by the Holy Ghost. Because the Holy Ghost is the record of heaven, or carries the record of heaven, it would be correct to say . . . it was given to abide in him, the record of heaven. That would be true of each of us that has received the Holy Ghost, wouldn't it?"

"Yes," Frank said, and yet for the most part, we receive so very very little of what the Holy Ghost has to offer. Our poor reception to his infinite capacity is probably the nucleus of what the Lord meant when he said of the Lamanites, they were:

3 NEPHI 9

20 . . . baptized with **fire** and with the **Holy Ghost**, and they *knew* **it** *not*.

. . . baptized with **light** and with the Holy Ghost, and they knew **it** not.

"They received the gift of the light through the Holy Ghost, but they never came to know it, or in other words, they were baptized into the record of heaven but never lived worthy enough to have it opened unto them. In Facsimile Number Two, Figure Seven, which we talked about earlier, the Holy Ghost is represented as holding out the 'eye' or the 'light' of the 'record of heaven' to all who qualify.

D&C 77

4 Q. What are we to understand by the eye?

A. [The] eye [is] a representation of **light**.

"If we return again to that first scripture we found in our search, we will find a definition of the record of heaven."

Moses 6

61 The **record** of **heaven**; [is] the peaceable things of immortal **glory**; the **truth** of all things; that which **quickeneth** all things, which maketh **alive** all things; that which **knoweth** all things, and hath all **power** according to **wisdom, mercy, truth, justice,** and **judgment.**

"Now I can see how another of those verses we found fits into the picture," Steve said. "Moses 1:24 says, in effect, 'Moses lifted up his eyes into heaven, being *filled* with the Holy Ghost, which carries the "record" of the Father and the Son."

"It makes me want to hurry up and qualify to know what these prophets learned when they saw into the record of heaven," Joan said. "The scriptures tell us many things, but I want to know more, and sometimes it is hard to be patient."

"Let's concentrate, then, for a few minutes on learning more about the 'record of heaven,'" Frank said. "Let's look at these verses."

---

3 Nephi 27

26 And behold, all things are **written** by the Father; therefore out of the **books** which shall be **written** shall the world be judged.

Revelation 5

1 And I saw in the right hand of him [the Father] that sat on the throne a **book** written within and on the backside, sealed with seven seals.

3 And no man in heaven, nor in earth, neither under the earth, was able to open the **book**, neither to look thereon.

Revelation 5

7 And he [the Son] came and took the **book** out of the right hand of him that sat upon the throne.

The first reference says that all things are written by the Father. This is referring to the words of his mind (scriptures) that have been recorded since the beginning of his Godhood by the Holy Ghost. The Lord, on one occasion, said to Sidney Rigdon:

D&C 35

20 And a commandment I give unto thee—that thou shalt write for him; and the scriptures shall be given, even as they are in mine own bosom, to the salvation of mine own elect;

"It is from this record in his own bosom that all earthly books of scripture are written and from which the final judgment will be made. The vision shown to Joseph Smith, for example, in D&C 76 was a manifestation from this record.

D&C 76

12 By the power of the Spirit our eyes were opened and our understandings were enlightened, so as to see and understand the things of God—
13 Even those things which were from the beginning before the world was, which were ordained of the Father, through his Only Begotten Son, who was in the bosom of the Father, even from the beginning.

"Because this vision is about things that are by-in-large still future to us (the judgment, the degrees of glory, exaltation, and so forth), we tend to think of it as a vision about things that do not yet exist. Yet Joseph says he was seeing things that were 'ordained from the beginning before the world was.' These things are part of the record of heaven written by the Father from the beginning of his Godhood.

"The next verses make reference to a time before the beginning of creation showing the Father on his throne holding a book in his right hand which no man could open. This book was his Plan, his Gospel, his Mind, and Will for the creation of all things—the record of heaven. When the Only Begotten of the Father agreed to make a sacrifice for the children of men, he was able to take the book out of his Father's hand and put it into operation."

"When we think of the Holy Ghost as the record," Steve said, "we must also think of him as being a recorder. What can you tell us about that, Frank?"

"The principle of the Holy Ghost as a recorder in the presidency of heaven is mirrored in every presidency in the church. Every presidency has a secretary or clerk whose duty it is to record, take minutes, validate, remind, recall, verify, and to witness. The Oxford English Dictionary gives this definition of a legal record:

> An authentic or official report of the proceedings of any case that has come before a court of law, together with the judgment given thereon; entered upon the rolls of the court and affording indisputable evidence of the matter in question. (Oxford English Dictionary [New York: Oxford University Press, 1971], 266)

"While the minutes of the proceedings of a Church presidency may not be a legal record in the strictest sense of the word, the record made by the Holy Ghost in the heavenly presidency is. Look at this verse:

D&C 59

24 I, the Lord, have spoken it, and the Spirit beareth record. Amen.

"I see what you mean," Steve said. "When the Lord speaks, the Holy Ghost makes and carries a faithful record of what he has said."

"We get an insight into the serious nature of being a faithful recorder from the Prophet Joseph Smith," Frank said.

D&C 128

2 I wrote a few words of revelation to you concerning a *recorder*. I have had a few additional views in relation to this matter, which I now *certify*. That is, it was declared in my former letter that *there should be a recorder, who should be eye-witness, and also to hear with his ears, that he might make a record of a truth before the Lord.*

3 Now, in relation to this matter, it would be very *difficult for one recorder to be present at all times*, and to do all the business. To obviate this difficulty, there *can be a recorder appointed in each ward of the city, who is well qualified for taking accurate minutes; and let him be very particular and precise in taking the whole proceedings, certifying in his record that he saw with his eyes, and heard with his ears, giving the date, and names, and so forth, and the history of the whole transaction; naming also some three individuals that are present, if there be any present, who can at any time when called upon certify to the same, that in the mouth of two or three witnesses every word may be established.*

4 Then, let *there be a general recorder, to whom these other records can be handed, being attended with certificates over*

---

their own signatures, certifying that the record they have made is true. Then the general church recorder can enter the record on the general church book, with the certificates and all the attending witnesses, with his own statement that he verily believes the above statement and records to be true, from his knowledge of the general character and appointment of those men by the church. And when this is done on the general church book, the record shall be just as holy, and shall answer the ordinance just the same as if he had seen with his eyes and heard with his ears, and made a record of the same on the general church book.

"Speaking of this same thing, Elder Parley P. Pratt of the Quorum of the Twelve Apostles, said:

Here, in the holy temples and sanctuaries of our God, must the everlasting covenants be revealed, *ratified, sealed, bound and recorded in the holy records, and guarded and preserved in the archives of God's Kingdom,* by those who hold the keys of eternal Apostleship, who have power to bind on earth that which shall be bound in heaven, and to record on earth that which shall be recorded in *the archives of heaven, in the Lamb's book of life.* (Parley P. Pratt, *Key to the Science of Theology* [Salt Lake City: Deseret Book, 1965], 163; emphasis added)

"If men on earth in the Lord's kingdom are required to go to that extent to ensure accuracy in recording," Steve said, "just imagine what that tells us about the Holy Ghost."

"I imagine when God began his creations," Frank continued. "He first appointed the Savior to be the administrator of all the works of his hands; then he appointed the Holy Ghost to become a recorder. The job of this recorder was to be an eyewitness to all that the Father and the Son would ever say or do. Every issue that would come before them—with their judgment upon it; every word of counsel, every commandment, every journey, every creation, every meeting or visitation, and so forth, was to be eyewitnessed, recorded, and stored in a sacred retrieval system. This would not only cause the information to be present with them at all times. but enable the Holy Ghost to bring it forth for the benefit of the kingdom whenever it was needed."

"How do you think he makes the record?" Steve asked.

"Well, first of all," Frank replied, "going along with what we learned in Moses 6:61, the Holy Ghost, like the Savior:

D&C 88
6 . . . [is] in all and through all things, the **light** of **truth**;
D&C 88
41 . . . comprehendeth all things, and all things are before
him, and all things are round about him; and he is above all
things, and in all things, and is through all things, and is
round about all things;
D&C 88
13 [is] the **light** which is in all things, which giveth life to
all things, which is the law by which all things are governed,
even the **power** of God . . . who is in the bosom of eternity,
who is in the midst of all things.
D&C 85
6 . . . [is] the still small **voice**, which whispereth through
and pierceth all things,

"The light that goes forth from the Holy Ghost, that is in all things
has a very remarkable quality; it reveals the true nature of everything it
enters into."

EPHESIANS 5
13 All things . . . are made manifest by the **light**: for whatsoever doth make manifest is **light**.
JOHN 14
13 Every man's **work** shall be made manifest: for the **day**
shall declare it, because it shall be revealed by **fire**; and the
fire shall try every man's **work** of what sort it is.

"So the record," Steve responded, "comes about as a result of the members of the Godhead initiating the action of light in and upon all things.
The light manifests the true nature of all those things and transmits that
knowledge back to the Holy Ghost, and hence to the Father and the Son."

"Yes," Frank said. "That is what the scripture says."

MORONI 10
5 By the **power** of the Holy Ghost ye
may know the **truth** of all things.

MORONI 10
5 By the **light** of the Holy Ghost ye
may know the **light** of all things.

"Why do the scriptures always say that the Holy Ghost knows everything and will reveal what is necessary, when both the Father and the Son also know everything and could reveal it?" Joan asked.

"The Father and the Son could do that, but they work through the Holy Ghost," Frank said. "The Holy Ghost has the special mission to regulate the manifestation of the light of God to men on earth. Look at these insightful scriptures."

D&C 8

2 Yea, behold, I will tell you in your mind and in your heart, by the Holy Ghost, which shall come upon you and which shall dwell in your heart.

MORONI 8

7 For immediately after I had learned these things of you I inquired of the Lord concerning the matter. And *the word of the Lord came to me by the power of the Holy Ghost, saying*:

8 *Listen to the words of Christ, your Redeemer,* your Lord and your God. Behold, I came into the world not to call the righteous but sinners to repentance; the whole need no physician, but they that are sick; wherefore, little children are whole, for they are not capable of committing sin; wherefore the curse of Adam is taken from them in me, that it hath no power over them; and the law of circumcision is done away in me.

9 And *after this manner did the Holy Ghost manifest the word of God unto me*; wherefore, my beloved son, I know that it is solemn mockery before God, that ye should baptize little children.

"The Lord says he will speak to men by the Holy Ghost. The bottom line of this principle is that what he needs to say to us, he may already have said to others at other times in other places under similar circumstances—even in other worlds. Because the words he spoke then were faithfully recorded and remain on the record, the Holy Ghost in his wisdom can search them out and bring them forth to us in the exact moment when they are needed. If you will look at the experience of Mormon in the verses above, you will see that is precisely what is happening. The Holy Ghost delivered the words of Christ to Mormon. The Savior may not have been actually 'saying' those words at that moment. Those words were on record. The work of the Holy Ghost bringing forth the words of the Savior in this manner frees him up to be doing other things in other places while the work goes on here." *(Note: The same type of experience happened to Adam; see Moses 5:9.)*

"That helps me understand why the Holy Ghost has all power according to wisdom, mercy, truth, justice, and judgment," Karen said. "Because he knows all things, it is his call what words to bring forth and in what manner and under what circumstances. It's like the Prophet knowing which scriptures to share with us in general conference. The Lord says 'his word ye shall receive as if from mine own mouth' (D&C 21:5). I'm sure that's the principle the Savior was trying to emphasize when he said the following of the Holy Ghost."

JOHN 16
14 He shall glorify me: for he shall receive of mine, and shall shew it unto you.

He shall **illuminate** me to you: for he shall receive of my **light**, and shall show it unto you.

"We talked a few moments ago about the great vision shown to Joseph Smith and Sidney Rigdon in D&C 76," Frank continued. "It was a look into the record of heaven that was narrated by the Holy Ghost—the recorder himself. We don't have time to read it all, but you can see the flavor of it in these verses:

D&C 76
12 *By the power of the* **Spirit** our eyes were opened and our understandings were enlightened, *so as to see and understand* the things of God—
13 *Even those things which were from the beginning* before the world was, which were ordained of the Father, through his Only Begotten Son, who was in the bosom of the Father, even from the beginning;
23 We heard *the voice bearing record . . .*
40 The *voice out of the heavens bore record unto us*—
49 And we *heard the voice, saying: Write the vision,*

"Notice that the recorder told them to write the vision. It was to be recorded on earth as it is in heaven. This was an instance of a book being written out of that book in which the Father has written all things, and by this recorded vision (section 76), the world will be judged (see above, 3 Nephi 27:26). Many prophets such as Enoch, the brother of Jared, and Nephi were given the privilege of seeing into and writing from the record of heaven. The Book of Mormon itself is a book written from the greater book of the record of heaven." (See 2 Nephi 27:6-10,14. Pay particular attention to the difference between the book, which refers to the whole record of the plates containing the sealed portion, and 'the words of the book' which refers only to that part which Joseph was permitted to bring forth as the Book of Mormon.)

"The Holy Ghost also records and sets seals on promises made by the Lord," Frank said.

D&C 98

2 Waiting patiently on the Lord, for your prayers have entered into the ears of the Lord of Sabaoth, and are **recorded** with this seal and testament—the Lord hath sworn and decreed that they shall be granted.

3 Therefore, he giveth this promise unto you, with an immutable covenant that they shall be fulfilled; and all things wherewith you have been afflicted shall work together for your good, and to my name's glory, saith the Lord.

"Here is the Lord and the Holy Ghost at work. The Lord has made a promise to his Saints on earth. The Holy Ghost has recorded it in heaven and set a seal and testament upon it. This has made it a sworn and decreed law in heaven. Attached to that law is an immutable covenant that the promise will be fulfilled."

"That sounds very formal and official to me," Steve said. "It's like the seal of a notary on a legal contract."

"You made a statement about a 'sacred storage and retrieval system,'" Karen said. "Would you care to comment on that?"

"The knowledge and power and glory of God of course reside in him," Frank responded. "But as he works and expands, the Holy Ghost keeps an archival record of all that is done, and there is a specific place where that record is kept. It is not kept on earth, for it is the record of heaven. Heaven is the only safe place for it. You can imagine that many would like to destroy that record. The last scripture we found in our Gospel Explorer search (see D&C 128:7) tells us that the record which is kept in heaven is the book of life. Let me show you some scriptures about the book of life.

Revelation 3:5
5 He that overcometh, the same shall be clothed in white raiment; and I will not blot out his name out of the *book of life*, but I will confess his name *before my Father, and before his angels.*

"From this verse we learn that the book of life is before the Father and before his angels.

D&C 62:3
3 Nevertheless, ye are blessed, for the testimony which ye have borne is *recorded in heaven for the angels to look upon.*

"Here we see again that things done on earth are recorded in heaven for the angels to look upon. You might wonder what these things have to do with helping us identify where the record is kept, but let's look at these next few verses."

D&C 130
6 The angels do not reside on a planet like this earth;
7 But they reside in the presence of God, on a globe like a sea of glass and fire, where all things for their glory are manifest, past, present, and future, and are continually before the Lord.
8 The place where God resides is a great Urim and Thummim.
9 This earth, in its sanctified and immortal state, will be made like unto crystal and will be a Urim and Thummim to the inhabitants who dwell thereon.

"I get the message!" Joan said. "The record is kept on the planet where God resides which is a great Urim and Thummim. It is a place where all things are manifest before the face of the angels, for their glory, and are continually before the face of the Lord."

"Just look at the intensity in the references to light in the words of those verses," Steve said. "Angels, presence of God, globe like a sea of glass (or crystal) and fire, glory manifested, past, present, and future continually present, Urim and Thummim, sanctified, and immortal. It's mind boggling! We know a little about the principles of Urim and Thummim and how they relate to light + light and perfection + perfection, but what is a planet that is like a sea of crystal and fire?

"The word *sea* might refer to its immensity and vastness," Frank said. "The idea of crystal and light might have reference to a computer-chip quality. Imagine a Urim and Thummim larger than this earth, larger than the sun. After all, it is a receiver and a transmitter. President Spencer W. Kimball once said:

> We are near appalled by the discernment of the scientists whose accumulated knowledge awes us, but there is greater knowledge; there are more perfect instruments; there is much more to learn. We can but imagine how the great truths have been *transmitted* through the ages. Exactly how this precious instrument, the Urim and Thummim, operates, we can only surmise, but it seems to be infinitely superior to any mechanism ever dreamed of yet by researchers. *It would seem to be a receiving set or instrument. For a set to receive pictures and programs, there must be a broadcasting set.* The scriptures above quoted [D&C 130:6-9] indicated that the abode of God is a *master Urim and Thummim, and the synchronization of transmitting and receiving apparatus of this kind could have no limitation.* (President Spencer W. Kimball, Conference Report, April 1962, 60)

"The Prophet Joseph, commenting on these things, said:"

> The angels do not reside on a planet like our earth, but they dwell with God, and the planet where he dwells is like crystal, and like a sea of glass. . . . This is the great urim and thummim whereon all things are manifest—both things past, present, and future—and are continually before the Lord. *The urim and thummim is a small representation of this globe.* (Ehat and Cok, *The Words of Joseph Smith*, BYU 1980, 169–170)

"Wow!" Karen and Joan said almost in unison. "The enlightenment never ends."

"But there is more," Frank said. "The Urim and Thummim on which God resides has another name. I want to show you three scriptures and see if you can pick it out."

ABRAHAM 3

2 And I saw the stars, that they were very great, and that one of them was nearest unto the throne of God; and there were many great ones which were near unto it;

3 And the Lord said unto me: These are the governing ones; and

the name of the great one is Kolob, because it is near unto me,
Book of Abraham, Facsimile No. 2
Fig. 1. Kolob, signifying the first creation, nearest to the celestial, or the residence of God.
D&C 130
8 The place where God resides is a great Urim and Thummim.

"I see it," Steve said. "It is the throne of God! This is entirely new information for me. I am completely amazed. The planet is his throne—he sits on a Urim and Thummim."

"That amazes me too," Karen said.

"President Kimball in the talk we have already quoted confirms that observation." Frank continued:

> Unto every kingdom is given a law. (See D&C 88:37–8.) He knew the bounds set to heaven, earth, sun, stars, their times, revolutions, laws and glories—which orbs borrow their light from Kolob, the greatest of all the stars. (Abraham 3.) *He actually tells us about the throne of God and that he resides "on a globe like a sea of glass and fire, [which]—is a great Urim and Thummim"* (D&C 130:7–8). (President Spencer W. Kimball, Conference, April 1962; scripture references in original)

"A few verses about the throne help us appreciate it's majesty:

D&C 76
92 And thus we saw the **glory** of the celestial, which excels in all things—where God, even the Father, reigns upon his **throne** forever and ever;
93 Before whose **throne** all things bow in humble reverence, and give him **glory** forever and ever.
108 Then shall he (Christ) be **crowned** with the **crown** of his **glory**, to sit on the **throne** of his **power** to reign forever and ever.
D&C 88:13
13 The **light** which is in all things, which giveth life to all things, which is the **law** by which all things are governed, even the **power** of God who sitteth upon his **throne**, who is in the bosom of eternity, who is in the midst of all things.
40 . . . **judgment** goeth before the face of him who sitteth upon the **throne** and governeth and executeth all things. (See also Alma 36:22 and D&C 76:21.)

"To give us a greater view of the role of this planet-throne of God in the great scheme of things, let's look at these next verses and see what principles they contain."

PSALM 9

7 But the LORD shall endure for ever: he hath **prepared** his **throne** for **judgment**.

2 NEPHI 28

23 All . . . *must stand before the* **throne** *of God, and be* **judged** according to their **works**,

ALMA 11

41 The day cometh that *all shall rise from the dead and stand before* **God**, and be **judged** according to their **works**.

44 Now, this restoration shall come to all, both old and young, both bond and free, both male and female, both the wicked and the righteous, and even there shall not so much as a hair of their heads be lost; but *every thing shall be restored to its perfect frame, as it is now, or in the body, and shall be brought and be arraigned before the* **bar** *of Christ the Son, and God the Father, and the Holy Spirit, which is one Eternal God*, to be **judged** according to their **works**, whether they be **good** or whether they be **evil**.

JACOB 6

13 Finally, I bid you farewell, until I shall meet you before the pleasing **bar** of God, which **bar** striketh the wicked with awful dread and fear. Amen.

ALMA 12

15 But this cannot be; we must come forth and stand before him in his glory, and in his power, and in his might, majesty, and dominion, and acknowledge to our everlasting shame that all his judgments are just; that he is just in all his works, and that he is merciful unto the children of men, and that he has all power to save every man that believeth on his name and bringeth forth fruit meet for repentance.

D&C 1

2 There is *none to escape*; and there is no eye that shall not see, neither ear that shall not hear, neither heart that shall not be penetrated.

"Viewing these things from the 'language of light' perspective," Joan said, "I see that the Lord has lighted his 'Urim and Thummim-Throne' for the purpose of judgment and that all men will be brought to stand before that throne to be judged."

"That's a bit overwhelming to think about," Karen said, "that we will all be taken to his throne to be judged."

"I guess there won't be any choice in the matter," Steve said. "The Atonement of Christ guaranteed that every soul would be brought back into the presence of God to be judged (see Mormon 9:13). This places them, in effect, before the record. Each must stand in the light and let it reveal what they really are."

"It's certainly not possible for us to discern in this world what men really are," Joan said. "Our physical bodies shield what light we have, and our physical eyes could not see it if they didn't. So the judgment has to take place where the true light of each person can be revealed."

"It's intriguing to see that the throne of God is called the bar," Frank said. "A bar is a legal term that comes from a court of law; for example, the bar of justice signifies trial and investigation. It can also mean the desk of the judge—the place where the law is kept and administered. The desk of a judge is like a barricade beyond which a person may not go unless judged innocent. It's also interesting to note that being summoned to this bar will be pleasant to the righteous but will strike the wicked with awful dread and fear."

"I'm impressed to understand that the arraignment before the bar of the Godhead will take place *after* the Resurrection." Karen said. "I guess it ensures that every person will be able to endure the experience if even for only a short time during their judgment. That it is the bar of the *Holy Ghost*, as well as of Father and of the Son, confirms what you've taught us, Frank, that the 'bar-throne' is the place where the Holy Ghost has kept the record."

"It's interesting to me to see that coming to this throne constitutes standing before God in all his glory, and in his power, and in his might, majesty, and dominion," Joan said. "In that place it would be easy to see how every soul could be brought to see and made to feel that all his judgments are just and that he possesses all power to save every man that desires to repent."

"I think there is something else that comes through to me in all this," Steve said. "A court of law seldom takes place at the scene of a crime. Even so, the judgment of men will take place, not on earth where they have sinned, but in the courts on high where the record has been kept. It is also worth considering that it was probably within those heavenly courts that we, in our pre-earthly state, made the initial decision to follow Christ. It was there that we were given to know the outcomes and blessings of the faithful execution of that decision. It seems fitting, therefore, that we be *brought* back to that very place to compare the state in which we are now with the state we were in then, to see if our works will bear the scrutiny of the light of the record."

"It is not without significance," Frank said, "that those who are faithful:

D&C 132

19 . . . *shall inherit throne*s, kingdoms, principalities, and powers, dominions, all heights and depths—then shall it be written in the Lamb's Book of Life . . . they shall *pass by the angels*, and the gods, which are set there, to their exaltation and glory in all things, as hath been sealed upon their heads, which glory shall be a fulness and a continuation of the seeds forever and ever.

"You mean that the faithful will one day have a throne like God's?" Joan said.

"Look at what the Lord said about Abraham," Frank said.

D&C 132

29 Abraham received all things, whatsoever he received, by **revelation** *and* **commandment**, by my **word**, saith the Lord, and hath entered into his exaltation and sitteth upon his **throne**.

37 And he abode in my **law**; as Isaac also and Jacob did none other things than that which they were commanded; and because they did none other things than that which they were commanded, they have entered into their exaltation, according to the promises, and sit upon **thrones**, and are not angels but are **gods**.

"And then he said this to Joseph Smith:

D&C 132

49 For I am the Lord thy God, and will be with thee even unto the end of the world, and through all eternity; for verily I seal upon you your **exaltation**, and **prepare** a **throne** for you in the **kingdom** of my **Father**, with Abraham your father.

"The future surely holds out a lot more for us than I thought," Steve said. "I knew that the faithful could one day become like God, but I didn't know anything about them possessing a throne in the 'Urim and Thummim' sense of the word."

"Yes, and that throne will actually be this earth in its glorified state," Frank said.

D&C 130

9 This earth, in its sanctified and immortal state, will be made like unto crystal and will be a Urim and Thummim to the inhabitants who dwell thereon . . . and this earth will be Christ's.

REVELATION 3

21 To him that overcometh will I grant to sit with me in my throne, even as I also overcame, and am set down with my Father in his throne.

"How exhilarating to contemplate," Karen said. "By the way, that verse you just used from D&C 132:19, about inheriting thrones, and passing by the angels, reminded me of what President Brigham Young said about the endowment."

> Your endowment is, to receive all those ordinances in the House of the Lord, which are necessary for you, after you have departed this life, to enable you to *walk back to the presence of the Father, passing the angels who stand as sentinels*, being enabled to give them the key words, the signs and tokens, pertaining to the Holy Priesthood, and gain your eternal exaltation in spite of earth and hell. (*Journal of Discourses* 2:31)

"Thank you for that insight, Karen," Frank said. "That should alert us to the relationship of the temple to the throne of God. In fact, the temple is an earthly extension of the throne of God. Notice how the throne of God is called a temple in the following verses."

PSALM 11

4 The Lord is **in his holy temple**, the Lord's **throne** is in heaven: his eyes behold, his eyelids try, the children of men.

REVELATION 7

15 Therefore are they before the **throne** of God, and serve him day and night in his **temple**: and he that sitteth on the **throne** shall dwell among them.

"Are there any scriptural references that show the earthly temple is an extension of the throne of God?" Joan asked.

One of the earliest scriptural references we have that bind the earthly temple and heavenly throne together is in descriptions of the Ark of the Covenant in the Tabernacle of Moses. There the 'Mercy Seat' is equated to the Throne of God.

---

1 SAMUEL 4
4 The ark of the covenant of the LORD of hosts, which dwelleth between the cherubims:
EXODUS 25
22 And there I will meet with thee, and I will commune with thee from above the mercy seat, from between the two cherubims which are upon the ark of the testimony, of all things which I will give thee in commandment unto the children of Israel.
NUMBERS 7
89 And when Moses was gone into the tabernacle of the congregation to speak with him, then he heard the voice of one [God] speaking unto him from off the mercy seat that was upon the ark of testimony, from between the two cherubims: and he spake unto him.
EXODUS 25
21 And thou shalt put the mercy seat above upon the ark; and in the ark thou shalt put the testimony that I shall give thee.

MERCY SEAT: The golden covering of the Ark of the Covenant in the Holy of Holies. It was the place of the manifestation of God's glory and his meeting place with his people (Exodus 25: 22; Leviticus 16: 2; Numbers 7: 89); *and was regarded as the Throne of God* (1 Samuel 4: 4; Exodus 30: 6; Numbers 7:89). (Bible Dictionary, 731)

D&C 130
6 The angels do not reside on a planet like this earth;
7 But they reside in the presence of God, on a globe like a sea of glass and fire, where all things for their glory are manifest, past, present, and future, and are continually before the Lord.
8 The place where God resides is a great Urim and Thummim.

"Notice in these descriptions of the Ark of the Covenant and the mercy seat, we have the main elements of the literal throne of God as we saw in D&C 130. It was the place where God dwelt (the residence of God). It was the place of the presence of God. It was the place of the angels of God (cherubims). It was the place of the manifestation of God's glory. It was the place of the ark as a vessel in which to keep the testimony or record of God.

"The ark was made of wood gilded with pure gold; the mercy seat and the cherubims were made of pure gold (see Exodus 25:11, 7–18). Gold is a representation of pure light and resplendent glory. Even so, the Lord sent fire down from heaven to sanctify these things and his glory filled the house, and he put his name there and his eyes and his heart were there perpetually (see 2 Chronicles 7:1–3,16; see also Psalm 11:4 above). Also we must not forget that the High Priest used the Urim and Thummim in connection with the Holy of Holies, and the Ark of the Covenant may have been the place where it was kept. We know it was kept there in the temple of Solomon. (See Bruce R. McConkie, *The Mortal Messiah: From Bethlehem to Calvary*, vol. 1 [Salt Lake City; Deseret Book], 103).

"Thinking of the temple as the earthly throne of God, where glory, angels, Urim and Thummim, and sacred records come together we must not forget the Kirtland temple and what happened on the eve of its dedication:

> The same evening the Prophet met the quorums in the temple. Brother George A. Smith stood up and began to prophesy, when a noise was heard like the sound of a mighty rushing wind which filled the building. All the congregation rose in an instant, being moved upon by an invisible power. Many began to speak in tongues and prophesy, others saw glorious visions. The temple was filled with angels. People from the neighborhood came running toward the temple, having heard an unusual sound and seen a brilliant light like a pillar of fire rising above the structure. These spectators were amazed at what they saw and heard. (George Q. Cannon, *Life of Joseph Smith the Prophet* [Salt Lake City: Deseret Book, 1964], 206–7)

> Members of the Church saw heavenly messengers in at least ten different meetings, and at five of these gatherings different individuals testified that they had beheld the Savior himself. (CES, *Church History in the Fulness of Times, Religion 341–43* [Salt Lake City: The Church of Jesus Christ of Latter-day Saints, 1993], 164)

"Joseph had a room specifically constructed in the temple, which was called the 'most holy place' (HC 2:429) and the 'translating room.' (*Parley P. Pratt Autobiography*, 1985, 48) There he kept the sacred records of the book of Abraham and the Seer stone with which he translated. (J.M. Todd, *Saga of the Book of Abraham* [Salt Lake City: Deseret Book, 1969], 196–200.) It was in this very room where he had the vision that is now section 137 of the Doctrine and Covenants:

D&C 137

1 The heavens were opened upon us, and I beheld the celestial kingdom of God, and the glory thereof, whether in the body or out I cannot tell.

2 *I saw the transcendent beauty of the gate through which the heirs of that kingdom will enter, which was like unto circling flames of fire;*

3 *Also the blazing* **throne** *of God, whereon was seated the Father and the Son.*

"Brigham Young said: 'Do we need a Temple? We do, to prepare us to enter in through the gate into the city where the Saints are at rest.' (*Journal of Discourses* 9:240)

"It is significant that there is a Holy of Holies in the Salt Lake temple and in other temples on the Wasatch front, as well as in Washington, and—we mustn't forget the consecration of the Prophet Joseph Smith's seer-stone on the altar of the Manti temple at its dedication by President Wilford Woodruff. (B. H. Roberts, *Comprehensive History of the Church*, vol. 6 [Provo: BYU Press], 230) And of course there is the all-seeing eye of God on the east face of the Salt Lake Temple, a constant reminder that the temple is the seat of his presence, the expression of his mind, the revelation of his record, the house of his light.

"All these things, as we said, connect the temple with 'the presence of God, the presence of angels, an environment associated with a Urim and Thummim, and with the keeping of sacred records.' (For a further discussion of angels, the Urim and Thummim, and their association with the temple, see Elder Orson Pratt, *Journal of Discourses*, 16:261)

"Understanding that," Joan said, "makes me feel like when we enter the temple, we're walking into a living Urim and Thummim, a stone of light where the record of God is manifest and where the ordinances of God are given that bind us to the throne of God. Perhaps we are even a little like the angels who dwell there."

"I appreciate how you feel," Frank said. "I have felt the same way. Speaking of having the record of God manifest, I want to return to Brigham Young's statement that Karen referred to a few moments ago. He said that in the temple we receive keywords, signs, and tokens. We are told there, and it has been commented on by President Hinckley that what we do there, is done 'in the presence of God, angels, and witnesses.' (See Gordon B. Hinckley, *Teachings of Gordon B. Hinckley* [Salt Lake City: Deseret Book, 1997], 331–332) That should teach us that these things relate to the throne of God. Now, what does President Young say we will do with these keywords, signs and tokens?" Frank asked.

"He says we will give them to the angels who stand as sentinels," Joan said.

"Why do you think we will do that?" Frank asked.

"I really don't know," Steve answered. "I've never thought about it."

"Keys open things," Frank said.

"Oh . . . I see," Karen said after a long pause. "They open the record! They are keys to the record of heaven."

"President Young described what one could do with these keys when dwelling upon the throne of God:

This earth, when it becomes purified and sanctified, or celestialized, will become like a sea of glass; and a person, by looking into it, *can know things past, present, and to come*; though none but celestialized beings can enjoy this privilege. They will look into the earth, and the things they desire to know will be exhibited to them, the same as the face is seen by looking into a mirror. (*Journal of Discourses* 9:87)

"Figure Number Three, in our Facsimile Number Two, also has something to say about this," Frank said.

BOOK OF ABRAHAM, FACSIMILE 2 EXPLANATIONS
Fig. 3. Is made to represent God, sitting upon his *throne*, clothed with power and authority; with a crown of eternal light upon his head; *representing also the grand Keywords of the Holy Priesthood*, as revealed to Adam in the Garden of Eden, as also to Seth, Noah, Melchizedek, Abraham, and all to whom the Priesthood was revealed.

Facsimile No. 2 Fig. 3

211

"Here we see a confirmation that the grand keywords of the Holy Priesthood are connected with the throne of God and that they have been revealed to the ancient prophets, and will be revealed to all faithful holders of the priesthood. That they are keys that open the record of heaven is affirmed by the Prophet Joseph when he said:

D&C 128

11 For him to whom these keys are given there is no difficulty in obtaining a knowledge of facts in relation to the salvation of the children of men, both as well for the dead as for the living.

"Can you tell us more about Figure 3?" Steve asked. "I can see an eye in there that looks like the eye the Holy Ghost is holding in Figure Number Seven."

"That's a great observation," Frank said. "Let's compare the two and see what we can learn."

First of all we must remember that the eye is a representation of light (see D&C 77:4), or, as we now know, of the record of heaven. We see three eyes in Figure 3. These eyes relate to the crown on the head of God which is called the crown of eternal light. This circle crown is the disk of the sun in its full shining power, as well as the pupil of the eye of God. This, you

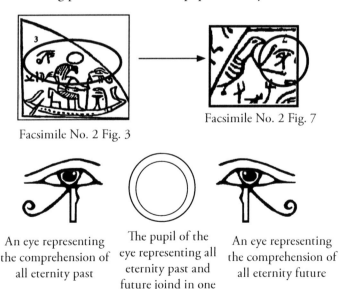

Facsimile No. 2 Fig. 3

Facsimile No. 2 Fig. 7

An eye representing the comprehension of all eternity past

The pupil of the eye representing all eternity past and future joind in one eternal "now"

An eye representing the comprehension of all eternity future

See Hugh Nibley, *One Eternal Round*, Lecture 11, September 19, 1990, FARMS, Tape: Side 1

will remember is what our Facsimile Number Two represents. (See Michael D. Rhodes, *The Joseph Smith Hypocephalus . . . Seventeen Years Later*, FARMS, 1994, 9.) Because the words *light* and *truth* are interchangeable, we can appreciate the nature of this crown of light if we apply the definition of truth to it.

D&C 93

24 And truth is knowledge of things as they are, and as they were, and as they are to come.

"Truth has three dimensions—that which was, that which now is, and that which is to come. The two eyes and the center pupil of the eye represent these three dimensions. The left eye represents all eternity past; the right eye, all eternity future; and the center eye, both of these eternities joined in one as 'one eternal now,' or as all truth encircled into one grand totality. This constitutes the record of heaven. This is the eye that the Holy Ghost holds forth and corresponds to the all-seeing eye we see on the Salt Lake Temple. We can get a small appreciation for the principle of these three dimensions as we in the center, kneel at an altar in one of the sealing rooms of our temples, and view the two mirrors stretching toward the eternities on either side of us.

"A much better Egyptian drawing of this same Figure Three of God sitting on his throne (see page 214) shows the eye-crown encircled with the body of a serpent. (See Richard Patrick, *All Color Book of Egyptian Mythology* [London: Octopus Books Limited, 1972], 30) The serpent is called Uraeus, which in Egyptian means "ficry light" and through an interesting tapestry is also associated with "words of power." (See: E. A. Wallis Budge, *An Egyptian Hieroglyphic Dictionary* [New York: Dover Publications, 1920,] 1:22-23) The Uraeus serpent is a spitting adder that spits venom into the eyes of those who get near it. In this case, as its name suggests, it spits a stream of fire into the faces of the enemies of God.[2] (See E. A. Wallis Budge, *Osiris & the Egyptian Resurrection*, vol. 2. [New York: Dover Publications, 1973], 233-4) This brings together a number of things:

"1. The eye, or light or record of God, is secure from any type of invasion by the wicked. To approach unlawfully is to die.

"2. The Egyptian word *ur-aeus* (light) associates with *ur* the root word of *urim* in the word *Urim and Thummim*.

"3. Coming to know what is in the eye, or light or record of God, is only revealed by fire and by words of power, or, as our Facsimile says, key words.

ABOVE: The "Uraeus" or "Flame-splitter" protecting the eye and showing forth its awesome power.

LEFT: Ra on the throne with sun-disk crown encircled with Uraeus

Courtesy of Jenny Carrington, www.geocities.com/SoHo/Nook/7916/ArtWorks

"This puts us in mind of a caution given of the Lord to those who would think to causally look into a Urim and Thummim, or to try for a look into the mercy seat as they did in 1 Samuel 6:19."

MOSIAH 8

13 And no man can look in them except he be commanded, lest he should look for that he ought not and he should perish.

"If the serpent represents the keywords, why is it not shown in Figure 3?" Steve asked.

"Original drawings like Facsimile Number Two—and there are many—were prepared for the dead and always show signs of being done in a hurry and are generally not very accurate. That's why it's important to look for similar, more accurate representations elsewhere in the Egyptian world. However, because the concept is not to be missed, the idea of keywords is emphasized in another way.

"Through the scepters?" Karen asked.

"They are," Frank answered. "Let's talk about the idea of a scepter for a moment. There's an interesting account in the book of Ruth that shows one of the meanings of a scepter."

ESTHER 4

11 All the king's servants, and the people of the king's provinces, do know, that whosoever, whether man or woman, shall come unto the king into the inner court, who is not called, there is one law of his to put him to death, *except such to whom the king shall hold out the golden sceptre, that he may live:* but I have not been called to come in unto the king these thirty days.

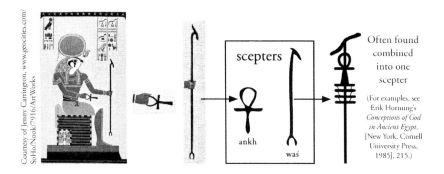

scepters

ankh

waś

Often found combined into one scepter

(For examples, see Erik Hornung's *Conceptions of God in Ancient Egypt*, [New York, Cornell University Press, 1985], 215.)

ESTHER 5

1 Now it came to pass on the third day, that Esther put on her royal apparel, and stood in the inner court of the king's house, over against the king's house: and the king sat upon his royal throne in the royal house, over against the gate of the house.

2 And it was so, when the king saw Esther the queen standing in the court, that she obtained favour in his sight: and *the king held out to Esther the golden sceptre that was in his hand. So Esther drew near, and touched the top of the sceptre.*

3 Then said the king unto her, What wilt thou, queen Esther? and what is thy request? it shall be even given thee to the half of the kingdom.

"What do you see in these verses about a scepter?" Frank asked.

"The king's holding out of his scepter granted a person power to enter into his presence," Karen answered.

"So how would you define 'scepter' as based on this experience?" Frank asked.

"It's like a permission granted or a key given to a person so he can advance."

"Another name for a scepter is a staff or a rod," Frank said, "and we all know from the Book of Mormon that the word of God is called a rod (see 1 Nephi 11:25; D&C 19:15). When these things come together, we can see that a scepter is a rod, which is a key; or in other words, it is a 'key-rod' or a 'keyword'."

"There is so much meaning in such small things," Joan said. "Thanks for helping us to see that."

"These things confirm," Frank said, "that those who inherit the throne of God and dwell on that celestial planet with him will be given keywords that enable the unlocking of the eternal record that is kept there. Incidentally one of the very scepters that we pointed out in the hand of God relating to these keywords is included in the inscription of Figure Eight, which speaks of the granting of these things to a temple initiate, which things, Joseph Smith emphatically states, 'cannot be revealed unto the world, but are to be had in the Holy Temple of God.'"

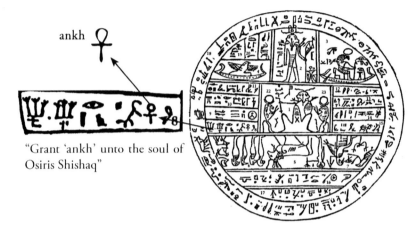

ankh

"Grant 'ankh' unto the soul of Osiris Shishaq"

Fig. 8 contains writings that cannot be revealed unto the world but is to be had in the Holy Temple of God.

D&C 84
19 And this greater priesthood . . . holdeth the *key* of the mysteries of the kingdom, even the *key* of the knowledge of God.

D&C 107
18 The power and authority of the higher, or Melchizedek Priesthood, is to hold the *keys* of all the spiritual blessings of the church—
19 To have the privilege of receiving the mysteries of the kingdom of heaven, to have the heavens opened unto them, to commune with the general assembly and church of the Firstborn, and to enjoy the communion and presence of God the Father, and Jesus the mediator of the new covenant.

"This has been a most enlightening discussion," Karen said. "I have been to the temple time and time again and never understood the things that have been made so plain today. You amaze me, Frank. You have never shared these things with me before."

"They have all come together in a remarkable way. It amazes me too."

"We have been so blessed to be a part of this," Joan said. "We have all contributed in our small way, and look at what has happened. We have been blessed with the Holy Ghost that has enlightened all of us beyond what any of us has understood individually."

"We have been stretched, and I am sure it will be a long time before our minds and hearts come down from this," Steve said. "Thank you for the journey!"

When they had cleaned up the room and put all things back in order, they parted with reluctance and appreciation and vowed to keep on learning and growing. They again expressed love and admiration for the efforts of each other as they said their good-byes.

Notes

1. Another interesting use of this wording is found in the following scripture:

Moses 6	Moses 6
63 All things are created and made to *bear* **record** *of me*, both things which are temporal, and things which are spiritual; things which are in the heavens above, and things which are on the earth, and things which are in the earth, and things which are under the earth, both above and beneath: *all things bear* **record** *of me*.	63 All things are created and made to *carry my* **light**, both things which are temporal, and things which are spiritual; things which are in the heavens above, and things which are on the earth, and things which are in the earth, and things which are under the earth, both above and beneath: *all things carry my* **light**.

2. We see interesting parallels in Numbers 21:6–7, where "the LORD sent fiery serpents among the people, and they bit the people; and much people of Israel died." Also see 1 Nephi 17:41; 2 Nephi 25:20; Mormon 8:24; Ether 9: 31,33; 10:19; Deuteronomy 8:15.

The Light that Is in You

Over the next few weeks, Frank and Karen were often deep into their studies. Karen was sitting at her desk, pondering her recent discoveries and sorting printed pages and notes from her laptop computer. At that moment, Frank walked into the room.

"What have you got going, dear?" he asked.

"I have just uncovered another incredible layer of meaning in the scriptures—at least for me," she said.

"Have you time to share it with me?" Frank asked.

"Sit here and let me find the best place to start. The insights have come from a number of things we have discussed. You'll remember that we talked earlier with Steve and Joan about section 93. Let's turn to that and study it once more."

D&C 93

21 And now, verily I say unto you, I was in the beginning with the Father, and am the Firstborn;

23 Ye were also in the beginning with the Father; that which is **Spirit**, even the **Spirit** of **truth**;

24 And **truth** is knowledge of things as they are, and as they were, and as they are to come;

25 And whatsoever is more or less than this is the **spirit** of that **wicked** one who was a liar from the beginning.

26 The **Spirit** of **truth** is of **God**. I am the **Spirit** of **truth**, and John bore record of me, saying: He received a fulness of **truth**, yea, even of all **truth**;

"Here Jesus is saying, in effect:

- The Father is the Spirit of truth,
- Jesus is the Spirit of truth, and,
- We are the Spirit of truth.

"In other words," Karen continued, "we are one and the same thing. We are on the same continuum. As you showed with the spiral on the Egyptian crown, God is the greatest, and man the least, but both are of the same substance and of the same origin and design."

"In other words," Frank added, "the same light that quickens the Father quickens the Son, and to a much lesser extent, quickens us."

"Yes," Karen said. "Now, let's go one step further.

D&C 88
50 I am the true **light** that is in you, and that you are in me; otherwise ye could not abound.

"Here we see a confirmation that the light from the Father that fills the Son is the same light that is in us; otherwise we would not even be alive."

"I guess that is why we are called a temple—for that light to dwell in," Frank said.

"The light could refer to our spirits, or the light that comes through inspiration but another sense that keeps coming to me is that it could refer to the light that gives our bodies life in the first place. This verse keeps impressing me."

JOHN 15
5 I am the vine, ye are the branches: He that abideth in me, and I in him, the same bringeth forth much fruit: for without me ye can do nothing.

"At first I thought it was only speaking about producing the fruits of goodness. For example, 'Without me you can do nothing good or worthwhile.' But then I read it again, and then I said it out loud:

"Without me ye can do nothing! You can do nothing without me! You can't do anything without me! That got my full attention. I then remembered another verse.

D&C 88

41 *He comprehendeth all things*, and all things are before
him, and all things are round about him; and he is above
all things, and *in all things*, and is *through all things*, and
is round about all things; and all things are by him, and of
him, even God, forever and ever.

"You remember that you taught us that a 'body which is filled with
light comprehendeth all things,' so the Savior by the light that is in him
comprehends all things, and through that light is 'in all things, and
through all things.' What do you think that means, Frank?"

"If you are thinking what I am thinking, I think he is telling us that
his light is the very power by which our bodies operate and we can't do
anything without that light."

"Or conversely, we do everything by that light," Karen added. "Here
is one more verse.

D&C 88

12 Which **light** proceedeth forth from the presence of God to
fill the immensity of space—
13 The **light** which is *in all things*, which *giveth life to all
things*, which is the law by which *all things are governed*, even
the **power** of God who sitteth upon his throne, *who is in the
bosom of eternity, who is in the midst of all things*.

"What this tells me is that while the light of God is giving us life, it
is also the means by which he sees and comprehends us in our very core
or center or in our very cells and tissues. I have imagined a conversation
with him:

> The Savior: You can't do anything without me.
> Me: What do you mean?
> The Savior: Without me being in it with you, without me
> being the source of your power to do whatever it is that you
> do. I am the vine, you are the branch. I am the life, you are the
> liver. I am the engine, you are the vehicle. I am the power to
> go wherever you want to go. Where you steer, we go.
> Me: What about my privacy?
> The Savior: You have your agency, but you use my
> power to make it work. And remember, there is nothing
> you can do without me being there and aware; you can do

nothing separate and apart from me; you cannot shut me out. Whatever you do forces me to be in it with you; whatever you do, I am present in it with you—I see it, I feel it, I experience it—from within you.

Me: Even when I sin?

The Savior: There is no other power available to you to sin with. Where would you get it? I have all power both on earth and in heaven.

Me: You mean that people who turn away from you to sin do it with your power?

The Savior: I give them what ever power they have. They use it according to their desire.

Me: But I am sure you withdraw from them when they sin.[1]

The Savior: I withdraw the Holy Ghost and the powers of enlightenment, but I do not and cannot withdraw my Spirit—the Spirit of Christ—from them, for in me they live, move, and have their being. I in them and them in me; otherwise there is no existence.[2]

Me: So is that why you get so upset when people sin?

The Savior: And why I have so much joy when they keep my commandments. Whatever they do they do it to themselves and to me. That is why I have often said that my people have committed grievous sins against me, and why I have destroyed some people—to hide their wickedness and abominations from before my face (see Hosea 7:2; 3 Nephi 9:7–9, 11).

"That is quite a conversation," Frank said.

"Have you ever thought that the whole body operates on light?" Karen said. "The very atoms, molecules, and cells of the body function with electro-magnetic energy. Light in every atom, molecule, and cell of our bodies constitutes the magnitude of the comprehension of God in our person. He can see and comprehend through our eyes, feel, and comprehend through our fingers and hearts, and understand through the very tissues of our minds."

"So much for the theory that he simply looks down on us from time to time," Frank quipped. "But it does add a new dimension to the idea of his all-seeing eye."

"It certainly does," Karen added. "How often I have heard people say with great emotion that God knows us by our first names? What an understatement!"

"From what you say, the Savior's teaching about our behavior becomes clearer to me:

MATTHEW 25

40 Inasmuch as ye have done it unto one of the least of these my brethren, *ye have done it unto me.*

45 Inasmuch as ye did it not to one of the least of these, *ye did it not to me.*

"He is not only in us, but in the person we serve or don't serve, and our actions to them constitute our action to him."

"I think that is why he takes our behavior so personally and seriously," Karen said. "As the scripture says, we really do everything we do, before him, in him, through him, by him, of him, and to him, and we don't even realize it."

"It's breathtaking to try and imagine the nature of God and how incredible it would be to be like him," Frank said.

"I'm not so sure about that," Karen said.

"What do you mean?" Frank responded.

"I had an experience last night that made me wonder if I ever really want to become like God."

"Tell me about it," Frank said. "You've got me curious."

"Well, in the light of the scriptures we have just read together, and some others that I read last night which are right here, I began to think very seriously about it:

D&C 38

2 The same which knoweth all things, for *all things are present before mine eyes*;

D&C 38:7

7 *Mine eyes are upon you. I am in your midst and ye cannot see me*;

ISAIAH 3:8

8 Their doings are against the LORD, to provoke the *eyes* of his **glory.**

D&C 121:24

24 Behold, *mine eyes see and know* all their works,

"I sat back on the sofa and began to ponder the implications of all this. I tried to imagine that I was God and what it would feel like. In my thoughts I found myself on top of the Empire State building in New York City, looking down at the sight below me. You remember we were there a few years ago. I imagined that I could see and hear the people on the street below and could discern their conversations and actions. Suddenly I found myself comprehending their emotions and thoughts. I could sense their expectations, their joys, their frustrations, and their anger. It frightened me. I could sense such darkness in some of them, such hatred. I didn't want to listen any more, but it wouldn't stop. I wanted to put my hands over my eyes and ears.

"Suddenly my awareness began to increase. I was now comprehending things outward from the immediate street below. I could see and hear into the buildings around, and I could discern the same things about those people. I was almost beside myself with the accumulation of stimuli that was coming into my awareness. The more I wanted to shut it off, the wider and wider in the city became the circle of my discernment. I could see the suffering and the cries of pain and anguish. I could hear every conversation—good and evil—and I could see into every heart and mind. With astonishment I saw more and more. I discerned the animals and the birds and the insects; I could see the parks and the water; I saw millions of people. Then, at that moment when I was almost ready to faint from the overpowering presence of all that I was seeing, I could see that another city was coming into my awareness. I could not imagine how I would handle it. And yet it came and others came and I was powerless to stop it.

"After what seemed an endless time, all the cities of the earth had come before me, and I was caught up and up and up and I was seeing the whole earth beneath me. And yet it was not beneath but around me and above me and I was in it and it was in me and I could discern it all (see Moses 1:27–29). I could even see into other dimensions of the world of spirits. You can imagine my feelings when again I suddenly became aware that there were other earths, hundreds of them, and they were moving into my presence.

"I slumped on the couch. My head ached, my body shook, and my mind felt like it would explode or already had. I was in the highest state of emotional shock that I have ever experienced, and I pleaded that it would end. Gradually it began to fade, and I lay down and sobbed. Was this what it was like to be God? Was this where I was headed through the pathway of the gospel? Was I doomed in eternity to feel like this over the actions and behavior of my posterity? Could I possibly endure it? And then with clarity, these thoughts came into my mind:

D&C 122

7 And if thou shouldst be cast into the pit, or into the hands of murderers, and the sentence of death passed upon thee; if thou be cast into the deep; if the billowing surge conspire against thee; if fierce winds become thine enemy; if the heavens gather blackness, and all the elements combine to hedge up the way; and above all, if the very jaws of hell shall gape open the mouth wide after thee, know thou, my son, that all these things shall give thee experience, and shall be for thy good.

8 The Son of Man hath descended below them all. Art thou greater than he?

D&C 121

8 If thou endure it well, God shall exalt thee on high; thou shalt triumph over all thy foes.

"Suddenly I knew that enduring all these things is what true love is. It is what light is. I wanted to shut them out; God never does and never could. His light is justice and judgment and mercy and the power to bless and to bring about the immortality and eternal life of man. And then I grasped that all men are the personal offspring of God, his very sons and daughters. And then I realized that God could be God in no other way than to be in the midst of all his children all of the time in every possible way and his light is the means and the foundation of doing so."

Frank and Karen sat in silence for a long time. Finally Frank spoke.

"You know, Karen, I have studied light for a long time, but I have only concentrated on the doctrine—on the theory of it all, but you have been able to see into it's reality and practicality. I truly appreciate what you've experienced and what you've shared. It's made me realize that the purpose of light is to do good and to discern and to help bring about peace and kindness and to give relief to the suffering and the poor."

"Right now, I am the suffering and the poor," Karen said. "I have such a long way to go."

"Don't we all," Frank whispered. "But we are on our way, and we will do it together."

"We will," Karen whispered back.

As they prepared for bed, Frank noticed that his laptop computer was still on and Gospel Explorer was still running. As he was about to exit the program, he, on a whim typed "all-seeing eye" in the search-box and hit enter.

His eyes fell upon one of the quotes that came up on the screen, and one in particular caught his attention:

> God searches the hearts and tries the reins of the children of men. He knows our thoughts and comprehends our desires and feelings; he knows our acts and the motives which prompt us to perform them. He is acquainted with all the doings and operations of the human family, and all the secret thoughts and acts of the children of men are open and naked before him, and for them he will bring them to judgment. [We] believe in an All-seeing eye which penetrates and is enabled to weigh the actions and motives of the children of men.
> (President John Taylor, *Journal of Discourses*, vol. 16, 302. See also D&C 121:24; Moses 1:27–8; D&C 33:1; 1 Corinthians 2:10.)

Notes

1. It is a common idea that God withdraws from men when they sin. In one sense that is true and in another it is not. It is man who withdraws from God. God withdraws the Holy Ghost from those who have received it and withholds enlightenment of the Spirit of Christ from those who have thereby been enlightened (see D&C 1:33), but the Spirit of Christ itself—Christ's personal omniscience, omnipresence, and omnipotence—is never withdrawn. It is the sustaining, communicating, and awareness power of his Godhood. It is like a one-way mirror through which he views all things. Note the following scriptures:

D&C 88
67 That body which is filled with light comprehendeth all things.

D&C 6
21 Behold, I am Jesus Christ, the Son of God. . . . I am the light which shineth in darkness, and the darkness comprehendeth it not.

D&C 14
9 Behold, I am Jesus Christ, the Son of the living God, who created the heavens and the earth, a light which cannot be hid in darkness;

Psalm 139
7 If I ascend up into heaven, thou art there; if I make my bed in hell, behold thou

art there. If I take the wings of the morning, and dwell in the uttermost parts of the sea; even there shall thy hand lead me, and thy right hand shall hold me. Yea the darkness hideth not from thee; but the light shineth as the day: the darkness and the light are both alike to thee.

HEBREWS 4

13 Neither is there any creature that is not manifest in his sight: but all things [are] naked and opened unto the eyes of him with whom we have to do.

HEBREWS 4

12 [He] is a discerner of the thoughts and intents of the heart.

As these scriptures attest, he is a being of light who (1) comprehends all things, (2) shines (or penetrates) into the darkness and the darkness doesn't even know he is there, (3) cannot be kept or blocked out of the darkness, (4) has manifested in his sight every creature, and (5) discerns every thought and intent of their hearts.

It might be meaningful to cite just two examples of his omniscience in the scriptures. We are all aware of the Lords instructions to Joseph Smith in the tenth secton of the Doctrine and Covenants about the loss of the 116 pages of the Book of Mormon manuscript. Verses 10–37 contain a discussion by the Lord about the actions of the men who stole the pages and the influence of Satan upon them.

Who would deny that those who stole 116 pages of the manuscript of the Book of Mormon were bereft of the spirit of God? God himself says that "their hearts are corrupt and full of wickedness and abominations; and they love darkness rather than light," yet these verses show that the Savior, by his spirit, the presence of which they were totally ignorant, had complete and perfect access to their hearts, thoughts, and reasoning power as well as their actions, not to mention what their very words would be, in the future, if certain things were to happen. Moreover, it demonstrates that he has total and complete access to the workings of the mind and the doings of Satan—even to the thoughts that he placed into the minds of those who were doing this work in darkness. If that were not enough, he says that in a future time, he will make all things about these events known to the inhabitants of the world.

A second example comes from D&C 76:43–49 where the Lord speaks of the sufferings of the ungodly. Their suffering is called endless and eternal punishment, where the ungodly "reign with the devil and his angels in eternity, where their worm dieth not, and the fire is not quenched, which is their torment" and "the end thereof, neither the place thereof, nor their torment, no man knows" and "the end, the width, the height, the depth, and the misery thereof, they [men] understand not." Now, just when we are feeling that this must be the darkest, the most repugnant, the most hidden of all conditions in existence, and that God in all his righteousness and holiness would never lower himself to penetrate into such a place, we learn that "endless" and "eternal" are his names, and the punishment given in this place is his punishment.

D&C 19:10

10 For, behold, I am endless, and the punishment which is given from my hand is endless punishment, for Endless is my name.

Moses 7:35

35 Endless and Eternal is my name, also.

D&C 19:

11 Eternal punishment is God's punishment.

12 Endless punishment is God's punishment.

Moreover, he says, "I, the Lord, show it by vision unto many, but straightway shut it up again." How could he show the "end, the place, the torment, the width, the height, the depth, and the misery" of such a condition if he did not comprehend it?

These examples, out of many that could be cited, show that God is truly in all things. President Spencer W. Kimball once said:

> God is omniscient. There are no corners so dark, no deserts so uninhabited, no canyons so remote, no automobiles so hidden, no homes so tight and shut in but that the all-seeing One can penetrate and observe. The faithful have always known this. The doubters should take a sober look at the situation in the light of the electronic devices which have come into increasing use in the last few years and which are often delicate and tiny but so powerful as almost to annihilate man's personal privacy." (*The Teachings of Spencer W. Kimball*, edited by Edward L. Kimball, 5)

God has given men his light and their agency and they are free to act for themselves, but, he warns, for all their works they will be brought to judgment.

2. Elder Boyd K. Packer of the Quorum of the Twelve Apostles confirms this:

> The Light of Christ existed in you before you were born, (see D&C 93:23; 29–30) and it will be with you every moment that you live and will not perish when the mortal part of you has turned to dust. It is ever there. The Spirit of Christ is always there. It never leaves. It cannot leave. (*Ensign*, April 2005, 10 and 13.)

CHAPTER 12

The Light of the Atonement

It was a beautiful, crisp evening when Frank and Karen came out of the temple. They were walking toward their car when they heard familiar voices calling to them. It was Steve and Joan on their way to the seven o' clock session. The two couples were overjoyed at seeing each other. They chatted for a moment and then Joan said, "Sorry we can't visit longer, but Tuesday is a holiday, and our children will be at their grandparents' house. Why don't you come over for supper and we could enjoy another visit together?"

"I think that would work out fine for us," Karen replied.

"Karen's sister and her children are taking our children to a movie," Frank added, "so that frees us up. We would love to come."

"We can eat about five-thirty," Joan said.

"What can we bring?" Karen asked.

"A little ice cream would be fine," Steve said.

"A little ice cream has never been enough for you," Joan said with a teasing smile.

"Nor for Frank!" Karen added.

"Well, five-thirty it is," Frank said. "We'll be looking forward to it—and we will bring a reasonable amount of ice cream! Oh, by the way, what should we talk about?"

"We could talk about the Atonement of the Savior," Steve said. "It's certainly been on our minds lately."

"That will be fine with me. Does that suit everyone?"

Joan and Karen agreed, and with warm and friendly smiles they hurried on their separate ways.

The meal was excellent, the ice cream delicious, and of course the menfolk ate more than their fair share. The foursome had spent a good deal of the time sharing insights they had been learning since the last time they had been together. It was evident that they were all moved by their studies and were delighted to hear each other's experiences.

"One of the reasons I suggested talking about the Atonement," Steve said, "is that we've learned so much about the Savior, and our love for him has steadily increased. I thought if we concentrated on the Atonement itself, we could learn to love and understand him more. Frank, perhaps you could begin and give us a sense of direction here."

"Thanks, Steve. Karen and I have also given this a great deal of thought and discussion. Let me just lay a little background here. Our studies to date have centered on light and the fact that it is the very nature and power of God. One of the reasons the study of it is so meaningful is that it is a real substance, and its action upon us is real and significant, and no matter what key word in the scriptures we study, we are studying about a real and living substance and influence. God the Father's person is the source of all light in our universe—there is only one light and it is his!"

"Before we go on," Joan interjected, "remind us how there is just one light when we know there is the light of God, the light of Christ, and the light of the Holy Ghost, and that there are three degrees of glory, and every spirit and exalted person seems to have their own light."

"That is all true in one sense, but you will recall that it is by the light of the Father that all of these things come about. We discussed earlier that God the Father is the fountain of all light. He has given a fulness of that light to his Son so that the Son says of himself:

ETHER 12
28 I will show unto them that faith, hope and charity bringeth unto *me—the fountain of all* **righteousness**.

"The Holy Ghost also uses and ministers by the Spirit or light of Christ as attested by Moroni:

MORONI 10
17 And all these **gifts** [of the Holy Ghost—see verse 7] come by the **Spirit** of **Christ**.

"It is also true that every being who exists is his offspring, whose light derives from his own, and every ounce of light that they receive in their journey toward him comes by his good pleasure (see D&C 76:7).

"What it amounts to is that there is only one issue or release of eternal light, just as there is only one issue of everlasting darkness. We don't know how that came about, but there are not three or four different kinds of light any more than there are three or four different kinds of darkness. There may be different intensities or penetrations or organizations of light or darkness, but light is light, and darkness is darkness. God is the source of the one, and godlessness is the source of the other. They are not compatible and are at war with each other all the time. You recall the scripture that says:

---

2 Nephi 2
11 There is an opposition in all things . . . And if these things are not there is no **God**.
2 Corinithians 6
14 What communion hath **light** with **darkness**?

"With that background let's concentrate for a few minutes on the Savior's light and how it relates with darkness and why there was a need for an atonement.

"The nature and magnitude of the Savior in his pre-existent state was supreme. He was God! That station he received from his Father. He had a fulness of light and power. That 'light proceeded forth from his presence to fill the immensity of space' (see D&C 88:12). He created this earth and many more like it (see D&C 76:24; 93:10; Moses 1:33, 35). He created suns and galaxies. It is hard for us to appreciate that there is enough light that generates from his person to light suns and stars, and yet the scriptures attest to that very fact.

D&C 88
7 *He* is in the sun, and the **light** of the sun, and the **power** thereof by which it was made.
9 As also the **light** of the stars, and the **power** thereof by which they were made;

"As we learned when we were together last, Christ and his Father together with all of the spirit-family of God reside on a resplendent

231

planet. Do you recall what we learned about that?"

"It is a great Urim and Thummim," Joan answered.

"It's also God's throne and the place of the record of heaven," Steve added.

"We also learned:

D&C 130

6 [The planet-throne of God is] . . . a globe like a **sea** of **glass** *and* **fire**, where *all things* . . . are *manifest, past, present, and future, and are continually before the Lord.*

"One of the reasons we have returned to this line of study," Frank continued, "is so that we can see another thing that is happening. You remember that there was opposition to the plan of God in that premortal state. What happened?"

"Lucifer didn't want to follow the plan of God," Steve answered, "and tried to get others to follow him in that desire."

"This scripture tells us what happened," Frank said.

D&C 29

36 The devil . . . rebelled against me, saying, *Give me thine* **honor**, *which is my* **power**.

"Wow!" Steve exclaimed. "I've seen that verse before, but I didn't realize that Satan was after the very light of God."

"Very few have ever imagined just exactly the extent of Satan's design," Frank said.

D&C 88

115 For Michael shall fight their battles, and shall overcome him who seeketh the **throne** of him who sitteth upon the **throne**, even the Lamb.

"You mean Satan actually wanted to steal away the Urim and Thummim-planet of God?" Joan interjected.

"Here are some other witnesses," Frank said.

D&C 76
28 We beheld Satan, that old serpent, even the devil, who rebelled against God, and sought to take the **kingdom** *of our God and his Christ*—

Isaiah 14
12 How art thou fallen from heaven, O Lucifer, son of the morning! how art thou cut down to the ground, which didst weaken the nations!
13 For thou hast said in thine heart, *I will ascend into* **heaven**, *I will exalt my throne above the* **stars** *of* **God**: I will sit also upon the *mount* of the congregation, in the sides of the north:
14 I will ascend above the heights of the clouds; *I will be like* **the most High**.

"That is frightful!" Joan said. "I would never have imagined it. He wanted the record of heaven! No wonder such stringent means were taken to protect it from wickedness. What could ever have persuaded him to think that he could do such a thing?"

"I suspect he didn't know what he was up against," Steve said. "I think there is a scripture that says that."

MOSES 4
6 Satan . . . knew not the mind of God, wherefore he sought to destroy the world.

"It sounds to me like he wanted to destroy a lot more than the world," Karen said.

"That is true," Frank said. "Hence we see the action of the Savior against him."

MOSES 4:3
3 Wherefore, because that Satan rebelled against me, and sought to destroy the agency of man, which I, the Lord God, had given him, and also, that I should give unto him mine own **power**; by the **power** of mine Only Begotten, I caused that he should be cast down.

"I just had a question," Joan said. "You indicated that Jesus has created more worlds than this one, and I just wondered when in the timeline Satan was cast out. Was it in the beginning before any of the worlds were created, or was it in connection only with our world?"

"We don't know the complete answer to that question, but Lucifer and Christ seemed to have been contemporaries with each other in the beginning before any worlds were created. The mission of Christ was to create worlds for the Father and to save them through his atonement. The following verses help us to see this."

D&C 76

24 That by **him**, and through **him**, and of him, *the worlds are and were created*, and the inhabitants thereof are begotten sons and daughters unto God.

41 He came into the world, [this world] even Jesus, to be crucified for the world, and to bear the sins of the world, and to sanctify the world, and to cleanse it from all unrighteousness;

42 That through **him** all [worlds] might be saved whom the Father had put into his power and made by him.

"I see what you mean," Joan said. "In order to complete this mission, he would have had to have been chosen before any world was created."

"So it must have been in that pre-creation time," Steve added, "that the council was held where Lucifer was cast out."

"These verses seem to confirm that," Frank said.

MOSES 4

1 *Satan . . . is the same which was from the beginning*, and he came before me, saying—Behold, here am I, send me, I will be thy son, and I will redeem all mankind, that one soul shall not be lost, and surely I will do it; wherefore give me thine **honor**.

2 But, behold, *my Beloved Son, which was my Beloved and Chosen from the beginning*, said unto me—Father, thy **will** be done, and the **glory** be thine forever.

"So if Christ is the Savior of all the worlds," Karen said, "then Lucifer must be the Satan of all the worlds. And if that is so, why does he seem to be so busy in our world?"

"The answer to that question is the key to understanding a large part of the Atonement," Frank said. "The complex of world-systems that the Savior has created is vast. Look again at these verses we read earlier about Kolob and try to appreciate the enormity:

Abraham Facsimile No. 2 Explanations
Figure 1. Kolob, signifying *the first creation*, nearest to the celestial, or the residence of God. First in government, the last pertaining to the measurement of time.
Abraham 3
9 And thus there shall be the reckoning of the time of one planet above another, until thou come nigh unto Kolob, which Kolob is after the reckoning of the Lord's time; which *Kolob is set* nigh unto the throne of God, *to govern all those planets which belong to the same order as that upon which thou standest.*

"There are additional insights in section 88 of the Doctrine and Covenants. We won't read it all but here are some of the key elements:

D&C 88
42 And again, verily I say unto you, he hath given a **law** unto all things, by which they move in their times and their seasons;
43 And their courses are fixed, even the courses of the heavens and the earth, which comprehend the earth and *all the planets.*
44 And they give **light** to each other in their times and in their seasons, in their minutes, in their hours, in their days, in their weeks, in their months, in their years . . .
45 The earth rolls upon her wings, and the sun giveth his **light** by day, and the moon giveth her **light** by night, and the stars also give their **light**, as they roll upon their wings in their glory, in the midst of the power of God.
46 Unto what shall I liken these kingdoms, that ye may understand?
47 Behold, all these are **kingdoms**, and any man who hath seen any or the least of these hath seen God moving in his **majesty** *and* **power.**
51 Behold, I will liken these **kingdoms** unto a man having a field, and he sent forth his servants into the field to dig in the field.
61 Therefore, unto this parable I will liken all these **kingdoms**, *and the* **inhabitants** *thereof*—every **kingdom** in its hour, and in its time, and in its season, even according to the decree which God hath made.

"Understanding that there are many worlds and many kingdoms, we now want to consider your question, Joan, as to why Satan is so busy in our world.

"We discovered that the mission of Christ was to create worlds and to save them. In order to do that, he had to come to a world, become mortal, take upon him the sins of all men, suffer for them, die, and be resurrected. In doing this he would have to descend below all things so that it could be said of him:

D&C 88

6 He descended below all things, in that he comprehended all things, that he might be in all and through all things, the light of truth.

"He would have to go down to a world, but which one? He would have to descend below them all, but which one was below all?"

"I can see where this is going!" Joan said. "This world is the most wicked of all the worlds. I read that in my study a few days ago."

MOSES 7

36 Wherefore, I can stretch forth mine hands and hold all the creations which I have made; and mine eye can pierce them also, and *among all the workmanship of mine hands there has not been so great wickedness* as among thy brethren.

37 But behold, their sins shall be upon the heads of their fathers; *Satan shall be their father,* and misery shall be their doom; and the whole heavens shall weep over them, even all the workmanship of mine hands;

"There's another scripture that adds more to that," Steve said.

---

2 NEPHI 10

3 It must needs be expedient that Christ . . . should come among the Jews, among those who are the more wicked part of the world; and they shall crucify him—for thus it behooveth our God, and there is none other nation on earth that would crucify their God.

"So there we have it," Joan said. "Christ had to come to our world because it was the only world he had created that turned out wicked enough to kill its own creator."

"Why do you think it's so wicked?" Karen asked.

"I don't know," Frank said, "but I have a suspicion that it has to do with Satan himself. It seems reasonable that after he and his host were cast out, they would begin to try to inhabit the worlds that were created. I can imagine where he would have wanted to concentrate his efforts."

"Oh, I see," Karen said. "On the world where the mortal ministry of Christ would be."

"That's just what I've thought," Frank said. "His great plan was to destroy Christ while he was in the flesh; therefore it seems that he would have spent a great deal of his time on this earth preparing and getting ready to destroy him."

"It's kind of a double-edged sword," Steve said. "The Savior sets things up on this earth to work out the atonement, and Satan sets up here to try and destroy him."

"The Prophet Joseph affirmed that," Frank said. "'When God set up his Kingdom on the Earth Satan always set up his in Opposition.'" (*The Words of Joseph Smith: The Contemporary Accounts of the Nauvoo Discourses of the Prophet Joseph Smith* [Salt Lake City: Book Craft, 1980], 372)

"It sounds like our poor little earth was an arena for a showdown," Karen said.

"Satan has made great claim on power," Frank said. "He has called himself 'the god of this world' and 'the prince of this world' (see 2 Corinthians 4:4; John 14:30). He has appeared as an angel of light (see 2 Corinthians 11:14; D&C 128:20) and has even claimed to be Christ and God himself:

MOSES 1
19 And now, when Moses had said these words, *Satan* cried with a loud voice, and ranted upon the earth, and commanded, saying: *I am the Only Begotten, worship me.*
2 THESSALONIANS 2
3 ... that man of sin (shall) be revealed, the son of perdition;
4 Who opposeth and exalteth himself above all that is called God, or that is worshipped; so that *he as God sitteth in the temple of God, shewing himself that he is God.*

"Enoch describes his haughtiness and rage against God:

MOSES 7
24 The power of Satan was upon all the face of the earth.
26 And he beheld Satan; and he had a great chain in his

237

hand, and it veiled the whole face of the earth with darkness; and he looked up and laughed, and his angels rejoiced.

"Let's turn now to the coming of the Savior to the earth," Frank suggested. "Who can tell us about his birth and what he inherited?"

"I can," Steve said. "He was different from any other mortal ever born. From his mother he received a mortal body that could suffer and die. From God, his Father, he received power to live forever."

"Thanks for that, Steve. Joseph Smith said of him:

> When still a boy he had all the intelligence necessary to enable him to rule and govern the kingdom of the Jews, and could reason with the wisest and most profound doctors of law and divinity, and make their theories and practice to appear like folly compared with the wisdom he possessed; but he was a boy only, and lacked physical strength even to defend his own person, and was subject to cold, to hunger and to death. (*Discourses of the Prophet Joseph Smith*, 302)

"We know," Frank continued, "that Jesus grew up without sin or darkness of any kind (see Hebrews 4:15), and Luke gives us this tiny glimpse into his growing life:

LUKE 2
52 And Jesus increased in **wisdom** *and* **stature**, *and* in **favour** with God and man.

"John the Baptist tells us essentially the same thing.

D&C 93
12 And I, John, saw that he received not of the fulness at the first, but received **grace** for **grace**.

"Then something very interesting happened. Jesus arrived at the point where he was to begin his actual ministry. Though he had been without sin and had received light + light in a consistent manner all his life, he did not possess the power necessary to embark upon or perform that ministry. That's not unusual, however, for we are all like that. If one of us were to be called to a position by God, there is no way that we could perform his work with our present level of knowledge. We would have to be endowed with power from him to accomplish it. That is what happened to Jesus but in a spectacular manner, for he had a spectacular assignment. John describes it this way:"

D&C 93

15 And I, John, bear record, and lo, the heavens were opened, and the Holy Ghost descended upon him in the form of a dove, and sat upon him, and there came a voice out of heaven saying: This is my beloved Son.

16 And I, John, bear record that he received a *fulness of the* **glory** *of the Father*;

17 And *he received all* **power**, *both in heaven and on earth*, and the **glory** of the Father was with him, for he dwelt in him.

"Spectacular to Jesus and to John," Joan exclaimed, "but apparently not to those who stood around. No one else even seemed to notice. How could the fulness of the glory of the Father come upon Jesus and not destroy everything physical on the planet? How could such a light burst forth upon him and not be visible to everyone?"

"How can light go forth from God to fill the immensity of space and it still be dark at night?" Karen responded. "And how did the bush that Moses saw burn and not be consumed?"

"Those are good questions, Karen," Frank said. "Jesus, you will remember, had a body of flesh and bone received from an immortal Father. It was tailored from his conception to receive this glory, whereas our bodies would have withered and died (see Moses 1:11). The whole experience was withheld from everyone at that time except for John, and his eyes were opened to be able to see it.

"Nephi and Alma saw his mortal ministry in vision and look at their descriptions:

---

1 NEPHI 11

28 And I beheld that he went forth ministering unto the people, in **power** *and great* **glory**.

ALMA 5

48 I say unto you, that I know that Jesus Christ shall come, yea, the Son, the Only Begotten of the Father, full of **grace**, *and* **mercy**, *and* **truth**. And behold, it is he that cometh to take away the sins of the world, yea, the sins of every man who steadfastly believeth on his name.

---

50 Yea, kingdom of heaven is soon at hand; yea, the Son of God cometh in his **glory**, in his **might, majesty, power,** and **dominion**. Yea, my beloved brethren, I say unto you, that the Spirit saith: Behold the **glory** of the King of all the earth; and also the King of heaven shall very soon **shine** forth among all the children of men.

Alma 9

26 And not many days hence the Son of God shall come in his **glory**; and his **glory** shall be the **glory** *of the Only Begotten of the Father, full of* **grace**, **equity**, *and* **truth**, full of patience, mercy, and long-suffering, quick to hear the cries of his people and to answer their prayers.

"We almost have to shake ourselves to realize that Nephi and Alma are not speaking of the Second Coming of Jesus, but of his first coming. Later, Peter, James, and John on the Mount of Transfiguration were given the privilege, like John the Baptist, to see his glory.

MATTHEW 17

1 Jesus taketh Peter, James, and John . . . and bringeth them up into an high mountain apart,

2 And was transfigured before them: and his face did shine as the sun, and his raiment was white as the light.

2 PETER 1

16 For we have not followed cunningly devised fables, when we made known unto you the **power** and coming of our Lord Jesus Christ, but were *eyewitnesses* of his **majesty**.

"These men were not seeing something that Jesus lacked and would one day have; they were seeing him for what he was, and it was they who lacked the ability to see it, until authorized."

"It's incredible that Jesus had that glory in him all the days of his ministry and the people in his very presence didn't know it at all," Joan observed.

"Let me just share with you one more witness," Frank said. "On his second visit to the Nephites, the Savior invited his disciples to kneel down, and he prayed to the Father for them. A wonderful thing happened. The glory that was in him encircled them and:

3 Nephi 19
25 His **countenance** did smile upon them, and the **light** of his **countenance** did **shine** upon them, and behold they were as **white** as the **countenance** and also the **garments** of Jesus; and behold the **whiteness** thereof did exceed all the **whiteness**, yea, even there could be nothing upon earth so **white** as the **whiteness** thereof.

"This was a remarkable manifestation of his glory. The disciples were literally redeemed and brought back into his presence. Jesus then spoke to them of his ministry in the old world among the Jews and said:

3 Nephi 19
35 So great faith have I never seen among all the Jews; wherefore I could not show unto them so great miracles, because of their unbelief.

"Jesus did not say he wished he had had the power to show these miracles to the Jews. He said the Jews lacked faith to be shown these things—implying that he had the power in him to do these things all along.

"Another scripture bears this witness:

JST John 3
34 For God giveth him not the **Spirit** by measure, for he dwelleth in him, even the fulness.

"The Prophet Joseph Smith said of Christ:

"None ever were perfect but Jesus; and why was He perfect? Because He was the Son of God, and had the fulness of the Spirit, and greater power than any man." (*Teachings of the Prophet Joseph Smith*, 187–8)

"He also said: 'A spirit cannot come but in glory; an angel that is, a resurrected being has flesh and bones; we see not their glory.' (See D&C 129:6; Teachings of the Prophet Joseph Smith, p. 162) This implies that Jesus in some manner had the ability to shield his glory from the eyes of man because of his physical body in which that glory resided."

"It just goes to show that most of the things of God are not open to our observation in this world," Karen said.

ALMA 32
21 if ye have faith ye hope for *things which are not seen*, which
are **true**.
2 CORINTHIANS 4
18 The things which are seen are temporal; but the *things
which are not seen are* **eternal**.
D&C 38
7 Mine eyes are upon you. I am in your midst and ye cannot see me;

"Yet, Jesus constantly told the people that he had the glory of the
Father," Frank responded. "He would say, for example:

JOHN 5
36 I have greater witness than that of John: for the **works**
which the Father hath given me to finish, the same **works**
that I do, bear witness of me, that the Father hath sent me.

"On another occasion he said:

JOHN 10
30 I and my Father are one.
37 If I do not the **works** of my Father, believe me not.
38 But if I do, though ye believe not me, believe the **works**:
that ye may know, and believe, that the Father is in me, and
I in him.

"One of the reasons we have spent so much time affirming that Jesus
was filled with the light and glory of the Father is so that we can appreciate some of the great things that happened in the atonement. Let's turn
our attention to that now."

"I just have to interrupt again and ask another question," Joan said.
"Why did Jesus have to have the fulness of the Father? What is the sig-
nificance of that? I'm not sure I really understand it. Do you, Karen?
Do you, Steve?"

They both agreed they had only a meager understanding.

"We have touched on it a bit, but let me go back and explain as best I
can what the significance of that is," Frank said.

"When God the Father came to his station of Godhood, he had

already passed through the experience of mortal life, death, and resurrection, and was in possession of a perfect immortal body of flesh and bone—filled with light. Of him, Elder Russell M. Nelson of the Quorum of the Twelve Apostles, said:

> Our Heavenly Father has a glorified body of flesh and bone, inseparably connected with His spirit. Scriptures state that He is "infinite and eternal, from everlasting to everlasting the same unchangeable God." (Russell M. Nelson, *Perfection Pending, and Other Favorite Discourses* [Salt Lake City: Deseret Book, 1998], 225)

D&C 20
17 We know that there is a God in heaven, who is infinite and eternal, from everlasting to everlasting the same unchangeable God, the framer of heaven and earth, and all things which are in them.

"The greatest desire of our Father in heaven was to have spirit children and to provide them with a plan for their glory even as he had received glory. After fathering an innumerable company of spirit children, he assembled them and proposed to them a plan of mortal life. The majority of them were in agreement, as we know. He knew full well, however, that as soon as they left his presence and went to an earth, they would sin, and sin would cut them off eternally from his presence—for no unclean thing can dwell there. He knew also that the only thing that could atone for and satisfy the effect of those sins would be a sacrifice of suffering and death. Amulek in the Book of Mormon tells us something about the sacrifice that would be required:

ALMA 34
10 For it is expedient that there should be a great and last sacrifice; yea, not a sacrifice of man, neither of beast, neither of any manner of fowl; for it shall not be a human sacrifice; but it must be an infinite and eternal sacrifice.

"It could not be a sacrifice of a man, but rather must be the sacrifice of a God. Abinadi explained that 'God himself would have to come down among the children of men to redeem his people' (Moses 15:1–3).

"There was just one problem. God the Father was the only God, and he had a glorified body of flesh and bone that could neither be made to suffer nor to die. Here was a matter of great concern. How does God—who is infinite and eternal—perform the great and last sacrifice, when he is personally unable to do it?"

"You've got my attention," Joan said.

"This is just where we find the Father in chapter 5 of the book of Revelation. Would you please read verse 1 to 9, Steve?"

REVELATION 5

1 And I saw in the right hand of him that sat on the throne a **book** written within and on the backside, sealed with seven seals.

2 And I saw a strong angel proclaiming with a loud voice, Who is worthy to open the **book**, and to loose the seals thereof?

3 And no man in heaven, nor in earth, neither under the earth, was able to open the **book**, neither to look thereon.

4 And I wept much, because no man was found worthy to open and to read the **book**, neither to look thereon.

5 And one of the elders saith unto me, Weep not: behold, the Lion of the tribe of Juda, the Root of David, hath prevailed to open the **book**, and to loose the seven seals thereof.

6 And I beheld, and, lo, in the midst of the throne and of the four beasts, and in the midst of the elders, stood a Lamb as it had been slain, having seven horns and seven eyes, which are the seven Spirits of God sent forth into all the earth.

7 And he came and took the **book** out of the right hand of him that sat upon the throne.

8 And when he had taken the **book**, the four beasts and four and twenty elders fell down before the Lamb, having every one of them harps, and golden vials full of odours, which are the prayers of saints.

9 And they sung a new song, saying, Thou art worthy to take the **book**, and to open the seals thereof: for thou wast slain, and hast redeemed us to God by thy blood out of every kindred, and tongue, and people, and nation.

"If we follow this carefully," Frank explained, "we can see the events unfolding. The Father is sitting on his throne—this is probably a throne in the more traditional sense. He has a book in his right hand. What do you think the book is, and what is the problem with it, Joan?"

"Well, based on what we've learned, the book must be the plan of the Father for his children, and the problem is that the Father is looking for someone to open it."

"What happens, Karen?"

"A lamb that looked like it had been slain, which I assume was Christ, came forward and was able to take the book out of the Father's hand."

"Why was he able to do that?" Frank asked.

"Because of the blood that he would shed to redeem God's children from the fall," Karen answered.

"Notice how this whole thing is summed up by Nephi," Frank said.

---

2 NEPHI 11

7 For if there be no Christ there be no God; and if there be no God we are not, for there could have been no creation. But there is a God, and he is Christ, and he cometh in the fulness of his own time.

"What we see here is that God the Father faced the need to make an eternal sacrifice of suffering and death, and he knew that he was personally unable to do that. So how was the problem solved, Joan?"

"He chose Christ to do it."

"Not so fast. No, that cannot be," Frank said. "The Son did not have power of himself to make the sacrifice. Whose sacrifice is this?"

"It was a sacrifice required of the Father," Joan responded. "But you said he couldn't do it! Christ had to do it!"

"There was a way that the Father could do it," Frank said. "With the consent of his Son, the Father could literally fashion him into a carrier of his own mind and will and through his flesh and blood make an atonement. Elder Bruce R. McConkie of the Quorum of the Twelve, said:

> How is our Lord the Father? It is because . . . he received power from his Father to do that which is infinite and eternal. This is a matter of his Eternal Parent investing him with power from on high so that he becomes the Father because he exercises the power of that Eternal Being. (*Promised Messiah*, 371)

"Hence the scriptures say:

ALMA 12

33 But *God* did call on men, *in the name of his Son*, (this being the plan of redemption which was laid) saying: If ye will repent and harden not your hearts, then will *I* have mercy upon you, *through mine Only Begotten Son*.

"If we were to put these things into clearer language, Steve, how might they be said?"

"God is calling upon us through Christ, and says to us, 'I will have mercy on you through him.' Mercy belongs to the Father. Mercy is only in Christ because the Father put it there, and the Father is giving it to us through him."

"As Elder McConkie said, in order for this great plan of redemption to go into effect in that pre-earth existence, the Father gave the Son a fulness of his power, of his mind, and of his glory. This enabled the Son to become one with the Father so that the Father could work the plan through him. Speaking of Jesus in that situation, John said:

JOHN 1
1 In the beginning was the **Word**, and the **Word** was with God, and the **Word** was God.
2 The same was in the beginning with God.
3 All things were made by **him**; and without **him** was not any thing made that was made.

"The Prophet Joseph said:

The Father and the Son possessing the same mind, the same wisdom, glory, power, and fulness—filling all in all; the Son being filled with the fulness of the mind, glory, and power; or, in other words, the spirit, glory, and power, of the Father, possessing all knowledge and glory, and the same kingdom, sitting at the right hand of power, in the express image and likeness of the Father. . . .

Jesus Christ; possessing the same mind, being transformed into the same image or likeness, even the express image of him who fills all in all; being filled with the fulness of his glory, and become one in him, even as the Father. . . .

The Son partakes of the fulness of the Father through the Spirit. (Lectures on Faith 5:2)

"Of this same thing, Jesus said:

D&C 93
3 I am *in* the **Father**, and the **Father** *in* **me**, and the **Father** and **I** are one—
4 [I am] the **Father** because he gave me of his **fulness**.

"When Jesus was endowed with a fulness of the Father—all of his power, all of his knowledge, all of his glory, and so forth, he became as if he were God the Father. They become one. He was not only the Son now; he was also the Father—a substitute and sacrificial Father. Two Fathers reigned side by side. One was God the Father, and the other was Christ, the sacrificial Father. Both possessed the same mind and comprehended at the same time the same things, to the same degree. Their purpose was to work the Father's plan through the Son who was now the Father.

"There are many scriptures about the Savior that can only really be understood in the context of his role as a substitute Father.[1]

MORMON 9
12 Because of the fall of man came Jesus Christ, *even the* **Father** *and the* **Son**; and because of Jesus Christ came the redemption of man.

ETHER 3
14 Behold, I am he who was **prepared** from the foundation of the world to redeem my people. Behold, I am Jesus Christ. *I am the* **Father** *and the* **Son.**
ETHER 4
12 He that will not believe me will not believe the Father who sent me. For behold, *I am the* **Father**, I am the **light**, and the **life**, and the **truth** of the world.

ALMA 11
26 And Zeezrom said unto him: *Thou sayest there is a true and living God?*
27 And Amulek said: *Yea, there is a true and living God.*
28 Now Zeezrom said: *Is there more than one God?*
29 And he answered, *No.*
32 And Zeezrom said again: *Who is he that shall come? Is it the Son of God?*
33 And he said unto him, *Yea.*
35 Now Zeezrom said unto the people: *See that ye remember these things; for he said there is but one God; yet he saith that the Son of God shall come,*
38 Now Zeezrom saith again unto him: *Is the Son of God the*

very Eternal Father?
39 And Amulek said unto him: *Yea, he is the very Eternal Father of heaven and of earth, and all things which in them are; he is the beginning and the end, the first and the last.*

"Does that help answer your question of why the Son had to have a fulness of the Father, Joan?" Frank asked.

"Yes, but it is something I never knew."

"The Father plainly tells us of the oneness that he and his son have," Frank said, "in some of the verses that deal with the creation of the earth:

MOSES 1

32 And *by the* **word** *of my* **power**, have I created them, *which is mine Only Begotten Son . . .*

33 And *worlds without number* have I created . . . and *by the Son I created them*, which is mine Only Begotten.

35 There are many worlds that have passed away *by the* **word** *of my* **power**. And there are many that now stand, and innumerable are they unto man;

MOSES 2

1 By mine Only Begotten I created these things; yea, in the beginning I created the heaven, and the earth..

5 And I, God, called the light Day; and the darkness, I called Night; and this I did by the **word** *of my* **power**.

"These verses are witnesses to the total fusing of the identity and the power of the God the Father and Christ—the substitute-Father. Though they are two separate and distinct beings, they are one; they possess the same mind and the same glory. And this because the Son was to make his journey as Creator and Savior in first person as if he were the Father, so that it could be said that God himself had done these things (see Alma 42:15).

"Notice in the verses we just read how, when the Son acted, the Father claimed the Son's actions as his very own. Here the Father tells us that his creations are his very own work, that he performed them, but says he, 'I did them through my Son—I gave him power to act as if he were Me.' Hence, the Son is the Father's very own power.

"So completely, in the early patriarchal era, was the Lord's identity as the Son guarded, that it is almost with a start that he reveals himself to the brother of Jared in that role.

ETHER 3

13 Behold, the *Lord* showed himself unto him, and said: Because thou knowest these things ye are redeemed from the fall; therefore ye are brought back into my presence; therefore I show myself unto you.

14 Behold, I am he who was prepared from the foundation of the world to redeem my people. Behold, *I am Jesus Christ. I am the* **Father** *and the* **Son**.

15 *And never have I showed myself unto man whom I have created,* for never has man believed in me as thou hast.

"The Savior's statement that he had never shown himself to man before relates, it seems, not to his position as the Father, for he had made many appearances with the glory and in the name of the Father (see D&C 107:54–55; Moses 7:4, 16–17). This, however, is the first time he had ever appeared in his role as the Son, momentarily putting aside the glory of the Father and showing his personal identity as the Father who is the Son.

"Abinadi gives us another special insight that helps us understand more," Frank said.

MOSIAH 15

1 I would that ye should understand that **God** *himself* shall come down among the children of men, and shall redeem his people.

2 And because he dwelleth in flesh he shall be called the **Son** of God, and having subjected the flesh to the *will* of the Father, being the **Father** and the **Son**—

3 The **Father**, because he was conceived by the **power** of God; and the **Son**, because of the flesh; thus becoming the **Father** and **Son**—

4 And they are *one* **God**, yea, the *very Eternal Father of heaven and of earth.*

5 And thus the flesh becoming subject to the **Spirit**, or the **Son** to the **Father**, being *one* **God**, suffereth temptation, and yieldeth not to the temptation, but suffereth himself to be mocked, and scourged, and cast out, and disowned by his people.

7 Yea, even so he shall be led, crucified, and slain, the flesh becoming subject even unto death, the **will** of the **Son** being *swallowed* up in the **will** of the **Father**.

8 And thus **God** breaketh the bands of death, having gained the victory over death; giving the **Son power** to make intercession for the children of men.

"First," Frank continued, "he says that God himself, the Father, will come down and will redeem his people. We are almost shocked to hear this because we have always thought that it was the Son who is to come down. He then proceeds to tell us how the Father will do this. He says that the Father will come down and dwell in the flesh and be called the Son of God. We ask: How can the Father come down and dwell in the flesh? He answers: By putting his mind and will into the mind and will of the Son who is in the flesh, and by the Son giving up his own will to the will of the Father.

"What will that accomplish? we ask. The Son will then do nothing but the will of the Father. What will that do? we continue. The Father's mind and will, will then work through the flesh of the Son to bring about the Father's atonement. Abinadi then says that the Son was conceived by the light of the Father and through that conception, the flesh of the Son became subject to the light of the Father, and with that light the Son will suffer temptations and not yield to them and will be mocked, scourged, and disowned by his people. He then says that the will of the Son will be so much swallowed up in the will of the Father that when the Father requires the death of this flesh which he (the Father) has claimed, it will be done. And in this manner the Father will break the bands of death by gaining the victory."

"I had no idea that the atonement was such a function of both the Father and the Son," Joan said. "I guess I have thought of the Father being in heaven and the Son being on the earth and the atonement being done by the Son."

"We have a great tendency to separate the Father and the Son and to emphasize their distinctness, and that is as it should be. However, it often prevents us from seeing the extent to which they are one. Abinadi emphasizes that the will of the Son was so completely swallowed up in the will of the Father that it was as if a contract was made directly between the mind of the Father and the flesh of the Son. In other words, the Father would do his work directly through the body of his Son as if that body were his own—the flesh of the Son becoming the flesh of the Father, the mind of the Son becoming the mind of the Father, the lips, the voice, the eyes, the ears, the heart, the hands, and the feet of the Son becoming those of the Father. In short, the Father became the Son and the Son became the Father. Why? Because it was the only avenue open to the Father to do the work—which only he could do—in a mortal world. Hence we see the son say:

John 5

30 *I can of mine own self do nothing*: as I hear, I judge: and my judgment is just; because I seek not mine own will, but the **will** of the **Father** which hath sent me.

John 12

44 Jesus cried and said, *He that believeth on me, believeth not on me, but on him that sent me.*
45 And *he that seeth* **me** *seeth* **him** *that sent me.*

John 14

10 Believest thou not that **I** am in the **Father**, and the **Father** in **me**? *the* **words** *that I speak unto you I speak not of myself: but the* **Father** *that dwelleth in me,* **he** *doeth the* **works**.
11 *Believe me that* **I** *am in the* **Father**, *and the* **Father** *in* **me**: *or else believe me for the very* **works'** *sake.*

John 15

24 If I had not done among them the works which none other man did, they had not had sin: but now *have they both seen and hated both* me *and my* Father.

"This unity was so complete that Jesus on one occasion said:"

JST Luke 10

23 All things are delivered to me of my Father; and no man knoweth that the **Son** *is* the **Father**, and the **Father** *is* the **Son**, but him to whom the Son will reveal it.

"If people were to read these things without the spirit," Joan said, "it's easy to imagine how quickly a false idea of the Father and the Son being the same person could develop."

"That's really true," Steve said. "These are the hidden mysteries of God. At least they have been hidden from me until now. They can only be understood by revelation."

"So now we ask," Frank continued, "what was the great mission and purpose of the Father and the Son in the atonement?"

"It was to overcome sin and death and bring redemption to all mankind," Steve responded.

"So what happened?" Frank asked.

"I think a large part of it happened in the Garden of Gethsemane," Karen responded. "Jesus did most of his suffering there."

"What do you think caused that suffering?" Frank asked

"Well, we know that he took our sins upon himself," Steve said.

"That is true," Frank said. "If we were to put that experience into the perspective that we've been studying, we would see a whole new picture. Let me explain.

"Prior to going into the Garden of Gethsemane with his disciples, Jesus said:

JOHN 12
31 Now is the judgment of this world: now shall the *prince of this world be cast out.*
JOHN 14
30 The *prince of this world* cometh, and *hath nothing in me.*
JST JOHN 14
30 The *prince of darkness,* who is of this world, cometh, but *hath no power over me . . .*

"What do you think he intended to convey, Steve?"

"To me, it is saying that Satan—the prince of darkness—is on his way and that he has no place nor part in the Savior because the Savior is the 'light in which there is no darkness at all.'"

"That's beautiful, Steve," Frank said.

"Karen remarked a few minutes ago that our poor little earth was like an arena for a showdown. That showdown was to take place in this tiny garden between two princes—the Prince of Darkness and the Prince of Light."

"How did it happen?" Joan asked.

"No one knows for sure," Frank said. "But the doctrine of Christ gives us a good idea. Look at these verses and tell me what you see."

ALMA 42
22 But there is a **law** given, and a punishment affixed, and a repentance granted; which repentance, mercy claimeth; otherwise, justice claimeth the creature and executeth the **law**, and the **law** *inflicteth the punishment*; if not so, the works of justice would be destroyed, and God would cease to be God.
3 NEPHI 15
9 Behold, I am the **law**, and the **light**. Look unto me, and endure to the end, and ye shall live.

"The first verse says to me that the law or light of God has a punishment fixed to it," Joan said, "and if that light is not obeyed, it works against the person who has not obeyed and inflicts the punishment. The second verse indicates to me that Jesus himself is the light to which the punishment is fixed and that he inflicts the punishment."

"So the Prince of Light is to inflict punishment upon sin and darkness," Steve said, "brought about by the prince of darkness—the ultimate contest between light and darkness."

"If I can, I want to add another layer of meaning to the discussion by asking again where it happened," Frank said.

"What do you mean?" Karen replied. "It happened in the garden."

"Fortunately, because of some other scriptures, we can be more specific than that," Frank said. "What do these verses tell us?"

D&C 93
17 And he *received all* **power**, *both in heaven and on earth, and the* **glory** *of the Father was with him, for he dwelt in him.*
COLOSSIANS 2
9 For *in* **him** *dwelleth all the* **fulness** *of the* **Godhead** *bodily.*

"This says what we learned before that the fulness of the Father was in his body," Steve said.

"Now look at this verse," Frank continued.

1 PETER 2
24 Who *his own self bare our* **sins** *in his own body* . . .

"My goodness!" Joan exclaimed. "The contest was in his own body!"

"Just think of it," Frank said. "Here was the body of Jesus, filled with a fulness of the ultimate power and glory of the Light of the Father, and into that holy vessel he draws, in some inexplicable way, the fulness of the consequences of the sin and evil of the everlasting kingdom of the prince of darkness—the darkness in which there is no light at all."

"That is staggering to the mind," Steve said.

"Not only was it a horrendous struggle," Frank continued. "It was completely invisible. No mortal man could comprehend either the light (1 Timothy 6:16) or the darkness (D&C 76:43–48)."

"It is incredible that the total awareness and summation of all these things could flow into him," Steve said.

"It is, and that awareness was one of infinite proportion," Frank added. "It was not just for the past or the present that he suffered, but for the future, and for all worlds and souls that will ever be created by him and his Father."

D&C 38

1 Thus saith the Lord your God, even Jesus Christ, the Great I AM, Alpha and Omega, the beginning and the end, the same which looked upon the wide expanse of eternity, and all the seraphic hosts of heaven, before the world was made;
2 The same which knoweth all things, for all things are present before mine eyes;

"We see here that Jesus, in the premortal state, was able to look upon all the hosts of heaven before he created this world. He says that all things were then present before his eyes. That does not only mean all things were visible; it also means that all things which were visible were present to him. I read a quote the other day by the Prophet Joseph about this:

> The great Jehovah contemplated the whole of the events connected with the earth, pertaining to the plan of salvation before it rolled into existence, or ever "the morning stars sang together" for joy; the past, the present, and the future were and are, with him, one eternal "now"; . . . whether in this world, or in the world to come. (HC 4:597)

"Having comprehended and taken all sin, past, present, and future, upon him, Isaiah tells us that at that moment, Jesus . . . "

ISAIAH 53

12 . . . *was numbered with the **transgressors***; [because] *he bare the **sin** of many.*

"What an awful thing to think about," Karen replied. "Drawing the darkness into his own body."

"I could imagine that the effect might have been somewhat like what our own bodies do," Steve said. "The blood and various parts of our bodies are cleaning agents for disease. Perhaps his blood and body did to darkness and sin what our blood and bodies do to disease and infection.

They neutralize it and destroy it. We can suffer a great deal when our bodies are trying to destroy disease. Perhaps it worked in him like that, only on an infinite scale."

"That is very interesting," Frank said. "There is another aspect to think about in terms of his suffering. At the moment of contest between light and darkness, Jesus was in effect two people. He was a being of light and at the same time, a being of darkness. Within him now were the sins of all mankind from all the worlds ever created. The Father-Light side of him would be compelled to inflict punishment upon the dark side, whereas the son-dark side of him would be compelled to suffer the punishment. The application of that light to the darkness is described in scripture:

D&C 88
106 The Lamb of God hath overcome and trodden the wine-press alone, even the wine-press of the fierceness of the **wrath** of Almighty God.

"Here we see that the Son suffered the wrath of the Father. Or rather, the Son-part of him into which the darkness was drawn, suffered the wrath of the will of the Father that was also in him. He describes his suffering as the light inflicted the punishment."

D&C 19
18 Which suffering caused myself, even God, the greatest of all, to tremble because of pain, and to bleed at every pore, and to suffer both body and spirit—and would that I might not drink the bitter cup, and shrink—
19 Nevertheless, glory be to the Father, and I partook and finished my preparations unto the children of men.

"I want to weep when I think of it," Joan said. "It must have been so dreadful for him."

"When I think of the cataclysmic confrontation of the two forces in the Savior," Steve said, "I can't help but remember a story I read once about a man who had a great hatred for another man and wanted to do away with him. This man had been in the military and had access to some rocket fuel. The story described that rocket fuel is in two parts, neither of which is volatile unless they come together. The man put one component of the fuel in part of a plumbing-pipe of the other man's house, sealing it off with a fragile membrane in the pipe. He put the other component in the rest of the pipe on the other side of the membrane. When anyone in the house performed a task that introduced water pressure of any kind into the plumbing lines, a horrific explosion would take place, destroying the house completely."

"That's awful!" Karen said.

"But that same kind of thing happened at the time of the atonement," Steve replied.

"What do you mean?" Karen asked.

"Look at these scriptures."

MATTHEW 27
51 And, behold, the veil of the temple was rent in twain from the top to the bottom; and the earth did quake, and the rocks rent;
1 NEPHI 12
4 And it came to pass that I saw a mist of darkness on the face of the land of promise; and I saw lightnings, and I heard thunderings, and earthquakes, and all manner of tumultuous noises; and I saw the earth and the rocks, that they rent; and I saw mountains tumbling into pieces; and I saw the plains of the earth, that they were broken up; and I saw many cities that they were sunk; and I saw many that they were burned with fire; and I saw many that did tumble to the earth, because of the quaking thereof.

"I had forgotten all about that," Karen replied. "The repercussions were felt through the whole earth."

"An angel of the Lord told why," Frank said.

HELAMAN 14
28 And the angel said unto me that . . . these signs and these wonders should come to pass upon all the face of this land, *to the intent that there should be no cause for unbelief* among the children of men.

"And Elder Parley P. Pratt wrote:

When I am passing a ledge of rocks and see they have all been rent and torn asunder, while some huge fragments are found deeply imbedded in the earth some rods from where they were torn, I exclaim, with astonishment, these were the groans! The convulsive throes of agonizing nature, while the Son of God suffered upon the cross. (Parley P. Pratt, *A Voice of Warning and Instruction to All People or, an Introduction to the Faith and Doctrine of the Church of Jesus Christ of Latter-days Saints*, New Edition [Salt Lake City: The Church of Jesus Christ of Latter-day Saints, 1957], 88)

"It's hard to fathom the magnitude of that," Steve said.

"And that is only part of it," Frank said. "If you remember, we said earlier that the atonement of Jesus was in effect for all the worlds that God had created through him and that he would come to this earth to work out an atonement that would save all.

D&C 76

23 He is the Only Begotten of the Father—

24 That by him, and through him, and of him, the *worlds* are and were created, and *the inhabitants thereof are begotten sons and daughters unto God.*

41 That he came into the *world* [i.e., this world], even Jesus, to be crucified for the world, and to bear the sins of the world, and to sanctify the world, and to cleanse it from all unrighteousness;

42 That through him *all* [worlds] might be saved whom the Father had put into his power and made by him.

"Enoch gives us an expanded vision of the repercussions of the suffering of Christ:

MOSES 7

29–30 And Enoch said . . . were it possible that man could number the particles of the earth, yea, millions of earths like this, *it would not be a beginning to the number of thy creations*; and thy curtains are stretched out still;

56 And he heard a loud voice; and the heavens were veiled; and *all the creations of God mourned*; and *the earth groaned; and the rocks were rent.*

"I have always known that the wounds in the hands and feet of the Savior were a special witness to his creations that he suffered," Steve said. "I didn't understand that the wounds of the earth are also a special witness to the inhabitants of all the worlds that on this earth the Savior descended below all things. These are great insights."

"Speaking of insights," Frank said, "the early Egyptians in their imitation of the true and ancient order of the Son of God (see Abraham 1:26) have a representation of the mighty struggle between the god of light and the god of darkness. They show the great Egyptian god, Horus, who typified the greatest power of the heat of the sun, linked in one body with Set, the prince of darkness. The feet moving in the direction of Horus signify the glorious victory which the god of light gained over his opponent. (See *The Gods of the Egyptians*, vol. 1., 473, 475)

The double god Horus-Set

"That is very interesting," Steve said. "It shows that these things were known and understood from the beginning."

"Well, our time is about up," Frank said. "It's been great being with you. Our children should be arriving over at the house in about a half an hour. Let's just end with the other part of the atonement that we haven't touched on yet."

"What part is that?" Joan asked.

"The part that enabled Jesus to descend below all things. As we mentioned, the greatest part of the suffering of Christ happened in the Garden, and yet there were the beatings and the crown of thorns and the crucifixion. Near the end, as he hung on the cross he made a very curious statement:

MATTHEW 27

46 And about the ninth hour Jesus cried with a loud voice, saying, Eli, Eli, lama sabachthani? that is to say, *My* **God**, *my* **God**, *why hast thou forsaken me?*

"What could this possibly have meant?"

"For some reason or other, the Father withdrew," Joan said.

"Pardon me!" Frank said. "What did you say the Father did?"

"He withdrew."

"What did he withdraw?"

"I get the message," Joan said. "He must have withdrawn his light."

"Why would he have done such a thing?" Frank asked.

"I guess it had to be part of the Savior's experience," Joan said.

"The Savior once told Martin Harris, who had done wrong and had suffered for it, that his greatest suffering came. . .

D&C 19
20 At the time I withdrew my **Spirit**.

"The withdrawal of the spirit is described in this verse:

ALMA 34
35 The **Spirit** of the Lord hath *withdrawn* from you, and hath no place in you . . . and this is the final state of the wicked.

"In his descending below all things, the Savior needed to experience the opposite from all that he had ever experienced, and that was the darkness in which there is no light at all. He had to descend.

D&C 76
44 . . . into everlasting punishment, which is endless punishment, which is eternal punishment . . . where their worm dieth not, and the fire is not quenched, which is their torment—
45 And the end thereof, neither the place thereof, nor their torment, no man knows;
46 Neither was it revealed, neither is, neither will be revealed unto man, except to them who are made partakers thereof;
47 Nevertheless, I, the Lord, show it by vision unto many, but straightway shut it up again;
48 Wherefore, the end, the width, the height, the depth, and the misery thereof, they understand not, neither any man except those who are ordained unto this condemnation.

"I remember studying something about that punishment earlier," Joan said. "It affected me greatly."

"The people of the land of Nephi were greatly affected by it also," Steve said.

3 NEPHI 8
20 And it came to pass that there was thick darkness upon all the face of the land, insomuch that the inhabitants thereof who had not fallen could feel the vapor of darkness;
21 And there could be no light, because of the darkness, neither candles, neither torches; neither could there be fire kindled with their fine and exceedingly dry wood, so that there could not be any light at all;

> 22 And there was not any light seen, neither fire, nor glimmer, neither the sun, nor the moon, nor the stars, for so great were the mists of darkness which were upon the face of the land.
> 23 And it came to pass that it did last for the space of three days that there was no light seen; and there was great mourning and howling and weeping among all the people continually; yea, great were the groanings of the people, because of the darkness and the great destruction which had come upon them.

"I think that was a witness to them and to us also that there is only one light, and it is the light of the Father. All light, whether it is in a candle or a torch or a fire or in the sun or the moon or the stars, comes from him, and when his light withdraws there is not so much as a glimmer."

"It makes me shudder to think about it," Karen said. "There are things about the light and about the darkness of which we know nothing. We just have to trust in the Savior to lead us along and give us light + light until we are finally saved in the arms of eternal life. I surely appreciate what we have learned and experienced. It makes me want to continue studying forever."

"Can I just ask one more question?" Joan said.

"Sure you can," Frank responded. "What is it?"

"What about the blood of Christ? Many scriptures indicate that it is through his blood that we are cleansed from sin and also that our garments must be washed white in his blood to have eternal life. How can we wash our garments in blood and have them become white?"

"We don't know all the answers to all these things," Frank said, "but first of all we can surmise that our garments are our bodies. They clothe our spirits. They need to be cleansed. Speaking of blood, the Lord told Moses:

LEVITICUS 17
11 The **life** of the flesh is in the *blood*: and I have given it to you upon the altar to make an atonement for your souls: for it is the *blood* that maketh an atonement for the soul.

"If blood is the life of the flesh and life is light, then blood must be associated with light. And this would be more applicable to the Savior's blood than to any other, for he was a being of infinite and eternal light. If his blood was light, we can readily see how it can cleanse us from darkness, and how we could wash our bodies in it and they become white. This would be realized through baptism by water and also of the Spirit. Jesus also said:

JOHN 6
53 Except ye eat the flesh of the Son of man, and drink his *blood*, ye have no **life** in you.
54 Whoso eateth my flesh, and drinketh my *blood*, hath eternal **life**; and I will raise him up at the last day.
56 He that eateth my flesh, and drinketh my *blood*, dwelleth in me, and I in him.
57 As the living Father hath sent me, and I **live** by the Father: so he that eateth me, even he shall **live** by me.

"This process is of course the sacrament. The blood was originally represented by wine, which in the scriptures is called the blood of the grape (see Deuteronomy 32:14). Today we are commanded to use water. This represents the living water or spirit or light of his blood."

JEREMIAH 2
13 They have forsaken me the fountain of living **waters**, and hewed them out cisterns, broken cisterns, that can hold no **water**.

"In relationship to this, let me just quickly show you three other scriptures and then one final verse," Frank said.

MARK 5
30 And Jesus, immediately knowing in himself that **virtue** had gone out of him, turned him about in the press, and said, Who touched my clothes?
LUKE 6
19 And the whole multitude sought to touch him: for there went **virtue** out of him, and healed them all.
LUKE 8
46 And Jesus said, Somebody hath touched me: for I perceive that **virtue** is gone out of me.

"What do you see here, Joan?"
"That light went out of him and healed and blessed the people."
"Now look at this verse and tell me how it relates."

D&C 38
4 I am Christ, and in mine own name, by the **virtue** of the *blood* which I have spilt, have I pleaded before the Father for them.

"Well, that certainly answers my question," Joan responded.

"There are still many things about the atonement we could discuss," Steve said, "but we'll have to do that some another time. We've already studied about the resurrection, though, and its connection with light. That was a glorious study and one I will not soon forget. It can all be summed up in one verse:"

MORMON 7
5 Believe in Jesus Christ . . . that . . . by the **power** of the Father he hath risen again.

As the evening came to a close, there were expressions of appreciation and promises of getting together again soon. As Frank and Karen were going out the door, Joan said, "This has meant so much to us. The only way I can really express its significance is by saying that it has changed us. You have given so much of your time, and we have been so blessed. Steve and I were watching a television show the other night, and it was telling of a university that had been given a grant to study sandpiles."

"Sandpiles?" Karen responded with curiosity.

"Yes," Joan replied. "They discovered that as grains of sand fall on the top of a sandpile, the pile eventually arrives at a state of critical mass. That is a condition where, with the falling of the next grain of sand, the entire pile shifts and is unalterably changed. I think that is what has happened to us. Through our studies we have arrived many times at a state of 'critical mass,' and then with the reading of the next scripture we have been suddenly altered, never to be the same again. It is exhilarating, and like the Savior once said, 'Behold, canst thou read this without rejoicing and lifting up thy heart for gladness' (D&C 19:39)?'"

Notes

1 The idea of Christ becoming a substitute for the Father does not imply that he was anything less than the Father would have been if he had performed that mission himself. Jesus became all that the Father was when he was endowed with his fulness. The word *substitute* as it is used here more nearly relates to the idea of proxy—one standing in for or representing another to do what he would do if he were there himself.

End Words

I hope the studies in this book will have been sufficient to help illuminate the depth of the "mother-lode" scripture that we started with.

> **D&C 84**
> 45 For the **word** of the Lord is **truth**, and whatsoever is **truth** is **light**, and whatsoever is **light** is **Spirit**, even the **Spirit** of Jesus Christ.

It is my sincere desire that the spirit of this work will launch the reader into his or her own discoveries of scriptural treasure.

Allen J. Fletcher

About the Author

Allen J. Fletcher was born and raised in Alberta, Canada. After serving in the East Central States Mission, he met and married his wife, Elaine Hardy. He then attended Ricks College, and later earned a bachelor's degree in speech/dramatic arts from BYU and a master's degree in education from the University of Calgary.

Allen served for thirty-seven years in the Church Educational System in the United States and Canada. Now retired, he lives in Stirling, Alberta. He and his wife are the parents of seven and grandparents of sixteen.